DINE' DEFIANCE

ROCKY MOUNTAIN SAINT BOOK 14

B.N. RUNDELL

Dine' Defiance

Paperback Edition

Wolfpack Publishing
6032 Wheat Penny Avenue
Las Vegas, NV 89122

wolfpackpublishing.com

Paperback ISBN 978-1-64119-927-8
eBook ISBN 978-1-64119-926-1

DEDICATION

I have spent countless hours in the company and minds of the characters of the Rocky Mountain Saint series. I find I must dedicate this, probably the last book of the series, to those characters. Tate, Maggie, Sean, Sadie, and their friends, both two-legged and four-legged, have lived in my mind and heart for many months. Seldom has a day passed that I was not walking or riding those many trails of adventure with them, howbeit only in my imagination. Other characters, John Fremont, Kit Carson, and more, although real, stepped off the pages of history and walked with these others in my imagination and became more real than I ever imagined. Most of the historical events, I have endeavored to remain true to the happenings as they occurred and were recorded, although it was necessary to add the "fiction" to the "historical" for the stories to be followed. And to you, the readers, I am thankful for so many of you that have followed these adventures and read every word. You have given me the inspiration and determination to continue to sit at my laptop and try to give life to these characters and stories, thank you. And may we meet again, another time, another story, and perhaps another series.

DINE' DEFIANCE

gly, brownish-blonde hair hung to the collar of his blue uniform. He squirmed around, watching General Carleton take his seat behind the desk, "You think they'll come in?" he asked, skeptically.

"Prob'ly not. But Canby had the right idea when he fought with 'em the last couple years. He said the only way to get the raiding and murdering to stop was to 'seize and destroy the crops of the Navajos'. He kept them on the run, drove 'em into the desert and mountains; the Navajos called that time the *Nahondzod* or 'Fearing Time.' He was successful up to a point, even had over thirty chiefs to agree, but then the New Mexican Irregulars and the war back east put a stop to all that. I do think if he'd had more time, maybe a few more men, he might o' been successful."

The general leaned forward, putting his elbows on the desk and looked sternly at Carson, "You're still upset 'bout me callin' you back, aren't you?"

"You better be glad it's me sittin' here and not Josefa. If she'd had her way, your scalp would be hangin' from our front porch!"

Both men chuckled at the thought, but Carleton knew the fiery temper of Carson's wife and had no doubt she would have done exactly that. "But Kit, like I told you before, you're the best man, really the only man for the job. After the way you did things with the Mescalero, you proved that you're the only one that can do this; I just couldn't accept your resignation, and I knew you were and are committed to this great nation. If it was anybody else, they'd probably just make things worse an' we'd be at war with the Navajos and others for the next twenty years.

Kit, just in the last eighteen months, the Navajo have killed over three hundred, stolen half a million sheep, five thousand horses, mules and cattle, and they keep at it. We've tried makin' peace, but the way their people are, they do what they want, no matter what the chiefs say, they just aren't like other tribes you've

CHAPTER ONE
SANTA FE

"Now that we have Fort Wingate," began General Carleton, standing before the large, framed map behind his desk, "with Wingate and Fort Defiance, you'll have supply points for any foray you make into Navajo territory!" He waved his hand over the northwest portion that showed the part of New Mexico Territory known as the Land of the *Diné*. "The meeting I had with eighteen of their chiefs, just last month, I told them they could have no peace until they would give other guarantees than their word that the peace would be kept!" he smacked his fist on the desk top, showing his consternation with the Navajo. "I said we had no faith in their promises and that if they did not return, we would know they had chosen the alternative of war. In this event, the consequences rest on them!"

"So, what guarantees do you want from them?" asked Colonel Carson.

"Just that they would agree to go to Bosque Redondo, like the few that have already gone," explained Carleton.

Kit Carson sat back in his chair, looking at the general wi piercing eyes from under his thick eyebrows. His signature sc dealt with, even the Apache do a better job followin' the wishes of their leaders.

Why, even back in '46 when ol' Chief Narbona and a bunch of the other Navajo leaders signed that first treaty with Colonel Doniphan at Bear Springs, that lasted all of what, a few days? And every time since whenever we've tried a treaty, between the Navajo and the Mexicans and the Utes and others, nothing changes. But the Mexicans are just as bad, what with their raiding and taking captives. Why, it galls me to no end to see them gather after they have mass in church on Sunday and gather in the town square and have an auction of the Navajo captives! We're fighting a war back east and, slavery is at the core of the fight, and here it goes on in this territory, that's supposed to be a free territory! Blast it all!"

Carson dropped his eyes, sat back in the chair, and added, "I do think Canby was right about one thing, the *ricos* and the *ladrones* have to be separated. The *Ricos* are what others call rich, because they have herds and more, while the *ladrones,* or robbers, are the ones that do all the raiding and killing. Their attitude is that they let the Mexicans live to raise crops and herds for them to steal. Canby wanted to separate the two, taking the *ladrones* to a reservation far away and letting the peaceful ones remain and raise their crops and herds."

"Well, it might surprise you to know that it was Canby's idea to launch another campaign against the Navajo and for you to lead it, but nothing was said about separating them. This time it will be for all of them to surrender to the idea of going to Bosque Redondo," explained Carleton.

"That might be a bigger problem than you realize, General. The *Diné,* like other tribes, have their homeland that is bounded by what they call their four sacred mountains. They will not willingly leave that land, it is sacred to them," declared Carson. "Just how are you planning to conduct this campaign? You still believe we should kill as many as we can?" Carson paused, watching the reaction of the general, knowing that his orders during the round-up of the Mescalero Apache demanded that every warrior be killed on sight and capture only the women and children; an order that Carson amended by his actions of tempered battle.

"You know, Kit, when John Floyd was Secretary of War, his orders were to 'inspire the Indian with fear, by a few decisive blows for the destruction of life.' But the Navajo don't fight like the Apache, they don't go in for pitched battles. They'd rather steal the herds and kill only when it can't be avoided. They don't even take scalps, but you know that. No, I think Canby was on the right track. If we destroy their herds, flocks, crops, and keep after 'em, fight 'em when you can, but deprive them of the three vitals: subsistence, security, and sanctuary. And if that's done before winter and they must spend it cold and hungry, I think they'll be willing to come in peacefully."

"How many men?"

"You'll have a regiment of nine companies, six mounted, three foot, and there will be four more companies that will operate from Fort Wingate, under your command," answered the general, smiling at the numbers that he knew would impress Carson.

Carson didn't smile, but asked, "Scouts?"

"As many as you want. I assume you'll want Utes?"

"The way I'm thinkin' General, I'd like to have enough for a separate company of Utes. They're very brave, fine shots, excellent trackers, and energetic in the field. They've been the enemy of the Navajo long's anyone can remember, and I believe a hundred Utes would do more than double their number of troops."

"Then I'll forward that request to Washington right away. I don't foresee that being a problem. In the meantime, I assume you'll be staying at the usual place?"

"Yup, the boarding house next to Mama Ortega's! Best food in town!" declared Carson, licking his lips in anticipation. It had been a two-day journey from his ranch in Taos, and he had yet to check in with the boarding house, but he was all the more anxious to get to the eatery. It would be at least a couple of months before the companies were formed with both regulars and volunteers, some of the companies being all New Mexican Volunteers. The war in the east was still going strong, and it would be a long time before things could return to normal, if there was such a thing.

The men walked together to the covered boardwalk in front of the General's office. The long rambling covering hung loosely from the side of the adobe structure that sat on the corner of Washington Avenue and Paseo de Peralta, just off the Santa Fe Plaza. As they shook hands, Carleton said, "I'm mighty grateful for you coming down, Kit. This is not going to be a pleasant undertaking, but we can't allow this raiding and killing to continue. 'Course, you know that as well as I, you've lived here in the territory with your family for several years now. By the way, I understand you and Josefa had another young'un, that right?"

Carson grinned, pulling his uniform coat back to put his thumbs in the belt loops, and pridefully answered, "Number six! And if she has her way, there'll be more!"

"Then you need to keep up your strength! Tell Mama Ortega to fix you the Ranchero Filete! That'll fill you up proper!"

"I'll do it!" answered Carson, stepping off the boardwalk to cross the street and go to the boarding house. He looked at the sky, lanced with color from the setting sun, and pulled the coat around him and ducked his chin into the warmth, thinking to himself he was looking forward to spring but not summer.

CHAPTER TWO
JOURNEY

THE TWO WOLVES LOPED ALONGSIDE ONE ANOTHER, PLAYFULLY bumping shoulders as they ran, tongues lolling, with an occasional look behind them to ensure the others were following. Their 'pack' had two men, three women, and seven horses, two carrying full panniers and additional parfleches. It was a typical wilderness family, with Tate Saint and his redheaded wife, Maggie, in the lead, followed by their son, Sean and his wife, White Fox, and their daughter, Sadie.

It had been a long time since the entire family was together, with Tate scouting for Kit Carson in Mescalero Apache country, Maggie and Sadie in St. Louis for Sadie's education, and Sean scouting for Fort Laramie among the Sioux where he found his new wife, White Fox. But now they were together and bound for Santa Fe to reunite White Fox with her childhood parents, a couple that ran a trading post in the busy town of Santa Fe and had lost their daughter to a Comanche raid when she was about five years old.

They rode up and down across the ridges and gullies that pointed the way to the small settlement and civilization outpost,

South Pass Station. So-called because it was a stage station and telegraph post. It was a familiar face that greeted the group. The trader, Wooster, stood in the doorway, watching his visitors' approach and his broad smile told of his recognition. He lifted a calloused hand in a wave, motioning for them to step down. "Howdy, Sean, White Fox, and I see you brung yore family! Welcome ladies!"

Sean grinned at the man, "Howdy Wooster," and motioning to Tate, "This here's muh pa, Tate Saint."

Tate, having already stepped down, stretched his hand out to shake, "Good to meet'cha, Wooster."

The men shook hands, and Wooster asked, "To what do I owe the pleasure of this visit? Needin' supplies are'ya?"

"We could use a few, and Sean tells me the ladies were thinkin' 'bout your spare cabin, still empty?" asked Tate.

"No, sorry. We had a couple spend the winter with us, and I think they decided to stay on, they're in that cabin for now. But I reckon they'll be buildin' one o' their own, soon 'nuff. Their family's growin' and they need a little more room, if'n ya' know what I mean," chuckled the trader. He turned away, and with a wave over his shoulder, he muttered, "C'mon in an' sit a spell, got the coffee pot on, an' I think I might have a letter fer someone, round'chere some'ers."

Tate and Sean motioned the ladies to the door as they tied off the horses at the hitchrails and loosened the girths. They soon followed the ladies and were surprised to see them gathered around the only table, chattering, as Sadie slipped open the letter.

With a broad smile, she looked at the others, "It's from Lieutenant Whitcomb!" she declared and set about reading the letter. The other ladies grinned and sat back, watching Sadie read, smile, giggle, and read some more. Although anxious to hear what it was all about, they gave her the privacy needed and waited for her to share.

Her facial expression sobered, then looked to her father, "Where is Fort Marcy?"

"Fort Marcy? Why would you want to know about that?"

"Father!" she reprimanded her pa with a stern expression as he grinned at her. "Where is it? Josiah is being transferred there, and he won't be able to come see me, er, us."

"Fort Marcy, uh, let me think. Let's see, there's Fort Union, up there along the Santa Fe trail, an' there's Fort Sumner, where they sent the Apache. And the new fort they're buldin', Fort Wingate, an' Fort Stanton down south a ways. Humm, Fort Marcy, now, it seems like I heard of it, but where is it?" he cupped his chin as he considered and pondered. He peeked at Sadie and Maggie, tried to stifle a grin, then added, "Ya know, I think I do know where Fort Marcy is, by Jove, I do!"

"Father!" pouted Sadie, looking at the grin on Tate's face. Then looking at her ma, "Mother! Tell him to tell me!" she whined.

Tate chuckled, looking at Sean and White Fox laughing, then he answered, "If it's the one I'm thinkin' of, course they change the names of 'em all the time, but I think it's there at Santa Fe!"

Sadie sucked in a deep breath, lifting her shoulders and smiling, "That's where Josiah is going to be!"

"Who's Josiah?" asked Tate, frowning.

"That's the lieutenant she took care of when we came out and stopped at Fort Laramie," explained Maggie.

"Yeah, he's the one that she nursed all the while and pouted ever since she had to leave him behind! He was s'posed to come see her!" added Sean, grinning at his sister.

"Since we are going to Santa Fe to meet my family, you will get to see your lieutenant!" suggested White Fox, smiling at her new sister.

"Oh, you! The whole bunch of you are incorrigible!" she declared and stood to march out of the post, letter in hand.

White Fox started to follow, but Maggie said, "Let her be, she just wants to be alone to devour the news in the letter. I'm sure he probably said more than just that he's being transferred."

Wooster poured coffee all around, and Tate followed him to the counter to list the supplies they needed. As the man gathered things up and placed them on the plank, Tate asked, "Any news about Indians to the south of us?"

"Haven't heard a thing. The stagecoach just started runnin' again, after the snow began to clear, an' the driver tol' 'bout seein' some a couple days back, but nothin' recent. But far's south is concerned, ain't had no travelers comin' through yet. Prob'ly be a while 'fore any wagon trains reach this far, but soon, I reckon." Wooster placed the last of the supplies down, began tallying up the total and asked, "Goin' south, are ye?"

"Yup, for a spell anyway," answered Tate, seeing no reason to speak of their destination of Santa Fe, but knowing Wooster might have overheard Sadie and the group speak about Fort Marcy.

They made their camp just below the cabins on the banks of the Sweetwater River, and just before the ladies finished fixing supper, Tate and Sean returned with a fat mule deer to add to their larder for the trip. It was going to be a long one, more than three weeks of travel, and they knew it to be best to take game when it was easily had, for the further south where it was dry, game was not nearly as plentiful.

EVEN THE COOL of spring retreated from the hot sun across the Great Divide Basin. With the last water being the Sweetwater River, it was just shy of five days travel to the next, at the North

Platte. With the heat willing to take more than its toll, Tate wisely chose to travel by the light of the moon. Maggie delighted in the return of night travel; she loved the lullabies of the lonesome coyotes, the cicadas, the occasional questions from the burrowing owls, and the seldom heard nighthawk. The desert was different at night, and the shadowy figures of sagebrush, grease wood, and rabbitbrush contrasted with the skeletal forms of the cholla. A random jackrabbit spooked at the travelers, and it took a while for the horses to accustom themselves to being the visitors in this wasteland. Yet even they preferred the starlight to the stark hot sun of the day.

Their third night of travel from South Pass Station brought the distant forms of the Medicine Bow Mountains into silhouette on the southern point of their trail. Another two nights brought them into the cooler timber of the Medicine Bow and they chose to take a day's rest and replenish their larder of meat. White Fox and Sadie had become quite close, and when they volunteered to do the hunt, Tate and Sean leaned back on the grey log by the small fire and nodded their agreement with a grin. Tate looked to Sean, chuckled and said, "Looks like you're gettin' her trained right!"

"More like she's trainin' me! Now watch, they'll come back with either a deer or maybe even an elk, but we'll be the ones that have to do the butcherin' and such," commented Sean, locking his fingers behind his head and looking to his pa with a grin.

In less than an hour, the two hunters rode back into camp, seemingly empty-handed, but grinning. White Fox was the first to the ground and walked to Sean, "We knew you men needed a job so we left the elk there," nodding towards their back-trail, "and thought you big strong men would be happy to fetch it back for us, while we women help Ma with supper," she said coyly, smiling. Tate looked to a grinning Sean, and they both rose and mounted up, smiling at the ladies as they reined around to go after the downed elk, leaving Lobo and Indy in camp with the women.

In a short while, both horses stutter-stepped, heads up and ears forward, and began to side-step away from the trail. Tate and Sean both grabbed for their rifles as they dismounted, loosely tying the horses to a clump of sage. They heard a ruckus coming from the tree line, Tate spoke softly, "Sounds like a bear got to the elk 'fore we did!" He motioned for Sean to move to the right, and he took the left, both men stealthily approaching. Once the clearing allowed, they saw the big hump of a monstrous silver-tip boar grizzly, nose and jowls buried in the guts of the elk. He suddenly jerked back, both front feet on the ribcage of the elk, blood dripping from his jaws as he jerked his head side-to-side, searching for anything approaching. Sean and Tate froze in their tracks, partially hidden by the thin trees at the edge of the clearing. The big bruin rose to his hind feet and let a growl come that mimicked a crashing avalanche tearing out trees as it cascaded. The roar echoed back from across the wide valley as the beast pawed at the air, threatening any and all that would dare interrupt his meal.

He dropped to all fours, and with one last look around, buried his face in the bloody gore, lapping up blood and guts as his main appetizer. Tate caught Sean's eye and motioned for the two of them to back out and away and began to slowly move, backstepping all the way until the trees gave sufficient cover. He turned and trotted back, arriving at the horses just before Sean, and both were laughing, Tate spoke first, "I'm wonderin' if those two didn't already know that ol' silver-tip was on that elk, you?"

"You're prob'ly right. That sounds like somethin' either one of them'd do," agreed Sean, mounting his Appaloosa. Tate swung aboard Shady, and the men headed back to camp, chuckling at what they would say. As they stripped the gear from their horses, they caught the giggling girls at the fire looking their way, and they readied themselves for whatever the women had conjured up.

Maggie looked at the fearsome duo, held her hands palms up at her sides and with uplifted shoulders, asked, "Well, where's the meat?"

Tate and Sean, somber expressions both, ambled over to the log, took a seat and Tate said, "You girls musta not hit it like you thought. We saw some blood, but . . ." and shrugged his shoulders in response.

White Fox said, "What was that noise we heard, sounded like somethin' growlin'?"

Sean looked to Tate, back at the ladies, "Musta been our hungry stomachs! What's for supper?"

CHAPTER THREE
VISIT

THEY PUSHED SOUTH, STAYING IN THE FOOTHILLS AND PARKS between mountain ranges, took another elk they didn't have to fight a grizzly for, and enjoyed the springtime ride in the Rockies. The towering, granite-topped peaks were still shrouded in their winter-white blankets, but the lower realms were decked with patches of flowers. White Fox, although raised in the hills of Sioux country, gazed at the mountains that scratched the blue of the skies which were a delight to her less experienced eyes. But this was all familiar country to the Saint family, and everyone enjoyed the journey.

Most of the early blooming flowers that put on their show in the spring were white blossomed, chickweed, and yarrow, but occasionally the Creator chose to scatter some purplish shooting star clusters that hung their humble heads with a dark snout. Some Indian Paintbrush were trying to bust out of their buds but still struggled in the cool nights that kept them captive. Maggie reveled in the multitude of colors, happy to point them out and call their names for the continued education of Sadie and Sean. Most of the flowers were new to White Fox, but she recognized the yellow patches of Wallflower and Golden Pea and called them by their names in the Brule Sioux language.

Maggie's spirits were heightened when she began to recognize mountains and valleys she explored on her inaugural trip to the Rockies, and when she looked questioningly at Tate, he just grinned and waited for her to guess where they were going. "Are we . . .?" she began as he twisted around in his saddle to look at her with his mischievous grin.

"Are we what?" he answered.

"You know what, we're going to see my father, aren't we?" she said with a broad smile, trying to lean closer, wanting to kiss him. He gladly met her half-way between the horses, and they had a bouncing embrace.

"Hey! What are you two doing up there?" came a shout from Sean, riding beside White Fox, at the tail of the group.

Maggie twisted around and shouted back, "We're going to stop and see your grandfather!"

Sadie, riding directly behind Maggie, called out, "Really? And Little Otter too?"

"Of course, we can't very well see him without seeing his wife too!" answered Maggie.

Sean had turned to explain all about Maggie's father, Michael Patrick O'Shaunessey, who had come west searching for gold and Maggie came to find him. "When Pa was asked by Kit Carson to guide her into the mountains to search for her father, Pa thought both Kit and Ma had lost their minds; to try and find one man somewhere in the Rocky Mountains! But, of course, they did, and Pa and Ma ended up married, and Grandpa married a Ute woman, Little Otter, the same time!"

"Where will we find them?" asked White Fox.

"The last we knew, they were living with a band of the Yamparika Ute in Bayou Salado, but they could be 'bout anywhere,

I reckon. The band's summer encampment is in the south end of the Bayou, but as you know, the different bands don't always camp in the same place."

They bore southeast and crossed over a cut in the mountains, to sit on a shoulder of the hillside overlooking Bayou Salado, the fertile wide valley that held creeks, salt flats, wide meadows, lakes, and more. It was a breath-taking sight surrounded by mountains with the granite peaks behind and directly south, and rugged foothills on the eastern edge and to the south. Tate pointed out a ragged ridge below and farther into the valley, "That always made me think of the pictures I saw of them crocodiles or alligators. Don't it look like a giant one o' them, with the ridges showin'?"

Maggie shaded her eyes to see, then nodded her head, "Yeah, I s'pose, but it's a mighty big one!"

Tate chuckled and gigged Shady to move off the shoulder and through the aspen, just budding out, below them. When they cleared the trees, Tate turned directly south to round the knob of foothill coming from the shoulder of the line of mountains they had kept off to their right as they made it through the cut. But now he wanted to ride the tree line, watching for any sign of the Yamparika camp. When the group was strung out, rocking to the ambling gait of the horses, Tate suddenly reined up, holding his hand to the side for the others to stop. He looked to the sky off his right and above a long, tree-covered draw coming from high up the mountains. A big golden eagle had begun his descent, probably after a rabbit or something, but suddenly veered off and winged it away.

"Something spooked that eagle," spoke Tate, softly, watching. Three magpies squawked and took flight, prompting Tate to lead the others into the trees. Once hidden, he motioned Sean forward, "Something or someone's got those birds spooked. You move up through there," pointing to the thinning spruce and pine, "I'll swing around this away," pointing to the lower end of the narrow valley.

Sean nodded, motioned Indy to his side, and soon disappeared into the trees. Tate, with Lobo, picked their way toward the draw. Within just a few moments, Tate had crossed the trail of four horses, moving upstream of the Tarryall Creek and into the thicker timber. He began to follow when he heard the trill of a meadowlark, their agreed-upon signal to get together. He turned back to the trees and worked his way toward the sound of the mountain bird. Sean was crouched down behind a big ponderosa, Indy lying beside him. As Tate neared, Sean grinned, "It's some old prospector with an Indian wife. I think he's settin' up camp, probably to do some gold panning."

Tate suspected more than Sean said as he looked at his grinning son, then asked, "Anyone we know?"

"He does look kinda familiar, but it's been a long time," answered the younger man, displaying some of his inherited mischievousness.

Tate nodded his head and turned to walk back to the waiting women, Indy and Lobo trotting ahead. When they came to the horses, both Sean and Tate mounted up without saying anything, but Maggie said, "Well?"

Tate nodded to Sean and he repeated about a prospector, trying to keep a straight face. Then added, "But, maybe you women would like to check it out, just in case."

"In case what?" asked an exasperated Maggie.

"I got a better idea, how 'bout we send Sadie and White Fox? They could say they're lost and need help or somethin' and maybe get some of the old man's gold!" suggested Tate.

Sean chuckled, "Good idea! We could always use some gold!"

Maggie had caught on to the pranksters and slapped Tate on his arm, "It's my father, isn't it?!"

"Well, don't you think sending Sadie and White Fox would be a good idea? Just for fun?" he answered.

Maggie turned to Sadie, "It's your grandfather and Little Otter! These characters think you and White Fox should go into his camp and pretend to be lost or something. See what he does."

Sadie looked to White Fox, grinning, and she nodded back. The two nudged their horses past the others and started for the prospector's camp. As they neared, Sadie called out, "Hello the camp! Can we come in?"

After a short pause, a raspy voice answered, "Come in if your peaceable!"

As soon as the two women appeared, the old man looked, cocked his head to the side, began to grin and drawled, "Sadie, me girl. Step down an' give your Gran'pappy a big hug!" As a smiling Sadie scampered down and started for her waiting embrace, he asked, "An' where's the rest of 'em? Up to no good, I 'spect!"

The others had heard the response and moved out of the trees for the joyful reunion. After the introductions were made for the newest member of the family, White Fox, the men took the horses to strip the gear and picket them near some grass while the women chattered on with Grandpa and Little Otter.

It was a good visit, but all too short as far as the women were concerned. They had only taken a two-day break from their travel, but it was an enjoyable time together. Maggie was concerned, as all children are, at the way her father had aged. Always a big healthy man, he had slowed a little in his movements, added some grey to his hair and beard, but lacked nothing in his wit and humor. It was obvious he was happy with Little Otter and she with him her maturity showing as her hair had gained mature streaks of white as did his. They always seemed to be touching one another. As a wedding gift to Sean, he had stuck a pouch of placer gold in his saddlebags that weighed all of five pounds and would fetch a goodly sum in trade. When Sean tried to refuse, he argued, "I ain't been any place to spend it since I been here. You're the only white men we've seen! Take it and be happy!" he insisted.

Grandpa had explained the Ute had moved their summer camp farther upstream on the Arkansas, well away from the direction of travel for the family. Tate took the Trout Creek Pass out of the park and crossed the Arkansas River before turning south again, pointing toward the San Luis Valley and the backside of the Sangre de Cristo Mountains. Maggie asked, "We gonna stay in our cabin on this trip?"

"Maybe. When I came through last time, there was a family there, but they said they were moving on, so, if it's empty, we'll stop in for a while."

"That'd be nice. I love that place," she added, wistfully.

"Ummhumm, lotta memories," answered Tate, leaning on the pommel of his saddle, looking at his redhead, grinning.

"Oh you!" she answered with a playful slap at his arm.

CHAPTER FOUR
TAOS

Kit had been away from home for two months and was anxious to get back to his family. Even though his chest pains refused to slacken, he chose to make the two-day trip back to Taos. With the recruiting and assembling of the troops well-in-hand, at both Fort Marcy and the new Fort Wingate, he knew he could take a few days with his family before the warm weather dictated his campaign against the Navajo. He was tired as he rode up to their adobe house sitting among the trees, but it was a welcome sight to see his beloved Josefa waiting on the long veranda, anxious for his return with their youngest, Rebecca, sleeping in her arms.

On the long porch, Kit Junior and Teresina played tiddlywinks while Julian stood, leaning against a post, watching the younger ones play. When Josefa spotted her husband, she stood and waved, causing Julian to turn and jump off the porch to run and greet his returning father. Everyone swarmed around Kit, hugging and talking all at the same time, "Whoa, hold on here!" he protested, and stepped towards Josefa, taking her in his arms and hugging both her and the baby. He stepped back, pulled the blanket away from the infant's face, smiled, and looked at his petite wife, "Sure is a good thing she looks like you!" he declared, chuckling.

Charles was busy in the barn with chores and missed the arrival of his father but heard the commotion and met him at the door of the barn, "Hi Pa!" extending his hand for a man's handshake, which Kit knocked aside to wrap his arms around his oldest son, "You ain't too big for a hug!"

"Gonna be home long?" asked Charles.

"Long enough," answered Kit, anticipating what the boy wanted.

"So, we can shoot a little?" asked the anxious youngster.

"Sure, we'll work it out, long's you do your chores!" he admonished.

"Great!" declared Charles, leading Kit's horse to the stall to strip the gear.

Kit started to turn, then spoke up, "Don't forget to rub him down and give him some grain!"

"I know, I know. Don't I always?" answered Charles, starting to loosen the girth.

JOSEFA HAD ALREADY COMMANDEERED Kit Jr., age six, and Teresina, age nine, to help in the kitchen. She placed Rebecca in the cradle near the settee in the main room and sat beside her, as the two Navajo maids, Nascha and Ooljee, started with the dinner preparations. Kit's favorite chair was a barrel-backed armchair that sat next to Josefa's settee, and the two sat beside one another to catch up on the latest developments in Kit's new assignment.

"So, General Carleton expects you to quell this Navajo war that has been going on for almost a century in just a few months?" she asked, eyebrows lifted and eyes wide, feigning innocence. But she had experienced the continual fighting between the Mexicans and

Navajo most of her life as a life-long resident of what was now called New Mexico Territory. Even before the land was taken in the recent war with Mexico, the same problems prevailed.

Kit looked at his wife with a slow smile, "No, there's no timetable, and at least this time he's given me enough men to get the job done. We'll have between seven and eight hundred men and he's allowed me to recruit a whole company of Utes, not just to guide but to fight as well. I've met several of the officers, and there's some good men in the bunch. Of course, there'll be a lot of New Mexico Volunteers, but with the right officers, I think they'll do well. As a matter of fact, my second in command is Lieutenant Colonel Francisco Chaves. You've heard me mention him before, he was at Valverde."

"Is Kaniache going to scout for you again?" she asked.

"I've sent word for him and asked him to recruit some more Ute to fight with us, I'm confident he'll be here soon, hopefully with enough fighting men."

"And Tate?"

"I dunno if he'll respond. I sent a telegram to South Pass Station, but . . ." he shrugged his shoulders. "There's no way of tellin' for sure, he's not too interested in leavin' home. Can't say's I blame him though, if I hadn't signed up under Carleton, I wouldn't be doin' it either."

"You've been friends a long time. I don't think he would say no to you," she replied, absent-mindedly reaching over to rock the cradle as the baby stirred.

Kit looked at his wife, smiled, and asked, "So, how're the kids doin' in school? They don't talk about it much when I'm home."

"Well, Charles thinks he's getting too old and wants to not go anymore, but Julian and Teresina seem to get along well enough. Of course, Kit Jr., well, it's hard for him to sit still, but he learns quickly. I'm happy with their learning."

"Good, good!" he proclaimed, leaning forward, "I think dinner may be ready from the sound of things." He stood, offered Josefa his hand, and they walked into the dining room, leaving the baby to rest quietly in the crib.

KIT AND JOSEFA sat on the veranda, sipping their champurrado, enjoying the cool of the evening when several riders came into view before the house. Kit scowled, the lead rider looking familiar, then smiled and stood as he recognized his friend. "Tate! Welcome, my friend! And you've brought your family! Great!" As the others neared, both Kit and Josefa stepped from the veranda to greet their friends. Josefa had met Tate, but now she was especially pleased to see the women, for she had long wanted to meet Tate's family.

She smiled as she walked to the side of Maggie's horse, extended her hand, but Maggie was quick to step down and stretch her arms wide to embrace the smaller woman, "Josefa! I've heard my husband talk about you! It's so good to finally meet you!" she declared as the two hugged. Maggie stepped back to introduce White Fox and Sadie, and Josefa welcomed them with a hug and encouraged the ladies to join her on the veranda. When they were seated, Naascha offered each one a cup of champurrado which they each accepted, as the men took the horses to the barn.

"Mmmm, this is wonderful!" said Maggie as she leaned back in the chair, holding the cup close to feel the warmth and enjoy the aroma.

"I've never had this, what did she say this was called?" asked Sadie, looking to Josefa.

"Champurrado, it is a very old drink made with masa de maiz, water, and spices. It is a customary holiday drink, but we enjoy it whenever we can," explained Josefa.

The ladies continued their get-acquainted conversation as the men tended to the animals in the barn. While Sean helped the oldest boy, Charles, with rubbing down the horses and giving them grain, Tate and Carson stood leaning on the fence rail. "So, I didn't think I would see you so soon! You must have gotten my telegram!"

"Telegram? I didn't get a telegram. Musta come after we passed through South Pass Station. What did you send me one o' them for?" asked Tate, with a glance from the corner of his eye, knowing his friend, suspecting the worst.

"Carleton didn't accept my resignation and talked me into helpin' him clean up the mess Canby left behind with the Navajo," he drawled, watching for Tate's reaction.

Tate dropped his head, shaking it side to side, then looked up at Kit, "And you want me to join you on the campaign, was that what the telegram was about?"

"Ummmhumm. Only there's a lot more Navajo than them Mescalero we rounded up. But, the Mexicans and the Navajo have been fightin' each other for decades, and of late, it's gotten worse. What with all the troops sent back east and the attention of the rest bein' on the Apache, the *Diné* have kinda had a free run. This last year," he paused and shook his head as he thought about all the raiding that had been going on, "has been the worst. Carleton gave me a bunch of numbers 'bout how many people killed, stock stolen, and such. Makes what the Apache were doin' seem like child's play, 'ceptin' the Navajo ain't as cruel and bloody as the 'Pache.

"The Mex are better at takin' captives, they make slaves out of 'em, and the *Diné* are more prone to take stock. But they take captives too. There's even a whole band of Navajo they call the Mexican Band, cuz most of 'em were captives and raised like Indians."

"So, ever'body back east is fightin' a war 'bout slavery, and here it's goin' on and has been for decades?" asked Tate.

"That's right. There's some o' the Mex that take orders for slaves, some folks want a certain type to work in their house an' such, then they go take 'em an' sell 'em."

Tate looked at the man, scowled, "Are those women in your house slaves?"

"No. They were captives, but when we got 'em, they didn't want to go back to the tribe. They said they had it better here and didn't ever wanna go back. They're free as you an' I, and we pay 'em for what they do, give 'em a place to live an' such, but they don't wanna go back. One fella said he thought there were some'eres around fifteen hundred, two thousand, just like 'em. But I think it's more like five or six thousand throughout the whole territory. But it's 'bout the same with captive Mexicans."

"So, what does Carleton say about the Navajo? Same as the Mescalero?"

"No, no, he's tried already to make peace, but won't know for a while if they take him up on it. He gave 'em a deadline of July. But he wants 'em rounded up and taken to Bosque Redondo."

"With the Apache? Ain't they enemies?" exclaimed Tate, surprised.

"Yeah, but he thinks they need to learn to live together. Thinks they can learn from each other."

"Well, one thing for sure, he ain't much smarter now than he was a year ago," mused Tate. He looked around, thinking, then turned back to Kit, "We came down to go to Santa Fe. Remember those two kids I left with the trader an' his wife?"

"Yeah, the ones that came from the wagon train?"

"That's right. Well, the family I left 'em with, they lost a daughter several years ago to a Comanche raid. Come to find out, that girl was taken from the Comanche by the Sioux, and when

Sean was scoutin' for Laramie, he met up with her and married her!"

Kit scowled, "You mean to say, Sean's wife," pointing toward the house, "is the girl taken from the trader by the Comanche?"

"Yup, same one!"

CHAPTER FIVE
RIO GRANDE

THE RISING SUN PAINTED THE BACKS OF THE RIDERS IN THE SAINT caravan, well on their way to Santa Fe. Leaving Taos, they bore to the southwest, staying on the high bank of the stream that came from the Taos Pueblo. Carson told Tate this was sometimes called the Low Road to Taos, as it followed the east bank of the Rio Grande instead of fighting the rugged trails of the mountains and foothills. With spring coming on, the weather was cool and the scenery colorful. The dark timber of the hillsides contrasted with green meadows filled with early blooming flowers.

Maggie enjoyed the ride through new country and made it a point to take it all in, but occasionally grew contemplative and quiet. When Tate noticed her pensive mood, he asked, "So, what's going on in that beautiful, red head with the glassy-eyed stare?"

Maggie looked to her man, smiling, and her laughter tinkled like tiny glass bells, or at least, that's what Tate thought. "Oh, just remembering our time at the cabin in the Sangres. I could have spent the entire summer there and been quite happy! But I was hoping to see White Feather. Have you heard anything about her or her people?"

"No, nothing in a long while. Maybe on our way back we can try to find them. It would be good to see her and her people." Just the mention of Feather's name brought a flood of memories pouring into Tate's consciousness. White Feather had become his friend when he helped her people, the Comanche, after the plague of smallpox hit their village. They had been friends for many years and early on, if she hadn't surrendered to the need of her village to become the shaman, they might have been married.

"When we left that cabin, it was cuz o' the Jicarilla, Ute, and Comanche all gettin' restless with the many settlers comin' through. But now, it's like that most ever'where. So, would you rather we live in the Sangre de Cristos or the Wind River Mountains?" asked Tate, grinning at Maggie, knowing that was a question she had asked herself several times before. Before she answered, he added, "Or would you prefer goin' back to St. Louis?"

"Oh no! Not St. Louis! I've had enough of the city. At least in the mountains, it's a little easier to tell who your friends are, most of the time, anyway," she declared.

"I agree with you, Mother!" came the unsolicited answer from behind them as Sadie leaned on her pommel to join the conversation.

Maggie twisted around in her saddle, "Really? I thought you liked the city!"

"Well, I did, at first anyway. And I enjoyed the school and learning, but the city is just too, well, noisy!" she answered.

Tate grinned as he listened, happy to hear his girls showing a preference for the mountain life. It had been a lonely time when they were gone, and he much preferred the time together with all his family. He looked back to Sean as he was leaning over to get close to White Fox, sharing their own intimate conversation.

The rattle of distant gunfire interrupted the family conversations, and Tate reined up to stand in his stirrups and shade his eyes to look toward the mouth of the Rio Grande canyon. With the sounds ratcheting off the canyon walls, it was difficult to tell where they originated, but Tate would take no chances. He pointed to an arroyo that cut the canyon wall and directed the group into the protection of the narrow gorge. "Sean, get everyone under cover, I'm goin' down to see what's happening!"

A simple wave of his hand and Lobo took off in the direction of the shooting, followed closely by Shady at a canter. As he came to the wide mouth of the canyon, Tate drew up to the side near a small cluster of gnarled cedar, and stepped to the ground, rifle in hand. With a loose wrap of the rein on a branch, he dropped to one knee at the edge of the trees to search the valley before him.

A Navajo raiding party of at least twenty warriors had attacked a small farm, leaving the barn and house burning. They drove off a small herd of sheep and goats, a handful of cattle, and several horses and donkeys. The fighting was over, and the smoke and dust from the melee made it difficult to see. Some of the horses were riding double, but Tate could not tell if they were carrying their wounded or captives. He watched as they went to the river crossing and skillfully moved the animals across with riders on both upstream and downstream sides. The sheep needed more prompting than the others, but they were sandwiched between the cattle and raiders and were soon across. Tate looked back to the buildings for any sign of life but seeing none he remounted and returned to the others.

"It was a raid on a small farm by some Navajos. It was all over by the time I got there so I didn't go any closer. We'll check it out before we find a place to camp for the night." Everyone mounted up and followed Tate back to the farm. As they neared, the stench of burning flesh and more filled the air, prompting everyone to cover their noses and mouths with whatever they had handy. "Sean, check around the barn. You women check by those other buildings, but be careful, if there's anybody left, make sure they know you're friendly!"

As the group scattered to survey the farm, Tate went to the remains of the adobe house. The roof had collapsed with the timbers still smoldering, the door hung by one leather hinge, the single window had been smashed and flames had licked the outside wall giving a gruesome grin with a black smirk emanating from the door and window. Tate stepped down, ground hitched Shady, and walked with Lobo at his side around the structure. At the rear door, a frail figure of a man with blackened linen britches and top, singed hair and bloody neck and face, was sprawled in the dirt, having crawled from the burning house.

Lobo paused, a low growl coming from deep in his chest as he bared his teeth and looked at the man. Tate dropped a hand to his neck and spoke softly, "Easy boy, easy." He slowly approached the still figure, dropped to one knee beside him and put a hand gently on a shoulder. "Can you speak?" he asked, but there was no response. Tate felt the figure, still warm, but whether from life or flames, it was hard to tell. Then the slight rise of a shoulder told of life. Tate put a hand to the side of the man's neck to feel for any pulse, although it was too faint, but another breath again showed life.

As he gently rolled the man over on his back, Maggie and White Fox approached, "Is he alive?" asked Maggie, quickening her pace.

"Barely, but he's hurt pretty bad," replied Tate, seeing a wound on the man's upper chest as well as the side of his head. Maggie knelt beside her husband, reached out to touch the farmer's face, saw the flutter of an eyelid, then looked up at Tate, "We need to get him where we can help him."

. . .

WHENEVER POSSIBLE, Tate always took to the high ground. A long flat-top mesa overlooked the mouth of the Rio Grande, and a shoulder just below the rimrock beckoned as a place for their camp. With ample shelter from a slight overhang, a smattering of juniper and piñon, plenty of dry wood for a fire, and a grassy basin to hide and feed the animals; it was just what he ordered. Maggie had yielded to White Fox and Sadie to fix the meal while she tended to the injured farmer. He had yet to regain consciousness, but with his wounds cleaned and bandaged, Maggie was optimistic as to his recovery.

It was the smell of hot food that stirred the man to wakefulness, and his moans brought Maggie and Tate to his side. He moved his head side to side, eyes wide and fearful, looking from Maggie to Tate, and he asked, "Isabella?!" He grew more frantic, "Francesca?!" he cried as he tried to sit up, but Maggie held him down.

Tate said, "There is no one but you, señor."

He struggled again, "¿Donde?" he asked, looking around, searching for anything familiar.

Tate pointed to the valley below, "Your farm's down there, but everything's gone or burned."

The man fell back, looked to Tate with wide eyes, and held out his hands questioning, "¿Mi familia?"

Tate dropped his head, shaking it side to side, then looked at the man as he let tears fill his eyes and begin to chase one another down the side of his face. Tate turned away and went back to the fire, motioning for Maggie to join him and let the man have his solitude to mourn.

When morning came, the man had roused himself and was sitting up, legs crossed, and watching the others at the fire when Tate came down from atop the mesa for his prayer time and usual survey of the countryside. He walked to the farmer and squatted down nearby, "How ya doin' today?" he asked, hoping the man could understand more than he did the night before.

"I am better, but I must find my family señor. The Navajos, they were too many. I thought I was dead!" he held his hand to the wound on his head. "My son, Miguel, died in the house and burned. They took my wife, Isabella, and my little girl, Francesca. I saw them ride away with them." He dropped his head, shaking it side to side, then looked up to Tate, "Can you get them for me, señor?"

Tate lowered his eyes and answered, "They are long gone, I'm afraid. There were probably twenty or thirty Navajo, and they took all your stock as well."

"It was that diablo, Nesjaja Hatali, he led them here before. They killed my brother and took his family. We have lived here all my life!" he exclaimed, hands to his side and shrugging his shoulders. "Now, I have nothing!"

Maggie had come near and said softly, "You have your life! You can start over."

WHEN THEY RETURNED to his farm, Mateo Santiago found the chicken coop was untouched, and his many chickens had also been left unharmed. Everything else was destroyed, though the walls of the adobe house still stood. As he looked around, he began to see what it could yet be, and he thanked Tate and his family for their help.

"Gracias, señor. I can do nothing but start over. I have no other place to go, and my family has been here for three generations," expressed Mateo. He smiled at Maggie as she handed him a sack of supplies to tide him over for at least a few days. "Gracias," he added, nodding to her.

"We will pray for you Mateo, and when we come back, we

expect to see you doing well," she admonished. Again, he nodded and smiled, then shook Tate's hand as he prepared to mount. "If you are to help Colonel Carson, and he needs more volunteers, I will come."

Tate had briefly explained to Mateo about what Carson had been tasked to do, trying to give the man a little hope about his family. He now answered, "I will tell him, Mateo. But in the meantime, you get this place back in shape just in case we can get your family back, understand?"

"Si, señor."

They parted with a wave, and Tate and family pointed their mounts to the south to turn from the Rio Grande and make their way to Santa Fe. But first they would pass through San Juan de los Caballeros, the historic capital of Nuevo México, and Carson had told of a place that had exceptional carrillada, and Maggie was convinced they had to stop for their midday meal before going on to Santa Fe. And Tate was not of a mind to disappoint his redhead.

CHAPTER SIX
SANTA FE

"Well, certainly, we have room for you and your family! I would love to have you join us. Will you be staying long?" asked the widow Wannamaker, looking Tate and family up and down.

Tate grinned and answered, "That depends, Mrs. Wannamaker, we might stay in Santa Fe longer. Would you know of a house we might use?"

The widow focused all her attention on the tall, lean man before her, "Weren't you here before? With Colonel Carson, wasn't it?"

"Yes ma'am, for a short while until we went into the field," he answered. "Do you? Know of a house, I mean?"

"As a matter of fact, I do, and it's a lovely home. It was my home before my husband, and I bought this," she motioned behind her to the large boarding house. "If you would prefer, I could let you have that for your family. That is, if it's more than a few days."

"That would be just grand, Mrs. Wannamaker. That way we won't be putting you out any here, and with more soldiers coming in, you'll have more room."

"More? More soldiers coming in, here to Santa Fe?" inquired the matronly woman, standing back with hands on her hips and eyebrows raised.

"Yes'm, from what the Colonel tells me, there will be quite a few," explained Tate, grinning at the greed showing in the widow's eyes.

It took just a short while for the widow to show her guests to their new accommodations and to quickly leave to return to her duties at the Inn. Maggie looked around, smiled, and said, "This will be very nice! Plenty of room for everyone and a nice kitchen, I love that stove!" she remarked, looking over her new domain.

"Well, while you all get settled in, I'll go to the trader and see how the youngsters are doing and kinda get the feel of things before we all drop in with White Fox."

"That's a good idea, although I'm anxious to meet them too and I know White Fox is quite excited as well, although she tries not to show it. I think she might be a little nervous about it too," suggested Maggie.

As Tate left the house, Maggie watched him as he walked down the walkway to the gate in the small picket fence, which looked even smaller next to her tall husband, and her shoulders lifted in a heavy sigh as she thought about what Carson would be expecting of Tate. She knew her man was loyal to a fault and would not disappoint his friend, but she wasn't anxious for him to be gone from her again.

The trader's store or post was on the south side of the plaza with a long, covered walkway in the front that shaded shoppers and tradesmen alike. Tate wrapped the rein around the hitchrail, patted Shady on the side of the neck, and stepped onto the boardwalk and into the store. At a glance, Tate saw two people were at the counter, talking with a female clerk, and another woman was fingering some cloth as she spoke with a male clerk. He stepped to a shelf of leather goods and bided his time as the other customers made their selections and paid for their goods. When the woman clerk came from behind the counter and approached Tate, she asked, "May I help you find something, sir?"

Tate turned to face her and asked, "Is Mr. or Mrs. Fraser around?"

The clerk smiled, "I'm Cherie Hobbs, their niece. My husband," motioning to the other clerk, "Scott, and I are tending the trading post while the Frasers are on their spring re-supply trip. We expect them back from Westport any day now. Is there something else I can help you with?"

Tate was surprised and disappointed to hear they were gone, but his curiosity bid, "Yes, did Ezra and Maribel go with them?"

The woman frowned, cocked her head to the side, and asked, "How do you know the children?"

"I'm the one that brought them to the Frasers. I just thought I'd check on 'em while I was in town."

She gave a smile of relief, "Yes, both the youngsters and my uncle and his wife were excited about them being able to make the trip back to the city."

Tate grinned and started to turn, then looked back at the younger woman, "I almost forgot, my wife gave me a list," he fumbled in his pocket a moment, "Here 'tis, if you'll fill that she'd be mighty pleased."

"Of course," replied Cherie, "I'll just be a moment."

Tate followed her to the counter, settled the bill and added, "If I'm still around when they come back, I'll check in on 'em. My family is with me, and they might stop in as well."

"That would be nice, and thank you, Mr. ?"

"Saint, Tate Saint, and my wife's name is Maggie. You won't

miss her, she's got a crown of red hair," he dropped his head as his face started to flush.

The clerk smiled, "I'll look forward to meeting her."

When Tate returned to the house with his armload of goods he shared the news about the Frasers, "So, I guess you'll be waitin' a spell for 'em to return."

"Oh, that's alright," answered Maggie, speaking to the rest, "we'll make the most of it. I'm sure there are some shops that might beckon," she looked to Sadie and White Fox, "right ladies?"

"So, Tate, my friend, can I count on you?" asked Carson. The two men sat on the veranda of Mrs. Wannamaker's boarding house, sipping their morning coffee. Tate and family had only arrived a day before Carson returned and he was quick to ask Tate to join him at the Inn.

"Well, Colonel, I ain't too anxious to get involved in another Indian war, but I can see how somethin' needs to be done. Like I told you about the Santiago place, it ain't right for either side to be takin' captives, breakin' up families an' such. There's just gettin' to be too blamed many people in the whole confounded territory!"

Carson chuckled, "I've thought that for several years now, but tryin' to stop all the settlers from comin' out west would be like tryin' to plug a beaver dam with your thumb! And the more people, the more problems."

"I think both of us are gettin' too old for this! But at least this time, my family is closer." spat Tate, shaking his head.

"Well, I ain't gonna admit to gettin' old, but it is gettin' harder to get around like we used to, that's for certain! Ain't never had so many aches an' pains!"

"So, how soon we headin' out?" asked Tate, emptying his cup and looking at Carson over the rim.

"Kaniache sent word he'd meet us on the way to Fort Wingate, prob'ly somewhere along the San Jose River. And the troops are garrisoned down at Los Lunas, so, it's just you'n me, an' a comp'ny from Fort Marcy. We'll go to Los Lunas, then head to Wingate. How's tomorrow sound?" asked Carson.

"Sooner we leave, sooner we get back." Tate stood, tossed the dregs of the coffee over the rail to the brush below, stretched, and went down the steps. Carson rose, watched Tate leave, then returned to the Inn. Both men knew what they faced, and neither was anxious for it to begin, but neither would shirk their responsibility.

"So, if you're going with Carson, are we to stay here in Santa Fe while you're gone?" asked Maggie, hiding her disappointment as she turned her head away and fidgeted with a button on her garment.

"I'd like it if you did. That way, I might get to come see you now'n again," answered Tate, hopefully.

Maggie smiled as she turned back to face her man, reaching her arms up and pulling his face to hers for a lingering kiss. When she leaned back, still smiling, "I was hoping you'd say that!"

Tate grinned, and pulled her close for another embrace, but was interrupted by Sean and White Fox. "So, you're goin' with Carson?" asked Sean.

"Yup, somebody's gotta keep him in line an' outta trouble," answered Tate, watching Sean and Fox seat themselves on a bench on the porch. Sadie stood in the doorway, listening and watching the others but stayed silent.

"That sounds like a full-time job. Does he need any more scouts?" asked Sean.

"No, he's got a bunch of Ute scouts comin' with Kaniache, but I tell you what you can do. You can watch out for your mother and sister, cuz I'm thinkin' keepin' them outta trouble will be harder than my job!"

Maggie playfully slapped him on the arm as she let a little giggle escape.

"But, there's somethin' else you and maybe you too, Fox, can do, and that's take a ride around the outside of town ever now'n then, kinda keep an eye on things. There won't be but a skeleton crew left at the fort, no patrols or anything, and the Navajo might see it as an opportunity to come sneakin' into town and raid the place."

Sean grinned, looked to Fox, and back to his pa, "So, while you an' all the troops are out in the hills chasin' after raidin' Navajo, an' they decide to storm the town, me'n Fox are supposed to fight off the whole Navajo nation?" He chuckled at the thought as he watched his pa's reaction.

With a wide grin, "What? You need reinforcements? Get'chur ma an' sister to help you!" suggested Tate.

Another playful slap from his wife, and he grabbed his arm in feigned pain. He laughed, as did the rest, then he added, "Well, problem is, many of the Mexicans have been raidin' the Navajo, and it's payback each time. That's why it keeps goin' on and on. But, yuh still need to be watchful anyway."

Sadie stepped from the doorway and looked to her pa, "Did you say the troops from Fort Marcy will be going with you?"

"Most of 'em, but there will be a few left behind to man the fort." Tate looked to his daughter and then to Maggie, who motioned with her eyes and eyebrows that there was more to her question. Tate remembered about Sadie's lieutenant, then with a slight nod to his wife, he turned to Sadie, "But maybe, you and your brother and Fox could go for a ride up by the fort and look things over. Nice afternoon for a ride, don't you think?"

Sadie let a broad smile split her face, and she practically hopped as she turned to her brother, "Want to?"

Sean and Fox leaned close and looked to one another, "Sure, sis, let's go!"

CHAPTER SEVEN
LOS LUNAS

"Carson, I've sent word again to Barboncito and his brother Delgadito. I told 'em to spread the word to other chiefs as well, that all the Navajos that say they have not murdered and robbed, that they were to come in and go to Basque Redondo. I told 'em we can't tell the good from the bad and any of those that don't come in, well, they will be treated as hostile and be dealt with accordingly. Their deadline is July twenty, after that the door will be closed and we'll start the round-up," declared General Carleton. He was intent on giving Carson his orders and was anxious for the man to get started. He believed the conflict had gone on long enough, and the people of New Mexico were tired of the continual raiding and killing.

"But General, I don't think the Navajo do very well at setting out dates on a calendar. What did Barboncito tell you after you gave him the deadline?" asked Carson, leaning back in the chair opposite the general's desk.

"He wanted a compromise. He said he and his people would remain peaceably near Wingate, but that even if he were killed, he would not move to the Pecos. But that's no nevermind. I want you to get those Ute warriors you mentioned and some other guides, Mexican or not, just get the best. We need to get this work done, and we need the good men to do it!" he slapped his fist on the desk to emphasize his frustration, stood, and started pacing around the office, glaring at Carson and out the single window. "Those blasted Navajo have murdered and robbed the people of New Mexico long enough, and they don't keep any of the promises and treaties they make! The only way to deal with them is to take them to Basque Redondo where we can control the bunch of 'em!" he smacked his fist into his palm and dropped back into his chair. He leaned forward, one elbow on the desk, and pointed at Carson, shaking his finger. "You have most of your men bivouacked at Los Lunas under command of Lieutenant Colonel J. Francisco Chaves and a couple majors besides. The rest of the men will be there by the time you're ready to leave. And of course, the four companies at Fort Wingate will be ready as well. Any questions?"

"I'll be meeting Kaniache somewhere along the Rio San Jose, he'll have some men with him and will probably already be scoutin' around. Tate Saint will be with me," and was interrupted by Carleton,

"Saint? Good man! He'll be an asset to you, go on!"

"There might be more volunteers coming into Marcy, and I'll have one of the officers there bring them to Wingate. But, that's about it, so, we'll be headin' out in the mornin'," declared Kit, starting to rise.

"Carson, let's get this wrapped up as soon as possible. You're in complete command, but I do want to be kept informed," admonished the general, remembering how much Carson dreaded the constant reporting.

THE PATTERN of the campaign was established on the first day of

March when they came upon a field of wheat and a store of already harvested grain. Carson ordered the men to have their horses feed on the standing wheat and to load the harvested grain into the wagons. Between the grazing and trampling by the horses, the field was totally destroyed. Whatever Navajo had planted or claimed the field had fled before the arrival of the troops, nor did they return. Near the end of the second day of hard marching and riding from Los Lunas, Tate met up with Kaniache and his warriors. The friendly greeting did little to distract Tate's attention from the small herd of sheep being driven by the Ute, and when Kaniache saw his expression, "One Navajo, Big Nose has his scalp."

Carson rode up and greeted Kaniache, "My friend! Good to see you," he commented, looking at the band of warriors that numbered about fifteen. "I see you've already taken some sheep, any Navajo captured?"

"One dead," responded Kaniache with no further explanation.

"Is this all your men?" asked Carson, leaning on his pommel.

"Yes, but there are other parties of my people, on their own, hunting Navajo."

"No big fights? No large parties of Navajo?" asked Kit.

"No. They do not fight like that. They choose to use small groups, sneak in and steal, kill when they can, and flee."

"Yeah, I know. But I thought with the ultimatum that Carleton gave 'em, they might try to get together to fight. But . . ." he shrugged his shoulders. "Well, Kaniache, we're headin' to Wingate, then we'll go on to Fort Defiance. I want you and your men to keep a scout well ahead of the rest of the column. If you run on any Navajo, do what you have to an' if you need help, send one of your men back for us."

Kaniache looked to Carson, then to Tate, nodded his head and reined around and with a short shout, took off at a canter, his men following. Tate looked to Carson, "They're plannin' on keepin all the stock and captives they take, you know that, don't you?"

"Yeah, although I didn't tell him it was alright, neither did I tell him they couldn't. I don't know yet what the general is going to allow for payin' 'em or if he is willin' to let me have as many as I want, but if they don't get paid, at least the bounty will be somethin' for 'em."

"What about captives?" asked Tate, showing his skepticism with a scowl and a growl.

"We'll just have to figger that out when we come to it."

FORT WINGATE WAS SITUATED in an austere area with basaltic formations to the north and northwest, alkali flats to the northeast and rugged arroyo scarred buttes to the west and south. The presence of a large spring garnered the name El Gallo but was later called San Rafael. The fort had four buildings and a wide flat, covered with canvas-wall tents to house the four companies of troops that awaited Carson's command.

Before entering the compound, Carson reined up for a good look-around, Tate at his side. He looked at his friend, "What'dya think?" he asked, knowing what to expect.

"It's a long way from the mountains. Those hills yonder," nodding to the north beyond the smaller malpais, 'are the only trees I've seen lately. This is mighty desolate country and if I lived here and somebody came to tell me to leave, all I'd do is say, 'point the way'!"

Carson chuckled, "Yeah, I know what you mean, but these Navajo, they see it as their sacred ground. Their four holy mountains corner what they see as *Dinetah,* their land. And most of it is desolate country, but they find all the good places, plant crops or orchards, raise sheep and goats, and live a good life. If they'd only keep to themselves and quit raidin' ever' where else, they'd do alright. But there's always gotta be troublemakers that make it hard on ever' body else.

"We'll be staying here, five or six days, maybe a little more, but Kaniache and his bunch will find their own camp and keep scoutin'. As for you, my friend, I'll need you to kinda keep an eye on Kaniache, as you can, and keep me informed about how and what he's doin'. We'll be movin' on to Fort Defiance, and all along the way, we'll be roundin' up *Diné.* But take a few days here, rest up, tend to your animals, an' do as you will."

"Suits me," answered Tate, "I wouldn't mind catchin' up on my sleep a little. Since I'll feel so safe an' secure among all these fine upstandin' soldiers an all."

Carson chuckled at Tate's cynicism, knowing he was referring to the lax discipline and morals among the men. Carson had never been a disciplinarian and preferred to command his troops by example rather than dictates, but sometimes, it had its drawbacks. With so many of these men being volunteers as opposed to the regular army enlistees, he had to rely on the conscripted Mexican officers to keep order among them. But with the Navajo and the Mexicans being long-time enemies, that order was quite lax.

Tate looked around, saw a narrow canyon that cut the hills to the west of the camp, and nodded in that direction, "I'll be camped up there. I'm gonna spend some time scopin' the valley and hills around here, get an idea of the lay of the land 'fore I head out on a scout. Looks like there's some green up there, so prob'ly some water and graze, so, if you need me, send somebody up there after me, alright?"

Carson nodded his head and with a wave of his arm, started the column of troops toward the makeshift fort and the many bivouacked troops.

As suspected, the green in the narrow draw yielded a small

spring. Although the pool of water was no more than two feet across and about five or six inches deep, it was cool and clear water that trickled out of a cracked stone, and disappeared less than ten feet down the draw, soaking into the gravel bottom. It was surrounded by a few stunted cottonwood, a small cluster of willow, and a nice patch of grass for Shady. The sandy edge of the patch was just the right size for Tate's bedroll, and once he finished rubbing down Shady, he rolled out his blankets and dropped the saddle and bags at the head. Not comfortable in knowing so little of his surroundings, he slipped the scope from the saddlebags and climbed the slope on the north edge to top out on the knobby hill, littered with granite rock and cacti.

He stretched tall and breathed deeply as he stood next to a gnarled cedar, looking around and enjoying the solitude and quiet. Picking a spot with a sizeable stone in the shade of a larger cluster, he seated himself and drew up his knees to start his survey. Taking one quadrant at a time, he started with the flat-top directly north of the small malpais and scanned the barren flat. It appeared empty, and he began to move the scope to the edge when movement caught his eye. Knowing it was easier to spot movement and familiar figures with your peripheral vision, he slowly scanned back, watching the edges of his sight. There! Shadowy figures in a cluster of rocks, similar to his own promontory.

He dropped the scope, snatched up a patch of buckskin he carried over his belt and held it over the end of his scope to obscure any sun glint. When he looked at the figures, they had stood and were pointing his direction, then ran to their horses and swung aboard and took off at a run, knowing they had been spotted. Tate grinned, recognizing the fleeing figures as Ute, but did not know if they were some of Kaniache's band. They posed no problem for the troops, so Tate continued his scan, chuckling at the fleeing Ute but admonishing himself for not using the buckskin hood on his scope before.

More movement caught his eye, but he was surprised to see any life around the black basalt of the malpais. He watched as a small herd of sheep disappeared into the rugged and ancient lava flow. He could only make out one man, probably some old Navajo sheepherder trying to protect his herd from both the Ute and the troops. But Tate also knew that for anyone that did not intimately know the malpais, it would be impossible to search. The black, sharp-edged lava would cut a horse's legs to pieces, and the uncertain footing could give way and break bones just as easy. And to try it on foot would risk getting injured and even lost, to never be found in the twists and turns of the black maize. He chuckled to himself at the simple and easy escape made by the old Navajo who probably knew the black basalt like the palm of his hand, and he also hoped the man and his sheep might never be found.

He rose from his perch and returned to his camp, to start a bit of a fire with the gathered cedar and anticipated some fresh coffee and maybe some Johnny cake. Then a quiet night by himself and away from the snoring contests usually carried on by the troops. Lobo lay quietly beside him, waiting for a tossed treat, obviously too tired to chase down a rabbit for his meal and preferring to wait for a hand-out. Tate stroked his thick fur at his neck and handed him a chunk of pemmican, which disappeared with one gulp of the big maw. "We're quite a pair, ain't we boy?" He looked to his grulla and said, "You too, Shady. I enjoy the company of you two more'n just about any other, 'cept'n maybe Maggie."

CHAPTER EIGHT
DEFIANCE

It was by any description, desolate country. Dry, cacti laden, brown grass, sagebrush, and greasewood dotted the desert. Squiggly lines of sidewinders through the sand, bigfooted cottontails leaving distorted tracks, scraggly coyotes panting in the heat, Gila monsters sunning themselves on hot rocks, and always the hot sun relentlessly bearing down to turn thin shirts into wet then dry blankets that weighted down hunched shoulders. Horses hanging their heads, dried mud at their nostrils, sweat tracks trailing down the cheeks of the men as they staggered in front of their mounts, everyone and everything with visions of streams or ponds of cool, clear water.

Lobo trotted with tongue lolling, seeming to be a living contradiction in his wool coat and showing no effect from the death-dealing desert and the sweltering temperature. Tate watched the big grey wolf glide across the flats, taking in everything and missing nothing. Suddenly he froze, mouth closed, head up, shoulders hunched, one front leg off the ground as he stared beyond a cluster of mesquite. Three javalina were grunting as they dug in the dirt for some tasty tidbit, oblivious to the visitors. Lobo looked back to Tate as if asking permission to pursue the quarry, but Tate spoke, "No, no, they're not worth the trouble. Not in this heat." He motioned with his hand for Lobo to continue on the trail, and with one more look to his friend, the wolf trotted on, ignoring the desert pigs.

It was the fourth day out of Wingate, and they should be coming up on the valley of Fort Defiance. The long, tan hogback, broken intermittently, was the last barrier to their quest. As Tate reined Shady to mount the ridge, he twisted around to get the scope from the saddlebags. Once atop the hogback, he stepped down near a twisted cedar, ground tying Shady, and bellied down on a sandstone slab. With a quick search, before and behind, he saw no obvious danger, and the trail in the bottom of the valley was easily seen as it bent around the long upthrust that obscured the upper end of the valley and Fort Defiance beyond. Behind him, about two miles distant, followed Carson and the troops, many afoot and struggling. Carson had said there should be some water on the west side of the hogback and no further than the piñon covered ridge that marked the upthrust of land. But try as he might, Tate could find no greenery that told of water.

Once off the hogback, he pushed on into the wide valley. The shoulder of the long ridge slid behind him to reveal a patch of greenery marked by stunted alder and oak. He gave Shady his head, and the horse quickened his pace to the scent of water. Even Lobo increased his ground-eating trot and the two animals, focused on the water, were unconcerned with anything else. Tate searched the trees and shrubs as they neared, looking for any danger, but being almost as anxious as the animals, he went to the water and slid off the saddle to put his face in the refreshing liquid. With his thirst slaked, he sat back on his heels and with both hands full of water, he splashed his neck and chest to turn the layer of desert dust into mud trails down his chest and back.

He sat back in the bit of shade offered by the alder and let Shady and Lobo enjoy the water and rest. It was less than an hour later when the column caught up, and Tate surrendered his patch of shade to the colonel. Fortunately, the trickle of water stretched into the valley, offering enough for the many troopers and their horses to drink. But they were soon back on the trail, pushing on to Fort Defiance, bound to make it before dark. Tate rode beside Carson as they talked about the days ahead.

"So, you're set on starting out right away for what'd you call it, Pueblo Colorado?" queried Tate.

"That's the plan. We're supposed to establish another fort, Fort Canby, further to the west and south from Defiance, and deeper into Navajo country," explained Carson. "I ain't never been there, so don't know what we're gettin' into, but I guess we'll find out. If it weren't for them wheat fields and corn crops, I don't think our horses would be able to go much further. But, they're doin' purty good, an' we got a good load of grain to take with us."

"How long we gonna rest up at Defiance?" asked Tate.

"No more'n a couple days. What day is this, anyway?"

Tate frowned, thinking, "Well, we're four days outta Wingate, an' we left there on the sixteenth, so, this is the twentieth of July."

Carson looked at Tate, "You sure? Cuz, the twentieth was the deadline Carleton gave the Navajo to turn themselves in at Defiance."

"Mebbe if we're lucky, when we get there it'll be overrun with Navajo waitin' to go to Bosque Redondo!" chuckled Tate.

"You don't believe that any more'n I do!" answered Carson.

The reds, tans, and greys of the sculpted terrain fascinated Tate, and his attention was captured as they passed some wind-carved red sandstone at the edge of the foothills. One part curved back towards the hill, but in the midst of the red stone, a large hole that made Tate think of the Great Creator poking his finger through the rock, just because He could. Tate smiled at the thought and stood in his stirrups to look at the streaked sandstone showing reds and tans in layers of colors and topped off with the deep green of the juniper and piñon. It was an amazing place, full of contrasts and contradictions, with its own kind of beauty. But as he let his eyes scan the vistas of wind carved formations, he was made to think, once seen, enough seen. He thought to himself, *Give me the mountains and the snow-capped peaks, green valleys, and broad vistas. That's my kinda country.*

Their first sight of the few buildings of Fort Defiance confirmed their suspicions when they saw no sign of the many Navajo that were to surrender. As they neared, they were greeted by Major Joseph Cummings, interim commandant of the Fort. "Welcome, Colonel! We've been expecting you!"

Carson stepped down, handed the reins of his mount to a nearby soldier, and motioning Tate to join him, walked with Cummings to the commandant's office. Before entering, both Carson and Tate used their hats to rid themselves of some of the trail dust, then stepped to the door. Once inside, Carson let the major take his seat behind the desk, and he and Tate seated themselves. "So, where's all these Navajo that were supposed to be surrenderin'?" asked Carson, skeptically.

Cummings chuckled, "If you believed that colonel, you've got a mighty long campaign ahead of you!" declared the major.

"That's what I figgered. Have you had any trouble with 'em?" inquired the colonel.

"Nothin' more'n usual. They pretty well keep to themselves. Any raiding done is mostly back toward Santa Fe or Albuquerque. Course, we do get some Mex comin' thisaway doin' their own raidin', justify'n it by sayin' their after their own stock or people that were taken by the Navajo," explained the major.

Carson sighed heavily, shrugging his shoulders, "Well, with the deadline bein' today, we'll be headin' out soon to start the round-up. First, we'll be goin' to Pueblo Colorado to see if it's a good place for another fort," but he was stopped by the uplifted hand of Cummings.

"Have you ever been down there? To see the area, I mean?" asked the major.

"No, I haven't. You?" asked Carson.

"Yeah, an' it's no place for a fort. No water, no graze, nothing."

"Any *Diné* down there that you know of?"

"Colonel, you're liable to find 'em anywhere and nowhere. They have a way about 'em that they can practically disappear right before your eyes! The only thing that stays anywhere is their crops and if they have a semi-permanent hogan. They can be herdin' a thousand sheep in a canyon that you'd think there wasn't enough grass for a javalina and have a field of wheat or corn or beans or squash, but you won't find them."

"Yeah, I know what'chu mean, major. But we've got it to do, so . . ." and he rose from his seat to leave, "Show me to muh quarters and such an' we'll get rested up 'fore we head out again. Most o' these men'll be stayin' here so I'll introduce you around an' you can get ever'body settled in, at least as much as you can. This is gonna be a long drawn out deal, I'm afraid."

Although it wouldn't be realized for some time, Carson's words would prove prophetic as the campaign began to try to uproot a people that had been established in this land for many generations. From the days of the Anasazi and the residents of the pueblos in the cliffs, even until this generation of semi-nomadic people, these people that seemed to live in the past, made the desert live.

CHAPTER NINE
PUEBLO

Before the rising sun could paint the eastern slopes of the buttes and mesas on the west side of the fort, Kaniache and his Utes had taken to the trail toward the area known as Pueblo Colorado. By late afternoon, the seventy soldiers with Carson and Tate had made their way through the scattered forest of juniper, cedar, and piñon to find the Utes stopped at a tank of semi-stagnant water, resting their horses as they waited. Kit and Tate walked to the side of Kaniache, "What did you find?" asked Kit, looking at the stoic Ute scout.

"Another band of Ute passed this way," he gave a sweeping motion of his arm indicating south to north along the tree line. "Mebbe twenty warriors. There," pointing to the west and the desolate cacti covered flats, "sign of sheep and Navajo."

"How many?" asked Kit.

Kaniache held up two hands, all fingers extended, "This many, mebbe few more."

Carson thought, looking around at the troops and the numbers of Utes, then to Tate, "I'll leave Captain Everett in charge of the troops, and I want you to stay with him and keep him outta trouble. I'm goin' ahead with Kaniache, see if we can catch up with those Navajo."

Tate nodded his head and looked at the colonel, "You want us to keep on the trail to Pueblo Colorado?"

"Yeah, if we get too far off the trail, at least you and Everett can get there 'fore dark tomorrow."

Tate waited a moment, then with a nod started toward the gathered soldiers, calling back over his shoulder, "I'll let the cap'n know you wanna talk."

KANIACHE SWUNG aboard his mount and was soon joined by Carson. They rode out ahead of the band of twenty Ute, none looking back at the soldiers still lounging in the shade, resting their horses. About an hour out, one of Kaniache's advance scouts came back at a gallop and slid to a stop beside his leader. Turning to Carson, Kaniache said, "The sheep and Navajo, down in the dry wash, there," pointing to a scar in the flatlands that told of a rain cut wash, probably with the only graze for hardy sheep and goats of the Navajo.

"Alright, let's take 'em," proclaimed Carson.

Kaniache nodded, motioned half his group to go to the north of the wash, and he led the others to the south. Within moments, they had launched their attack, rifles blasting without any warning and screams of war cries from the Ute, telegraphing fear into the hearts of the attacked. Bleating sheep and goats scampered up out of the wash, scattering in every direction, some run over by the horses of the Ute. Carson was in the middle of the melee, firing his pistol at a Navajo warrior clad in pants like a Mexican peon and a loose-fitting cotton drop-shouldered shirt. Red blossomed on his chest, forcing him to drop the spear that was used more as a shepherd's crook than a weapon. Several women were huddled, shielding children with their bodies, against the steep side of the wash. The attack lasted only minutes, but the noise of the animals and crying children, women wailing their mourning songs for their men, and Utes ordering captives out of the wash, filled the usually silent flats with a cacophony of sounds.

Of the small party of *Diné,* only three were men, all dead, and the others were women and children, but two were captive Paiute. When Carson spotted the captives, he approached the two on foot, addressing them in the language of the Ute and asked where the Navajo were hiding.

"Many Navajos, with sheep, cattle, and horses, there," pointing to the west, "canyon, past blacktop mesa. One, two days," answered the older of the two Paiute captives.

"How many Navajos?" asked Carson.

She thought a moment, held up both hands, all fingers showing, and flashed them four times. "This many."

"Many sheep and cattle?" asked Kit.

The woman enthusiastically nodded her head, "Many, many."

Kit turned to Kaniache, who had come to his side, "Let's go after them. Have two of your men take these captives and sheep back to Fort Defiance, we'll go on after the rest."

Kaniache frowned but nodded his agreement and quickly barked orders to two of his men to do as he was told. The rest mounted and started their pursuit. Once on the move, Kaniache told Kit, "The valley she spoke of is more than a day. If we ride in the night, mebbe we be there in morning."

"Then we'll ride tonight," agreed Kit.

TATE SAT on the crest of a low-rising knob, overlooking the sparse dull green of the valley beyond. He leaned on the pommel, scanning the flats for any sign of life, but nothing moved. What he saw was a large wheat field and, in the shadows of the buttes, the brighter green of corn and beans. He shook his head, knowing these would soon be destroyed, and he thought of all the labor that had gone into the tilling of the soil and planting of the seed, all with the hope of a bountiful harvest. But all that would soon be gone under the hooves of the soldiers' horses. He dropped his head and reined around to report to Captain Everett.

He watched from the same promontory as the seventy men rode into the fields. The men dismounted, and staked out their horses, giving them ample length of lead to graze as much as they wanted, then found a place in the shade of the rimrock at the edge of the butte to sit and rest. One man came to the shade, two ears of stubby corn in his hands and sat down to gnaw on the half-grown kernels. Others saw him and soon followed his example, and several were soon dining on the fresh corn. One man said, "It sure ain't like what we growed back in Missoura, but it ain't too bad!" He was answered by the grunts of others that chose to mumble and chew than talk.

With the nearby water available, Captain Everett chose to make camp in the lee of the buttes and fires soon flared as the men broke into their haversacks and brought out the coffee and more. Their spirits were lifted after a good meal, and the cool of the evening settled over their bedrolls. One man brought out his harmonica, another a jew's harp, and several gathered around to lift their voices around the campfire. Soon the strains of *Wait for the Wagon* filled the air.

Will you come with me my Phillis, dear, to yon blue mountain free,

Where the blossoms smell the sweetest, come rove along with me.

It's ever Sunday morning when I am by your side,
We'll jump into the Wagon, and all take a ride.

Wait for the Wagon, Wait for the Wagon,
Wait for the Wagon and we'll all take a ride.

It was a familiar tune to most, and all joined in, whether they could sing or not. Just the memories it brought bid each one join, and a surprising chorus of harmony carried into the night. Tate sat with Lobo beside him, listening and enjoying the camaraderie of men he didn't even know, but the pleasant sound of music in the lowering black of night was comforting. He lifted his eyes to the familiar night sky and picked out known constellations, traced the milky way across the sky and rolled into his blankets, staving off the unusual cool of the desert night.

"No, no water, ride three, four days, no water," declared Kaniache, looking off to the west. They had ridden most of the night and now stood in the valley told of by the Paiute captive. The sign of the passing of the large group of Navajo and their herds was everywhere, and there had indeed been at least forty Navajo with large herds, but they were long gone.

"If they can go there, there must be water!" proclaimed Kit, showing his exasperation with the stubborn Ute.

"No, because they go, no more water. The only water there," pointing to the west, "standing water in tanks. No fresh water. Herds," pointing to the tracks of the sheep and cattle, "drink all. Our horses cannot go that far and come back without water."

Kit looked at the sign, lifted his eyes as he shaded them with his hand, and saw nothing but dry land and rising heat waves. "Yeah, you're prob'ly right." He sighed heavily, turned back to his mount, and swung aboard. "Let's water'm here, and head back. We'll go to Pueblo Colorado and check that out for a fort, then back to Defiance."

Kaniache nodded and followed Kit to the small stream. They

turned to the south, cutting across toward the Pueblo Colorado wash, planning on joining up with Captain Everett and the rest of the troop. But once on the trail for no more than a couple hours, another advance scout reported seeing sign of more Navajo. The report had no sooner been given, when their group was under attack. The Navajo had spotted them and set an ambush. Rising up out of a dry wash, were at least a dozen mounted Navajo, and rifle fire sounded, driving the Ute and Kit to swing their mounts and try to flee, but they were cut off by a like number from behind. Kit ordered, "Dismount!" and the Utes, not used to the orders from Carson, milled about, trying to fire their rifles one-handed as Kaniache shouted, "Get down!"

Finally, all the Utes were on the ground, dragging their horses down by pulling their heads low and pushing on their sides. The horses laid down, and the battle raged. The Navajo raced towards the Ute but were easy targets for the rifles of the now stationary Ute, and the attackers began to fall. While the Navajo were experienced at the guerrilla tactics of hitting with small groups and fleeing, the Ute were more experienced at confrontational battle. The greater numbers and skill of the Ute soon took their toll, and the ground was littered with the bodies of Navajo and their horses. After the first attack, the losses were too great for the Navajo to continue and they quickly fled from the area, leaving behind eight dead warriors.

The echoes of gunfire had barely stilled when the screamed war cries of the Ute rattled across the flats as they went to the downed Navajo and pillaged and desecrated their bodies, taking scalps and plunder as they shouted and danced among the dead. Kit brought his horse to his feet, looked around at the remains, and shook his head as bile rose in his throat.

. . .

THE TWO FORCES joined at the site of the Pueblo Colorado wash, and all agreed it was not a place for a fort. Their return trip to Fort Defiance was without incident and no more sightings of fields or Navajo. The Fort was a pleasant sight, but one that would become dreary in the coming days. With one month behind them since leaving Los Lunas, the pattern of the campaign had been set. Tate had begun to believe this is what the next few months would be like: destroying crops, taking herds, and chasing an elusive enemy. How long would this take, he wondered. But no answer was forthcoming.

CHAPTER TEN
CAMPAIGN

"We've done as ordered by renovating the fort and now General Carleton says we're to call it Fort Canby. But we've got to be gettin' back to our original orders and round up the Navajo. Major Cummings, you'll be coming with me. Major Chacon, you and Captain Eaton, you'll take your company C and head straight north, then swing around to the east and back here. That loop'll take you 'bout a week, maybe a little more. Captain Pfeiffer, you and your company H, you make a swing to the south, come up to Pueblo Colorado and back here." Carson took the time to line out on the map a more detailed route of all the companies and within the hour, the commanders and their companies were moving out of the fort to their assigned patrols.

Kit turned to Lieutenant Colonel Chaves, "I'm leaving you here at the fort, and when the companies return, let 'em have a day or so rest, then send them out on these assignments," and he turned to the map to detail the additional orders.

"I'll be out a bit longer than the others, probably three or four weeks. We'll be covering this country to the west," he pointed out the area around the Zuni pueblo and the Hopi villages. "Then we'll come back toward the Canyon de Chelly and back here. But that's coverin' a lot of territory, so I'm not sure when we'll be back. I'm takin' more men than the others, and of course, I'll have the Utes. You hold things down here and keep the patrols going. Any questions?" asked Carson, looking to his second-in-command.

"No, colonel. I've copied down everything you said," answered Chaves, showing the scribbled notes to Carson, unaware that Kit was illiterate.

Carson nodded his head, turned away, and started to the door, putting his hat on as he walked out into the bright sun. He motioned to Tate and Kaniache, stepped to his horse and mounted up, and the remnants of the regiment lined out to follow.

Tate rode with Kaniache as the two men took the point well ahead of the band of Utes and the column of soldiers. Bound to the south through the juniper, cedar, and piñon, it was a meandering route, but one that offered some respite from the boiling sun of the high desert. By early afternoon, Kaniache reined up, pointing through a break in the trees to a valley showing green. Tate craned around to see a wide valley with an expansive field of wheat and others of corn, beans, pumpkins, and a few melons. They waited for the rest of the column, and Tate watched as Carson directed his junior officers to turn the animals into the fields to enjoy themselves and for the troops to pull some of the wheat to add to the packs of the mules. The remainder of the wheat field was put to the torch, and the black cloud rose over the flats, warning the Navajos of the heavy toll they would pay for failing to honor the promises of many of their leaders to surrender. This first day's destruction set the pattern for the patrol of Carson and company, pursuing the Navajo wherever they could be found, destroying crops, and confiscating livestock, leaving behind a desecrated landscape in their wake.

Captain Eben Everett began recording the events of the campaign in his diary as the march wore on and the miles were put behind them.

We left the fort on August 5 and within the first two days, came upon a vast farm which was subsequently destroyed. The animals continue to suffer the depredations of travel, and while we destroy vast crops, it is difficult to reconcile with the fact the fort, just fifty miles away, is so short of any grain for the animals. But it continues to be feast or famine as we travel. Day after day, the pattern is the same, dealing death and destruction on every front. I wonder if the patrols of the other officers are as destructive as Carson's?

TATE OFTEN FOUND himself retreating within, turning his mind from the campaign and improving his wilderness education, learning from majesty and splendor of nature. He marveled at the many formations of rocks and towers that seemed to have been fashioned by the loving hands of the Creator, taking special delight in the thin towers that stretched to scratch the blue of the sky with their narrow pinnacles of red sandstone. The pale tans of some of the faces of the buttes contrasted with the dull grey of sage-covered flatlands. But everywhere the colors were of muted tones but stark contrasts.

By the end of the first week, they left the land of the Zuni and were headed west toward the Hopi country. Tate was belly down on a long ridge when he saw the dust of a column approaching from the southwest and with the aid of his scope, he recognized the stiff form of Captain Pfeiffer at the head. He climbed aboard Shady and walked the grulla, stiff-legged, off the side slope to tell the waiting Carson of the approaching column.

"You're sure it's Pfeiffer?" asked Carson.

"It's him alright. You have any other officers that ride that stiff-backed like he does? You'd think this far from West Point, that boy'd relax a little, but he sits so straight, it's bound to hurt," answered Tate.

Carson chuckled, "Yeah, well, he didn't go to West Point, but he's a good officer, and we've been friends for some time. And I sure can't say that about all of 'em. One day I'll tell you a little about that man." It was a wistful expression that painted Carson's face as he looked into the distance.

When the column drew near, the captain came directly to colonel Carson and gave a sharp salute, "Captain Pfeiffer reporting sir! We have five prisoners and one hundred sheep!"

"Good job, Captain. Now, what're you gonna do with 'em?"

"Sir?"

"Well, you gonna take 'em all back to the fort, or you got somethin' else in mind?" asked the colonel, looking to the stiff captain.

"Just obeying my orders, Colonel. I didn't expect to meet you, and we are bound for the fort."

"Alright, Captain. Then I'll let you take one of these companies and the pack train back with you. We're headin' on to the Hopi villages. Some of Kaniache's scouts tell us there are several Navajos holed up near there."

"Yessir, colonel, sir."

When the two columns separated, the captain would have the easier time of it with only two days travel back to the fort. But Carson's larger column, of four companies, had a longer trek ahead of them. Captain Everett continued with his narrative in his diary. *We made it to the Hopi villages, but the large number of Navajos turned out to be no more than a small group. Carson fumed at the possibility that so many of his prey had either outwitted or simply escaped his pursuit. One Navajo was killed, two women and three children captured. However, the Ute captured 20 to 25 horses, and over a thousand sheep and goats. Carson and the Ute seemed to have a falling out when the Ute complained that he wanted all the property captured, but Carson refused. Kaniache was not happy, and he and his Utes left. However, I believe they will return.*

Now with Tate as the lone scout, Carson and company continued their pursuit of the Navajo. Just after midday on the third week out, Tate came storming back to the column, sliding Shady to a stop beside Carson. "Colonel, there's a bunch of Navajo 'bout four, five miles out, beyond that long ridge, 'fore ya' come to the flat-tops. Reckon there's twenty-five, thirty of 'em, and they're pushin' a good-sized herd of animals, cattle, horses, sheep, an' such."

Carson shaded his eyes, looking at the position of the sun, "Think we can overtake 'em?" he asked Tate.

"We'd have to push it, but mebbe so! Course, if they pick up their pace, they might lose us in those canyons!"

Carson turned to Cummings, "I'm goin' with Tate an' the few Utes we have left. You come along with the column, double timin' it!" he ordered. Carson dug his spurs into his mount's side, and the horse hunched his back and bounded ahead, as the colonel motioned to the handful of Utes that remained to follow. The small band, those that had chosen to stay with the troops instead of following the disgruntled Kaniache to take the stock to their camp, eagerly followed the colonel and Tate.

Cummings lifted his arm in the air, pumped his fist up and down rapidly, and commanded, "At a canter, Ho!" and the column lunged ahead. With a somewhat ragged double line, the troopers kicked their horses to a canter, and the dust rose around them.

Carson and Tate led off, horses at a lope, and the colonel

looked to Tate as he pointed in the direction of a long rimrock-topped ridge that made a blue and tan slash across the horizon. To the west of the ridge rose-red sandstone buttes and flat-top mesas that marked the *Dinetah,* the land of the Navajo. Tate set the pace but soon dropped Shady from a lope to a canter and then to a trot, slowly bringing the grulla to a walk. Lather painted the shoulders, chests, and flanks of the horses, heads were hanging and mouths were open gasping for air. The merciless heat yielded nothing for the anxious pursuers, and when Tate reined up to drop to the ground beside Shady, he took the reins and walked beside his loyal mount. Carson followed his example, and the blistering sun robbed them of enough spittle to make talking worth the effort. Dust lifted from every footfall as blue uniform britches turned to a faded red from the sands of the flats. Every step compounded the aggravation. Thoughts had turned from the fleeing Navajo to simple survival. Although this day's trek was little different than the preceding days, stamina had become a rare commodity.

Even the seasoned Ute were gasping for air, staggering under the heat and dust. Tate stopped near a shoulder of rocks, leaned against one and took his canteen, shaking it to hear the water within, judging what was left, and began to pour water into his hat for his horse. Shady nosed the wet, tonguing and licking until Tate lowered the floppy felt, added a little more and offered it to Lobo. Only after the animals had wet their lips did Tate take a sip. He replaced the cool hat to shade his eyes, looked to Carson, "As much as you wanna catch 'em, I think the horses vote against you."

Carson was holding his canteen above his face, tongue out, catching the last few drops of water. He capped the canteen, looked to Tate, "Find us some shade and water, if possible. We'll head back to the fort soon's we can."

With a nod, Tate took the scope from his saddlebags and

began to climb the slope at the shoulder of the butte behind them, staggering and clawing his way to the top. He seated himself and, with elbows on knees, he searched for any sign of water, stagnant or fresh, anything. They had been traveling south on the flanks of the Chuska Mountains, and the long, timber-covered ridge of foothills with many finger ridges pointing to the sandstone flats showed no sign of water. But due south, about another ten miles, a hint of green showed promise. Tate recognized the area as the origin of the Canyon del Muerto that lay to the north of Fort Canby. He slid down the slope, walked to Carson, "Colonel, 'bout eight- or ten-miles due south, along these finger ridges, there's some green that might yield some water. But that's the only thing I can see in any direction. I figger if we move o'er yonder," nodding his head toward the tree line of juniper about three hundred yards away, "an' rest up a mite. Mebbe we can make it 'bout dusk."

Carson looked in the direction Tate indicated, nodded his head, and started plodding his way to the line of shade. He had lost all concern about the fleeing Navajo, and now sought any relief for himself and his men, even if it was just a line of shade for a brief respite. They had been fighting the heat and lack of water for most of a month, their only relief coming when they found the fields of the Navajo and let the horses take their fill. But grain is a poor substitute for water, and the horses were showing the wear, patches of hair falling out, ribs showing, and more.

With the sun lowering in the west, the glare seemed to intensify, and men dropped hats askew to protect their eyes from the blinding light. A clatter of rocks up a narrow draw caught the attention of the Utes and with a glance to Carson, and an acknowledging wave from him, they took off up the draw as if they had never suffered from the afternoon's travail. The rattle of gunfire came echoing down the draw, but Carson and Tate didn't hesitate in their steps toward the greenery and the hoped-for water. Within moments, the five Utes came from the draw, three holding scalps and the others driving a small bunch of sheep and goats. Carson stopped, turned, and waved the men off, watching as the entire group high-tailed it through the trees, taking their plunder with them.

Tate stopped to wait for Carson, and when he came alongside, Tate pointed to a flat at the mouth of an arroyo where a field of ripening wheat waved in the slight wind. They felt the relief of the breeze but pushed on to the saddle of the slight ridge before them, and soon came to the cluster of alder and cottonwood that bordered a small stream that chuckled over the rocks inviting the thirsty travelers to partake. Both men quickened their pace and were face down in the water beside the lowered heads of their mounts. Lobo walked into the water, put his face under, and came up to shake the water from his coat, and splash the men and the faces of the horses. No one complained as Tate and Carson sat back on their heels, breathing deep of the cooler air among the trees.

Dusk was dropping all pretense of light when the rest of the troop caught up with Carson and Tate. Cummings and the men were just as fatigued as Carson and no one complained about stopping for the night. Before turning in, the Colonel gave Cummings orders to return to the wheat field and destroy it and any other crops before they left for the fort the next morning. "I'll be riding out with Tate, so you can go back and take care of that 'fore you head out. We're 'bout two days outta Fort Canby, so we might still run 'crost some more Navajos, or at least their fields. So, keep a sharp eye."

"Yessir," responded Cummings and Captain Everett with a salute.

"Tate and I are going to have a looksee at Canyon de Chelly on the way back, so we'll be taking a roundabout route. If you take the troop due south, after you round the canyon, you should make it by dusk day after tomorrow. But, I'll prob'ly catch up to you 'fore then."

"Very good sir," answered Cummings as he and the captain turned away to return to their troop.

CHAPTER ELEVEN
BARBONCITO

THE STEEP AND WINDING RAVINE TWISTED ITS WAY TOWARD THE crest of the mountain ridge. The Chuskas were rugged mountains littered with granite boulders scattered amok among the juniper and twisted cedar. Mesquite, scrub oak, ocotillo, and skunk brush holding sway among the gravelly slopes as bunch grass clung to the steep ridges, with prickly pear, hedgehog, and cholla lying in wait to snag any passersby with their needles. It was a tough land for a tough people and the Navajo called it *Dinetah* or the land of the people.

Well up the ravine, where it twisted around a stack of granite, a smooth shoulder protruded from a slight basin that cradled a hogan with an intricately patterned blanket hanging over the entryway, blocking the bright lances of sunlight that sought entry in the wee hours of the morning. Horses were tethered behind the hogan and several people, warriors and women alike were gathered near a fire, most with cups in hand as a woman, showing grey in her hair, poured greenthread tea into the upheld cups. Beyond the fire, several other women were busy preparing dishes for a meal for the entire group, and all were talking in low tones, conversations and expressions showing great concern.

Seated directly opposite the entry, cross legged with hands clasping his ankles, Barboncito, the respected leader and orator of the *Diné,* looked around the circle of leaders. To his right sat Manuelito and beyond him Delgadito. To his left sat Nesjaja Hatali, Hastii K'aayélii, and Armijo. Several other headmen of the Navajo joined the group, seating themselves, some with cups of Navajo tea, others sitting stoic and somber.

Barboncito began, "What is happening is not new to us. The medicine man, 'The man with young lambskins on his hat' from the 'One who walks around you' Clan, gave his vision of prophecy of the bluecoats attacking and burning the homes and fields of our people. Some prepared by putting up dried foods and more atop Fortress Rock, but many did not believe. Now, we believe." The headmen and leaders nodded and mumbled their agreement as Barboncito or Hástiin Dághá, continued. "Many have tried to make peace with the bluecoats, but still they come. I told the General Carleton that my people would stay by Fort Wingate and be at peace, but we would not go to Bosque Redondo. But he still gave his time that we must surrender and go to the Bosque, or he would send his man Carson and destroy all the *Diné.*"

"Ayee, Carson and his bluecoats have tried to do what Canby could not, and he has failed like Canby!" declared Manuelito, or Hastiin Ch'il Haajiní. "We fought them before, and they are easy to kill!"

"But now with crops burned and our herds taken, our people are afraid of the coming of the snow!" spoke Delgadito, brother to Barboncito.

Again, the leaders nodded their heads and mumbled as they agreed with the headman about the fears of the people.

"It is better to die of hunger than to become the captive of the bluecoats and go to Bosque Redondo to live with the Mescalero!" proclaimed one of the more militant headmen, Nesjaja Hatali. He had fought the bluecoats before by attacking and harassing the troops but never became involved in an all-out mass confrontation. With the bluecoats better outfitted and armed, he preferred the tactic of destroying or raiding and taking their supplies, much like the soldiers were now doing to the Navajo.

"It is easy to say that now, but when the cries of your women and children grow loud and you see them freeze in the snow, will you say it is better then?" asked Barboncito. He was known as a peacemaker and orator and was one of the most respected leaders of the *Diné.*

Hastii K'aayélii, spoke slowly but with a gravelly voice as he looked sternly around the circle of leaders, "Our people dwell north of most of you," he nodded to the other leaders, "and Carson has not found our fields. We will share as we can with you," he made a sweeping motion around the circle of leaders, "but what we have will not be enough for all. If we are found, we will fight, we will hide, we will do what we must to survive. My people are now putting supplies in some of our caves and other places of storage, but even if we are not found, it will be a hard winter. The signs show it will be long and I know many of our old people and weak ones will not live to see another summer. But, to live as captives with the bluecoats is not to live, but to die slowly. It is not the way of Beauty as our people must live."

Silence filled the hogan at the words of K'aayélii. Men often speak of war, battles, and times of conquest when they are alone, but when the images of women, children and old people starving or dying as captives of their enemies become real, bravado is replaced with caution and even wisdom is admitted into the discussion.

Barboncito looked around the circle, then looked to Manuelito, regarded as the most dominant war leader of the people, and watched as the man dropped his eyes to the ground, thinking. "My brother, you and I have seen the numbers of bluecoats that came to Fort Defiance with Carson. We have seen the soldiers go on their hunts and destroy the fields and even kill some of our people. You have fought the bluecoats many times. What do you believe we," he motioned to the entire circle to include all the bands of the people, "should do? Should we fight, try to hide, surrender? What is your council?"

Manuelito looked around at the others, "It is not the way of our people for one man to tell another what they must do, or even another village. From the times of the ancients when our people first came to this land of the sacred mountains, we have had to fight. We warred against the Apache, Ute, Pueblo, Comanche, and others. Always we must fight for our people to live. It is in fighting that a people are made strong. But the *Diné* have learned from others and become a people with herds and fields and with lodges that cannot be moved. Our people have lived well and grown fat from our way.

"Now it is hard to fight and still have our fields and herds. That is why the bluecoats destroy and take these things. If we cannot fight with these things, then we must surrender or learn to live without. There was a time when our people could live without these things, but that time is no more.

"This is our land, the *Dinetah*, and if we leave this sacred land, we will die slowly. Our people would not be in balance with Mother Earth and Sky Father and the spiritual people. This is our home, we belong here." Manuelito looked around the circle of leaders, then put his shoulders back and lifted his head, taking his eyes from the men. He dropped his eyes to the center of the circle, "We, those that follow me as their leader, will go to Canyon de

Chelly. We have fields and caves where we can live. Our fields need to be cared for and the herds we have left will do well on the grasses of the canyon. If Carson and the bluecoats come into the canyon, we can go to Fortress Rock and they cannot reach us there. If any choose to fight, we can raid the fort and other places from there."

Barboncito paused as he looked to the others, reading their responses, then agreed, "Manuelito speaks wisely. I and my people will also go into the canyon. Perhaps Changing Woman will give us a mild winter in the canyon, and we can plant again when greenup comes. We still have sheep and cattle and I do believe we can make it through the winter, but only in the canyon."

As Barboncito looked around the circle, waiting for each leader's response, they gave their decision. Nesjaja Hatali and Hastii K'aayélii both agreed to stay in the mountains north of the Canyon de Chelly, but that they would do what they could to help the others. Delgadito, Armijo, and the others chose to take their people into the canyon, preferring the portion called the Canyon del Muerto, but said they would also retreat to Fortress Rock if they were attacked. With the decisions made, the men continued their discussions regarding the time of their moves and more, mostly just biding their time until the women finished the preparation of the meal.

It is never a pleasant time when a family or an entire band or village of people chose to make a major move, but when they are forced to because of an enemy that destroys all they hold dear, everyone feels the pain. Even the children, that are usually so resilient as they approach every day with enthusiasm and optimism, sensed the somber mood of the leaders and drew silent. The women, knowing the work before them, appeared to be tired already, just from the anticipation of the change. But beneath all the brave faces and determined moves, lay a lingering fear of what might yet come at the hands of the bluecoats and the assault of winter.

CHAPTER TWELVE
RETURN

"First Sergeant! Come in here and take a report!" barked Carson as he walked to his office, dusting himself off with his hat. The troop just arrived from their month-long expedition and he was anxious to get his report in writing so he could hit the sack for some well-earned rest.

First Sergeant John Harvin grabbed paper and pen and followed the colonel into his office, uncertain of what was expected since this was his first time on duty with the colonel and he had heard some of the reports about the man. They varied from him being a coward because of his tactics, scuttlebutt being any officer that refused an all-out confrontation and full-on attack against any enemy which was considered the proof of physical courage, and that the colonel was lacking that essential male virtue. Others admired the man, for he had learned that kind of courage or blatant show of disregard for danger, would often result in the death of men. Because when Carson was staging an attack on the Navajo, he would never allow fires in camp and preferred to surprise the enemy with a cautious and stealthy approach, some thought he was afraid. But those who knew him best never questioned his bravery nor his leadership.

"Yessir, Colonel sir!" barked the seasoned sergeant as he seated himself at the end of the colonel's desk, pen in hand.

"General J.H. Carleton, commander, department of New Mexico, etc. etc.," began a weary Carson. He detailed the campaign, the different confrontations and the numbers of Navajo killed and captured, and the many livestock confiscated. "Regret to inform you of the loss of one of our officers, Major Joseph Cummings. While reconnoitering, he and one trooper were attacked and killed. His company pursued the attackers, killing two Navajo. We will now regroup and resupply before resuming our expeditions." Carson paused, lit a stub of a cigar, and added, "Sign it, and get it off right away!"

The sergeant jumped to his feet, "Yessir, right away sir!" He pivoted and started for the door and stopped, slowly turning around, "Uh, sir?"

"Yes, what is it, First Sergeant?" asked Carson.

"Uh, while you were away, the general sent Major Blakeney, one of those California officers. His orders are there on your desk, and I believe the general requested that the major be given a chance 'to distinguish himself', were the general's words, sir."

Carson looked at the seasoned fighting man, detected something lingering in his manner and asked, "What is it, Sergeant?"

"Well, sir, it's not my place to say, sir, but I believe you will be hearing things soon enough sir. I just thought you might be warned ahead of time sir. If you know what I mean, sir?"

"That bad, eh?" asked Carson. He always had a lot of confidence in the men like the sergeant that had worked up through the ranks. They were the backbone of the army and any officer worth his salt knew it was the rank and file that would make or break any command.

The sergeant dropped his eyes, then looked up at the colonel, "Worse, sir."

Carson lifted his head in a slow nod, "Thank you, Sergeant. I appreciate the heads up. Now, get that report off to the general."

"Yessir!" responded the man with a sly grin as he spun on his heels and left the office.

CARSON INTENTIONALLY PUT off talking with anyone as he left his office and went to the stables, hoping to catch Tate before he turned in for the night. As he entered, he saw his friend mounting the ladder to the loft where he preferred to roll out his blankets, choosing the company of horses and mules to the unkempt and noisy men of the troops. "Tate!" called Carson, seeing the man turn and descend the ladder to join him.

"Have you heard anything about problems goin' on here at the fort?" asked Carson.

Tate chuckled and sat on a bench beside a stall, "Aren't there always problems around a fort like this?"

"No, I mean something unusual. The first sergeant implied there might be problems with a new officer, and I couldn't get anything outta him, but I ain't likin' the idea of gettin' ambushed by my own men," grumbled Carson.

"Well, I did overhear a couple fellas that were shovelin' manure here. They were complainin' 'bout some new officer from the California bunch that was creatin' some kinda ruckus, but they didn't say what. Other'n that, didn't hear anything."

Carson shook his head, "I tell you what. Sometimes I feel more like a schoolmarm than a commander. Dealin' with some o' these men . . . makes me wanna turn 'em o'er my knee an' give 'em the whuppin' their daddies shoulda done! I'm guessin' this one the general sent out is goin' be a real pain in my backside!" The colonel sat down on the other end of the bench, "While I'm here, I'm thinkin', after you get rested up a mite, I might just have you do a scout by your lonesome. When we head outta here with all these troops its like sendin' one o' them new telegrams to the Navajo to let 'em know we're comin'. But if you go out by yourself, maybe you can find some o' the camps or hideouts before we even leave. Ya reckon?"

"To be honest with you Kit, I been wantin' to do that anyway. This scoutin' for the big troop seems to be a waste of time, cuz like you say, by the time the troop gets caught up, the Navajo are long gone."

"You wanna take anybody with you?" asked Kit.

"Nah, me'n Lobo can do alright by our ownselves. But how soon you wantin' me to head out?

"Ah, take a couple days if you want. Whatever supplies you need, just sign for 'em. Oh, an' by the way, there was a telegram waitin' in my office, seems another company of volunteer recruits will be comin' from Fort Marcy. They got 'em a scout name of Sean Saint, sound familiar?"

Tate grinned at the colonel, "You know it does. But I was hopin' he'd stay with the women folk, but I reckon he had enough of petticoats and perfume."

"The general sent orders with Major Blakeney that I was in command of the regiment, under you, of course, Colonel, but that the major was to be the post commander," explained Lieutenant Colonel Chaves, squirming in the chair in front of Carson's desk.

"Colonel, you have served me well and you have no need of any apology," explained Carson, "now, I don't know what the general was thinking, but you and I both know that just because a man has a star on his collar doesn't mean he's got anything inside his head. Now, explain to me just what happened."

Chaves took a deep breath and scooted to the edge of his seat, leaning forward as he began, "From the time he arrived, he had the attitude that he alone knew what had to be done. He started barking orders to everyone, treating all the officers like they were no different than the privates shoveling the stables. I have received many complaints from officers and enlisted alike about his 'conduct unbecoming an officer'! But the worst . . ." he hung his head, shaking it side to side, "was when the Navajos came in to surrender."

"Some Navajos came in to surrender?!" asked Carson, astounded by the news.

"Yessir. The first man, who had a flag of truce, said he had come 'to have a talk with his white brethren' but the major did not believe him and had him thrown into the stockade."

Carson listened patiently and shook his head, frustrated at this report of the Navajo being confined. "Go on," he encouraged.

"Then two days later, the major reported the Navajo had been shot while attempting to escape," explained Chaves, sighing heavily. "When I tried to find out what happened, the men would not speak to me, but I could tell they were afraid. I think the major had ordered their silence.

"Then about four days later, three more leaders of the Navajo came in," before continuing, Lieutenant Colonel Chaves stood and went to the office door, opened it and summoned the First Sergeant. "I'll have the first sergeant explain about those men."

With a nod from Carson, he began, "Well sir, the major told me to write a report, but what he ordered me to say was not what happened."

"He ordered you to lie?" asked Carson.

"He ordered me to write a report that wasn't true sir. You see, sir, he made it clear that I was to kill the prisoners as they tried to escape, but they hadn't tried to escape sir, they were still in shackles!"

"Are they still?" asked Carson, incredulously.

"One man is sir. One was killed and one did escape," mumbled the first sergeant.

"Did you do it, Sergeant?" asked Carson, sternly.

"Oh, no sir! It happened during second watch, and I was in my bunk, sir."

Carson was visibly angered as he stood to his feet and leaned on the desk. "Sergeant, bring that last prisoner in here right away!"

The sergeant hastened his departure and when the door was closed, Lieutenant Colonel Chaves said, "There's more, sir."

"Go on," ordered Carson, dreading what more he would be told.

"Blakeney had two of my officers, of the New Mexico Volunteers, arrested for insubordination, refusal to obey a direct order, when they would not release the Navajo. They knew what he had planned, and they would have no part of it, so he arrested them. I do believe he planned to have them executed in a similar manner," explained Chaves.

Carson dropped into his chair, shaking his head and slammed a fist into his palm. He took a deep breath, "Colonel, you go right now and have those men released! Tell Blakeney to report to me immediately. After he does, you arm those two officers and have them wait outside my office. You come back with the major, understand?"

"Yessir!" he stood and snapped a salute to Carson, who returned it and sat back in his chair.

. . .

THE NAVAJO CAME TIMIDLY into the colonel's office, but Carson stood, smiling and told the man to be seated. Once the man sat down, Carson followed suit and leaned on the desk and asked, "What is your name?"

"I am called Little Foot, I am of the *Diné,* born to the *Bít'aa'níí* or 'Folded Arms People Clan'."

"Little Foot, I understand you came under a flag of truce to speak about some of your people surrendering. Is this true?" asked the colonel.

"Yes, it is true, there are many that wish to surrender. We know the general said we must go to Bosque Redondo and we agree."

"Well, the man who had you confined was wrong. You have my apology for that. I am letting you go. I will give you twelve days to return to your people and bring them here. Will you promise to do that?"

"You will let me go? Will I be killed like the others?" asked Little Foot, fear showing in his eyes.

"Yes, I will let you go, and I promise you will not be killed. What happened to the others should not have been, but we, you and I, will go on from here. Agreed?"

Little Foot slowly stood, nodding his head and answered, "Agreed."

Carson called to the first sergeant, "Sergeant Harvin, I want you to personally escort Little Foot here to the edge of the camp. Return anything to him that he brought and make sure he safely leaves to return to his people."

The first sergeant grinned, saluted, "Yessir, right away sir!" and motioned for Little Foot to follow as he turned away and started to the outer door of the office. He stepped aside as Major Blakeney walked in, smiled as the major looked at him and the Navajo, but continued to the colonel's office.

"Major Thomas Blakeney, reporting, sir!" announced the man snapping a quick salute as he stood at attention before the colonel's desk. Carson looked up and saw a tall, sandy-haired man with broad shoulders, a handlebar moustache, lantern jawed and broad forehead, with what appeared a permanent smirk on his face. The colonel returned the salute, and when the man started to relax, Carson barked, "I did not say at ease!"

Blakeney stiffened but stayed at attention, looking straight forward, waiting. Carson began, "Major, I have heard some disturbing reports about your conduct since you have arrived at this post."

The major started to respond, "Stay at attention!" ordered Carson. Then he continued, "I will give you an opportunity to respond, but first you need to know that I am in command here, not General Carleton. And every officer under my command will conduct himself as a proper officer at all times. That means everyone you come in contact with, officers, enlisted men, even an enemy, will be treated with all due respect! Am I clear?"

"Enemies? You mean Indians, sir?" asked the man, showing surprise.

"I didn't stutter! You heard me, did you not?" barked the colonel. Major Blakeney stood a full head above Carson and outweighed him by at least seventy-five pounds. This was a man that had become accustomed to intimidating everyone by his size and force of personality and to have this man, barely over five and a half feet tall, scruffy hair and no bigger than a typical youngster still in his teens, shouting orders at him, a West Point graduate; it was unbelievable.

"Yessir," he answered, stammering to say more but stopped by the piercing eyes of Carson.

"Now, explain yourself!"

"Explain myself? About what, sir?"

"Start with the manner in which you treated your fellow officers."

"If you mean those men of the New Mexico Volunteers, surely you don't consider them proper officers sir, why, they're just Mexicans!" spat the major contemptuously.

Carson gritted his teeth as he folded his arms across his chest and glared at the presumptuous man before him. "And what about the Navajo?"

"Those dirty Indians? They tried to escape and were properly executed!" he spouted, puffing his chest proudly.

Carson jumped to his feet, both hands flat on the desk as he leaned forward. He lifted one hand to shake in the face of the man, "You pompous hypocrite! You sniveling, wet-behind-the-ears mama's boy! I should have you whipped! But you're not man enough to waste my time on! Any one of those 'dirty Indians' is twice the man you'll ever be!" He walked around the desk to stand directly in front of the major, "I am ordering you to be shackled in the stockade under the charges of insubordination, conduct unbecoming an officer, cowardice in the face of the enemy, and assault on a prisoner in confinement! And if I have my way, you'll be drummed out of the service like the jackal you are!"

He turned aside and shouted, "Officers!"

The two men that had been imprisoned by the major came into the office, one on either side of the major, both holding sidearms pointed in his direction and grinning.

"Take this man to the stockade and put him in shackles!" ordered Carson, shouting.

"Yessir!" responded the two officers in unison. They each grabbed an arm and hustled the major out of the office as he struggled to free himself. And both men were hopeful he would try just a little harder; they had a score to settle. But they were disappointed, as the major, as most men that blustered their way through life in the manner of a bully is, dropped his head and surrendered to the two determined officers.

CHAPTER THIRTEEN
PLAZA

THE TRADING POST ON THE PLAZA OF SANTA FE WAS THE OLDEST IN town. Started by an early settler, the Fraser's had owned and operated it for almost twenty-five years. Felix and Juanita had taken in the waifs from the wagon train that had been rescued from the Comancheros by Tate, and now the youngsters prided themselves in their duties in the store. While Ezra swept out the store and the boardwalk in front, Maribel arranged goods on the shelves that were usually askew after a day's business. Felix and Juanita watched the two as they busied themselves, and Juanita looked to her husband, "They are wonderful children, aren't they?" smiling at the thought that they now had the children she always longed for and couldn't have.

"Yes, they are, their parents did a fine job teaching them manners and responsibility. I will have to admit, I was a little apprehensive about taking them in, but now I'm glad we did."

They looked up as the first customers of the day pushed their way in the door. A redheaded woman and a young couple, the girl apparently an Indian by her dress and manner.

Maggie smiled as she looked to the storekeepers, "Oh wonderful, you're back!" she exclaimed as she led the others to the counter at the back of the store.

"Uh, yes, we got back the day before yesterday, but we've been mighty busy putting away all of our new stock. I take it you were in while we were gone?" asked Felix, looking a little askance at the woman, someone he had never met before.

"Yes, we were, and we've been waiting anxiously for your return," began Maggie. She extended her hand toward the store-keeper couple, "I'm Maggie Saint, perhaps you remember my husband, Tate?"

Both faces immediately wiped questioning frowns away with broad smiles. Juanita was the first to extend her hand, "Oh yes! It is wonderful to meet you, Mrs. Saint. We can never thank Tate enough for the wonderful gift he brought us in these two delightful children. Would you like to meet them?" she asked as she made her way around the counter. Without waiting for an answer, she called, "Ezra, Maribel, come here please. There's someone very special I would like you to meet."

In the short moment they waited for the children, Juanita glanced to the younger couple and Maggie said, "I would also like you to meet my daughter, Sadie, and my son, Sean, and his wife, White Fox." The three stepped forward, smiling, but Fox hung back slightly behind the shoulder of Sean as she looked at Juanita.

The woman smiled, extended her hand, "It is a pleasure to meet you, and you certainly take after your father!" Then Juanita turned to White Fox, "And you are lovely!" She said, "White Fox?"

"Yes, I was named White Fox by the man and his wife who raised me. They were of the Brule Sioux," answered Fox, timidly, dropping her eyes to the floor. She grabbed Sean's arm and leaned against him, looking around for someplace to sit. She was feeling weak and a little faint, her heart beating faster than she thought possible. Spotting a bale of furs against the wall at the end of the counter, she motioned and tugged at Sean's arm, "I need to sit down." They walked together to the bale and Fox sat down, just as the two children came to the side of Juanita, wondering what all the ruckus was about.

"Children, I want you to meet Mrs. Saint, she is the wife of Tate! And this is her daughter, Sadie."

It took a moment for Ezra to absorb what was said, then a grin painted itself on his face and he stepped forward, "Wow! You're Tate's wife? Where is he? Is he coming? I wanna see him!" he declared in a rapid-fire series of questions. Maribel also stepped closer, a mixture of timidity and anxiousness confusing her, but she smiled as she looked up at the beautiful redheaded woman and her daughter that was the mirror image of her mother.

"So, you must be Ezra!" exclaimed Maggie. "May I give you a hug?"

"Uh, I guess so," he answered, trying to look behind her hoping to see his rescuer and hero, Tate. Maggie bent down and drew him close, hugged him and looked to the girl, "And you must be Maribel!" as she opened wide her arms and waited for the girl to come forward. Sadie was also eager to give the children a hug and copied her mother in their embrace. It was a heartwarming scene, but the children didn't quite know what to make of these new people in their lives.

Maggie straightened up and looked to Juanita, "They are beautiful children. And they look very happy."

"Indeed they are," echoed Sadie.

"We are very happy they are a part of our family." She looked to the two and said, "Alright now, back to your chores."

"Yes Ma'am," they answered in unison and trotted off to their duties.

Juanita looked to Maggie, "Would you and yours like to come into our home and have a cup of tea, perhaps?"

"That would be wonderful," answered Maggie, as she turned to follow Juanita, Sadie at her side. Their living quarters were behind the store and they started to the back, but Juanita glanced over to see White Fox sitting on the bundle of furs, and she stopped, quickly putting her hand to her mouth as she gasped. She looked back to Maggie, "I'm sorry, I saw White Fox sitting on that bundle of furs and I saw my daughter, so many years ago, who loved to sit just like that and watch everything in the store. Of course, my daughter, Carmelita, was much younger and her feet dangled off the bundle. But my husband often bundled the furs he traded for and would stack them right there. It was her favorite place because she could see the whole store, and that's a lot for a little girl."

"My husband told me you had a child taken by the Comanches, is that right?"

The women walked toward the back as Juanita answered, "Yes, it was thirteen years ago, now. I will never get over it, but having these children is such a blessing. We, my husband and I, wanted more children, but I am not able, and we had almost given up hope, and then in walked the padre and your husband, and those two wonderful children. I can never thank him enough!"

"Did you ever think you might get your daughter back?" asked Maggie.

"I never gave up hope. We tried to find where the Comanches were, but they were long gone by the time any of the townspeople could get together to hunt for them. And the soldiers were too busy to be bothered over one little Mexican girl! I was so angry I wanted to line them all up against a wall and shoot them!" She spat the words as she relived the emotions of losing her child. "My husband went with some Comancheros to trade with the Comanches, but the ones they traded with denied any knowledge of the raid." As she spoke, she readied the tea and sat down at the table beside Maggie. Sean and White Fox had followed them into the living quarters and were also seated at the table.

"But I never gave up hope. I prayed time and again, went to the church and talked to the padre and prayed with him. And my husband offered a reward to the Comancheros for any information about the captives of the Comanche, but we never heard another word."

Maggie looked to White Fox, gave a slight nod, and in a quiet and timid voice, White Fox began, "I told you I was raised by the Brule Sioux. The only father I knew was Crow Dog, a chief among the Brule, and his woman Runs in Water, was my mother. But I was not always a Brule. I was taken in a raid by the Sioux when I was very young. They raided a Comanche village where I was held as a captive."

Juanita's eyes flared as she brought her hand to her mouth, holding her breath.

"I remember being taken by the Comanche when they raided Santa Fe. I am Carmelita."

Juanita jumped to her feet and went around the table as White Fox stood with open arms and the two embraced long and hard, tears chasing one another down their cheeks. When they drew back, Juanita turned her head and hollered, "Felix! Felix! Come in here!"

The door between the store and the home slammed open and Felix stood staring at the two women, still clutching at one another, "This is Carmelita! Our baby girl!"

Felix stood, a frown scrunching his forehead, and he stepped slowly into the room, a slight scowl showing his consternation. Juanita explained, "She is our Carmelita! She was taken by the Comanche and the Sioux took her from them! Now she has returned to us!"

A slow smile spread across his face, mouth dropping open just a mite, and a sparkle showing in his eyes as he drew near, then a quick step brought him to his wife and he wrapped his arms around both Juanita and Carmelita and hugged them both as tight as he could. Sobs came from the man as tears filled his eyes and the family embraced for the first time in thirteen years.

"Oh, Madre de Dios! That which I have prayed and hoped for so long, has come to pass! What a wonderful God we know! Oh, I'm so happy!" Juanita reached into the pocket of her clerk's apron and brought out a hanky, wiped at her eyes, and began to giggle hysterically. "Oh, Carmelita! How beautiful it is to say that name again. And look at you! You are all grown up, and beautiful, and married to this fine young man! Oh, how wonderful!"

She plopped back into her chair and looked at Maggie, Sean, and Sadie, all smiling broadly, happy for the family. Juanita reached across the table to take their hands, "And thank you for bringing her back to us! You are just as wonderful as your husband!"

"Well, Tate would have been here, but he's off gallivanting with Carson! But he wanted to be, but you folks were gone. So, we've been waiting for you now for almost two weeks. But the wait was worth it, wasn't it, Fox?"

White Fox was wiping tears as she vigorously nodded her head, forcing a smile. She reached for Sean's hand and squeezed it tightly.

"What's going on?" asked a little voice from the doorway. Maribel stood, twisting the corner of her little apron in her hands, as she looked to those at the table, wiping tears and talking.

Juanita turned to her charge, "Come here sweetheart, I want you to meet somebody very special." She drew Maribel close, saw Ezra in the doorway, and motioned him in. When they were beside her, "Remember me telling you about our little girl that was taken by the Comanche?"

"Ummhumm," answered Maribel.

"Well, this is her!" proclaimed the woman, nodding to White Fox. "Meet your sister, Carmelita, or as she is now known, White Fox!"

Fox twisted around in her seat and held out her arms. Both youngsters walked to her and she hugged them close, "Yes, I am your sister now! It is so good to have a family again!"

"Wow! I have an Indian for a sister," proclaimed Ezra as he leaned back from Fox.

Fox smiled at him and said, "Yes, I am known as a Brule Sioux. That is how I was raised, but this is my real mother and father," nodding to Juanita and Felix. "I was born here, in this home, and was stolen away by the Comanche. But now I am back."

The rest of the morning was spent enjoying the tea and conversation and the getting acquainted between families that would now be linked forever. When Juanita found out the Saints would be staying for a few weeks and maybe months, she was delighted about having new friends and family so near and vowed to spend much time together. When Sean, Fox, Sadie, and Maggie rose to leave, there were many hugs and more tears, but they were happy ones.

CHAPTER FOURTEEN
HOPIS

Frustration seemed to be the order of the day. With several excursions behind him, Carson had experienced greater frustration than at any time in his military career. Short supplies and little provision for the animals required the horses and mules to subsist on the little grain captured from the corn and wheat fields of the Navajo. The order had been to destroy the fields after they were looted of all that could be carried, but the stores at Fort Defiance, now called Fort Canby, were rapidly depleted as winter approached. The mounted patrols from the fort would often encounter Navajo but were unable to pursue them on horses that were exhausted and starving. To accomplish the mission, Carson was forced to send several smaller parties of dismounted men into the field to continue the harassment of the Navajo and to deny them any subsistence.

"Look at these reports!" growled Carson, stomping around his desk to the window. He was venting his frustrations to his one friend that would tolerate his grumblings, Tate Saint. "With Kaniache and his scouts on their own, they've had more success than the troops from here! Even the troops from Wingate are accomplishing more!" He stomped back to his desk and grabbed some papers, waving them before him, "There's New Mexican militia and other irregulars, Utes and Pueblos, all goin' without military supervision! That blasted Superintendent of Indian Affairs, Michael Steck, reported some Utes killed nine Navajo and captured forty children and the Pueblos killed two more! And that Ramon Baca, he had over a hundred men and left Ceboletta, went up there by Chaco Mesa, killed six, captured three, and some ponies." He pounded his fist on the desk and grabbed another report, "The troops from Wingate thought they'd get some Navajos near Sierra Datil, but they were beat by some Pueblos that killed sixteen and captured forty-four women and children an' over a thousand sheep!" He grumbled some more as Tate doffed his hat and hung it on the toe of his crossed leg, then Kit looked at his friend.

"I think the Hopi, those back there on those mesas west of here, have been keepin' the Navajos posted on the movements of troops here at Canby. They're a poor lot, an' with the Navajos all around 'em, it would be to their best interest to keep the *Diné* informed. So," he paused, leaning forward as if sharing some great secret, "I'm gonna go after the Hopi and stop that once an' for all!"

He looked at Tate, "I'm gonna have some Zuni scouts to go to the Hopi. An' I want you to make that scout we've talked about. One man can move around and the way you like to move at night, I think you'll have better luck. I wanna know where they are, where they're goin' and what we need to do to bring this to a head."

"You know it's winter out there, don't you?" asked Tate, not relishing a scout in the cold of the desert. He knew winters in the high desert could be insufferable at best, and he was anxious to get to Santa Fe to see his family, hopefully by Christmas.

"Don't you think I know it? The next excursion we make the

troops will be on foot! But that doesn't make any difference to Carleton. I've put in for leave to go be with Josefa, she's expectin' another child an' I'd like to be there. But Carleton bowed his neck cuz he thinks all we need to do is keep up the pressure on the Navajo and they'll come runnin' in to give themselves up!"

"So, you still thinkin' you want me to scout Canyon de Chelly?" asked a reluctant Tate.

"No, but maybe on your way back you can take a look. I still don't think there's any Navajo in there, it's just too dad-blamed wild! But Carleton is convinced an' I reckon he'll be back up on his high horse soon and demandin' we go in there. But I want you to scout to the north of there and a bit to the west, just wherever you think they might be hidin'."

Tate looked at the window, guessed the time to be mid-afternoon, and looked back at Carson, "Alright, guess I'll head out soon's I get my stuff together. Shady an' Lobo's been gettin' a little restless anyway, so, might as well, I reckon." He stood, stretched, and turned to leave. He turned back to face Carson, "So, you're goin' to those Hopi villages on those mesas to the west?"

"Ummhumm, that's the idea. So, we'll prob'ly be back 'fore you. Take your time, I ain't in no hurry to make another excursion very soon, maybe Carleton will come through on those furloughs for both of us."

Tate lifted his head in a skeptical nod, then turned away with a wave over his shoulder as he left the colonel's office. He headed to the sutler's to gather up the supplies he would need and began considering just how much of each item he would require. In less than an hour, Tate was mounted on Shady, Lobo trotting before him, and he led a blood-bay pack-horse and was pointed to the north along the low-rise ridge and headed for the crater basin. This route would provide good tree coverage and keep him out of the cold desert winds that blew snow and dust in equal amounts.

. . .

CARSON WAS STANDING before his wall map, mentally calculating the route and destination of his latest excursion, when a frantic knock came on his door, and he called out, "Enter!"

"Colonel, sir!" began a flabbergasted corporal, obviously winded and forgetting to salute, which was overlooked by Carson as he waved for the man to continue, "it's the mules and sheep! Judgin' by the sign, some Navajo run off several mules an' over a hunnert sheep!"

"An' just what sign convinced you it was Navajo?" asked an angry Carson. It was bad enough that his details couldn't find the Navajo on their excursions, but for them to flaunt their presence by raiding here at the fort was about as belligerent as they could get.

"Well sir, I figgered they was the only ones that'd dare do it!" he answered.

Carson shook his head, wanting to stomp his feet and beat his fists on the desk, but refrained from such a display in front of the corporal. "Alright, Corporal. Return to your unit and prepare to move out!"

"Yessir!" replied the man, saluting and spinning on his heels to leave the office.

The sun was just beginning to throw lances of red from the eastern horizon when five dismounted companies and some Zuni scouts followed Carson from the fort, bound for the

Hopi village of Oraibi in the mesas area about five days march to the west. As he rode beside his second-in-command, Major John Ayers, he thought about his plan and chosen route. Although the officers were mounted and most of the gear and provisions were carried in the wagons, it would be a difficult trek for the men. With about six inches of snow on the flat, the trail was broken by the oxen pulled wagons. Carson also knew that as the sun rose to its zenith, the melted snow and churned trail would be a mix of mud and slush that would be more challenging than the snow.

He looked to the major, "Major Ayers, I want a detail, to make a round-about an' see if they can find any sign of Navajo. The Zuni are well out front, but I'd like to see what's on our flanks."

"Yessir," answered Ayers, reining his horse around to select the 'volunteers' for the scout mission. As he rode along the column, he spotted a familiar sergeant, "Sergeant Andrés Herrera!"

The enlisted man fell out of formation and stood before the major, saluted, "Yessir!"

"Pick a detail of two squads, get another sergeant to lead the other, and make a scout of our right and left flanks. You know what to do!"

"Yessir!" he answered and turned away to carry out his orders.

That pattern continued, but each day Sergeant Herrera and Sergeant George Strong selected a different squad for the detail, but always led the men themselves. It wasn't until the third day out that Sergeant Herrera's squad finally spotted some Navajo. It was a small band and the few hogans were below the canyon walls, almost obscured by the overhang, but the thin trail of smoke gave away their location. When Herrera bellied down on the edge, he saw the cluster of hogans at the bottom of the wide canyon, about two hundred fifty feet below. He searched for a trail down and noticed a scar on the canyon wall to the north of their position.

"Lopez!" He spoke in a loud whisper, knowing how easily sound carried in the cool air. "You and Martinez check out that trail yonder. If it goes down to the bottom, wave us down and we'll go together against those Navajo!"

Within a few moments, he spotted the two men, waving their arms overhead, and he turned to his men, "Let's go!" They trotted along the rim, well back from the edge, and soon joined the others. As he gathered the men together, he scratched out his plan in the dirt, looked to each man for questions, and getting none, they started down the trail. It was just over a quarter mile from the village and around a bend in the canyon that protected them from the sight of the village. The twelve men spread out as assigned, and at the signal from the sergeant, they started for the village at a trot, holding their rifles across their chests.

It was over almost before it began. Most of the villagers were gone, having left behind four men, two of whom were now dead and two wounded, to guard their flight. Ignoring the pleas of the wounded men, Sergeant Herrera ordered, "Search all the hogans and look for any storage places. Destroy any supplies, food, blankets, and such!"

The pillars of smoke rose behind them as they drove the small herd of sheep away from the site. The one horse found at the village was loaded with two bags of grain and one of dried corn. This would be used to supplement the sparse rations for the animals. By evening, Sergeant Herrera and his squad were reunited with the company and Carson received the report of the destroyed village, complimenting the sergeant and his men on "a job well done!"

THE MORNING of the sixth day out from Fort Canby, Carson made a show of force as he marched the five companies of men into one Hopi village after another, stopping in each village to question the leaders and recruit additional scouts to accompany them through the other villages and against the Navajo. Carson soon learned the Hopi were not friends with the Navajo and prided themselves on having been settled in this land long before the Navajo or others came. He also discovered that one village of the Hopi, Oraibi, were friendly with the Navajo.

It was an impressive sight when Carson led the five companies of troops, numbering over three hundred, straight into the village of Oraibi. Although the Hopi were visibly impressed by the many men in blue, the women didn't leave their work. Several had the traditional squash blossom hairdo with large buns on either side, and they worked at basket weaving, pottery making and grinding wheat on the stones, seldom looking up at the many men that marched into their village.

Carson and his men were also impressed with the multi-tiered adobe pueblos that housed the people. Ladders leaned against the walls, giving access to the upper levels, some with old people sitting and watching the spectacle of intruders. The structures were obviously old, older than any structure seen before. It would be later when Carson discovered this village dated back to the first century A.D. and had been inhabited since its founding.

The show of force quelled any opposition, but Carson commanded Ayers, "Major, take that man," motioning to the one that appeared to be the leader or chief of the village, "and that man" pointing to the one beside him, "bind them and bring them with us!"

No one tried to stop them, although there was much mumbling and gesturing, but nothing appeared to be threatening. Carson wheeled about and led the entire regiment from the village and off the big mesa. Once on the flats, he stopped the column to give the men a rest, and with a Zuni scout as an interpreter, he began to question the Hopi leaders.

After Carson chastised the leader and his companion for assisting the Navajo and warning them to never support them again, the leader began, "My father, *Nakwaiyamtewa* met with your leader, James Calhoun, and asked for protection from the

Navajo. That is why your people built Fort Defiance. But the blue-coats have not protected us. We are the *Hopituh Shi-nu-mu* or the Peaceful People. We promise we will not assist the Navajo in any way, but you," he pointed at Carson, which among his people was a rude gesture, "must protect us from them." He crossed his arms in front of his chest and nodded his head that he was finished.

Carson grinned, "Well chief, I guess you got me there. Alright then, we will do our part and you do yours," he declared, and stretched out his hand to make the promise secure. He let the two men return to their village, both loaded with blankets and a bag of trade goods.

The return to Fort Canby was typical of their journey out. They captured four more Navajo, three horses, and just under a hundred sheep. They destroyed three camps and burnt some dry fields, but several times they saw signs of recent flights of Navajo, but because of the poor condition of their animals, they could not give chase.

When two days out of Fort Canby, the advance party of mounted soldiers were confronted by a handful of Navajo. One of the Indians fired his rifle into the air and approached the men, showing signs of wanting to talk. But the one man they allowed to come near was treated roughly and had his weapons taken away, but was allowed to leave. When one of the recruited Hopi saw the rifle, he told Carson, "That is the rifle of Manuelito!"

Carson looked at the Hopi, astounded by what he said, "You mean, Manuelito, the Navajo chief?"

The Hopi enthusiastically shook his head and Carson dropped his eyes as he gnashed his teeth. Major Ayers asked, "What is it, Colonel?"

"That man probably wanted to talk! He is one of the strongest leaders of all the Navajo!" He was practically shouting, "Maybe if I could have talked to him, we would've gotten this whole mess settled!" He smacked the pommel of his saddle with a balled-up fist, mumbling to himself, and shaking his head. "Major, that boy that was captured, get him up here!"

Once the young man came near, Carson stepped down and instructed him about how the Navajo had to surrender and go to Bosque Redondo, but they would be safe and fed. Once he was certain the young man understood, he set him free to try to find the leader Manuelito or any others that would be willing to surrender. He knew it was probably a foolish idea, but there was nothing to lose and if he convinced even a handful, that would be more than they had now and maybe many others would follow their example.

He looked forward to returning to the fort, but he also knew that Carleton would probably renew his determination to have Carson take the troops into Canyon de Chelly before he would be allowed to take a leave and visit his wife. But, he had to try, because Christmas was just around the corner.

CHAPTER FIFTEEN
SCOUT

Moonlight cast dim shadows as Tate rode past the wide crater-basin that held Buell Mountain, on the western part of the big bowl. With lunar light coming from the high eastern sky, the shadows of the crater rim held secrets that wouldn't be known on this journey. He pushed on through the scattered juniper and piñon, occasionally glimpsing Lobo leading the way toward the Sunsela Buttes. The Chuska Mountains loomed in the dim light off Tate's right shoulder, and the occasional cry of lonesome coyotes added to the symphony of the night. Cicadas, nighthawks, the seldom heard yeowl of a mountain lion, and the last struggling scream of a captured rabbit, chased away the solitary thoughts in the pale blue light of night. The sounds were comforting for the nocturnal traveler, each reflecting the cycle of life in the high desert.

As sun boy launched his javelins of red and gold to herald his coming, Tate rode through the Sunsela saddle to search for his day camp. He turned to a draw on the right, rode up the gravel bottom and into a grass bottomed basin that held a tank of collected water.

He smiled as Lobo stood waiting then stepped down from his saddle and began loosening the cinch to strip the gear from the grulla. He snatched up a handful of bunch grass and rubbed down Shady, then stripped the pack saddle from the bay and gave him the same rubdown. Both horses wasted no time as they rolled in the grass, then walked to the water to slake their thirst, reaching the end of their picket lines.

The only snow that remained after the warm day and Chinook wind of the night hid beneath the branches of the junipers or under the shadows of mountainous formations. Yet Tate found a sizable granite overhang that faced south and offered good shelter and wide-spread sand that had been worn away over the eons. He rolled out his blankets, gathered some dry, grey wood and started a small fire for his coffee and a little breakfast.

Lobo had disappeared on his usual scout of the morning and Tate sat by the fire, sipping the last of his coffee. The dim light of early morning chased the last of the stars from the sky and now reigned supreme horizon to horizon. Suddenly, the Owoooo ooo cry of Lobo carried across the wide valleys, the familiar call bringing a slow smile to Tate's face, thinking about his long-time companion. Lobo didn't often lift his voice except to answer another, unless he was feeling a little romantic and wanted to let the ladies of the mountains know there was a possible suitor in their land. The big grey wolf lifted his voice again and let it trail off as if he were sending the telegram of his presence as both a challenge and an invitation. But there were no answering cries and soon the big wolf padded into the camp and lay beside his friend, anticipating a hand-out. He wasn't disappointed. He caught the proffered bit of fried pork belly and downed it in one gulp, then stretched out with his head between his paws and promptly fell asleep. Tate made one last circuit of the camp, checked the horses, and made certain the camp could not be easily seen, then rolled into his blankets, Shady and Lobo nearby.

"AIIEEE! DID YOU HEAR?" asked the younger of the three hunters. They had left the village that lay southeast of White Cone Mountain on an early hunt for the people. But the cry of the wolf stopped them, and they looked from one to the other.

"Yes, it is Ma′ iitsoh, the grey wolf," said the second hunter. For the legend of Ma′ iitsoh, who was given by Changing Woman to be the protector of the Bitter Water Clan, was also the protector to Abalone shell boy and the Navajo Sacred Mountain Doko' o'osliid, San Francisco Peaks. All *Diné* knew that to hear the howl of a wolf was a signal to turn back. If they were on a raid or a hunting trip, or even bound for a battle, this was a signal to return to their hogans. The three looked to each other, and without any message shared, they turned back to the village.

Their excitement was somewhat abated as they walked to the hogan of Hastii K'aayélii, *One With Quiver*, the leader of their village. He was seated outside, watching his woman prepare their breakfast, and looked up as the three men approached. The hunters looked to one another and the oldest spoke, "Uncle, we left to go on a hunt, but we were at the mouth of the arroyo, near the base of White Cone, and the cry of Ma′ iitsoh came from the Sunsela Buttes." He paused, dropped his gaze to the ground, and finished with, "So, we have returned."

Hastii sat silent for a moment, then spoke, "You have done well. To proceed could bring the wrath of Changing Woman upon our people. Sometimes, Grey Wolf just calls the people to go to work in the fields, but it is winter, and there is no work in the fields. Perhaps he was sounding a warning, not just to you, but to our village. I have considered returning to the Bears Ears area, the land of my fathers. This may be the sign for us to go."

He dismissed the three hunters with a wave of his hand, and they quickly left to go to their own hogans and their women. Hastii looked up as his woman brought a platter of food and asked, "Do you believe this is a sign to return to our homeland?"

"Perhaps. I will consider it and talk with the elders."

"It is a long journey in the winter," advised his woman, quietly.

"Yes, and we have few horses. With the bluecoats destroying the fields and taking our animals, it would be a long walk and a difficult one."

Hastii fell silent and ate his breakfast, often pausing and looking to the distant peak of the White Cone. Although it was not one of the sacred mountains of the *Diné,* he always considered this a sacred place. And now to hear the cry of the chief ruler, Ma' iitsoh, just made it all the more sacred. They must prayerfully consider what Changing Woman would have them to do; he must summon the medicine man and discuss this before he meets with the elders.

THE SNOW BEGAN IN MID-MORNING, yet by late afternoon, the wind had drifted the big flakes and covered the buffalo robe that lay heavy on Tate. Although warm and cozy under the added layer of insulation, the random drifting flakes that found his exposed cheeks soon let him know that old man winter had returned. He rolled out of his blankets to a white landscape that lay quiet, hushed, with nothing moving save the last few flakes drifting down to take their place on the downy covering of a violent land. Peace reigned and nothing stirred. Even the horses stood stoic and still, heads hanging as they stood between juniper that struggled under the weight of the deep snow.

Tate wore his fur-lined, high-topped moccasins and he kicked away the fluff, making way for his fire. He knocked the snow from the wood stacked beside the fire ring, pushed aside the snow and gathered bits of bark, twigs, and once the little pyramid was set, pulled out a lucifer and struck it on the side of a rock. The match flared and he quickly held the little flame under the dry kindling, letting the small bits catch and soon had a fire going, sufficient to start his coffee.

With the pot balanced between two flat stones, he pushed some of the sticks under and let the heat melt the snow in the pot. Soon, the aroma of coffee assailed his senses, and he poured a cup of the black brew, anticipating the warmth to both his innards and his hands and face as he held the cup near. He warmed the leftover pork belly and Johnny cake, tossed a few morsels to Lobo and brought the horses near to gear up.

He stayed just in the tree line, knowing the snow and moonlight made him an easy target for anyone that might be watching. But the fresh snow also served to quiet any sounds of the trail. As he neared the White Cone Mountain, he noticed the hint of tracks leading into the trees and a wide arroyo to his right. He stopped, stood in his stirrups for a better look-see, and recognized the trail was made by more than one, moving sometime during the storm, but before the snow ceased. The tracks were no more than dents in the down, but a trail, nevertheless. He moved further into the trees, stepped down, and ground tied the horses. With a hand signal, he and Lobo moved up the slope, snaking in and out of the trees.

It was a clear night, the moon waxing to full, forcing Tate to move within the dim shadows. As he mounted the shoulder of the ridge, he saw the village. Six hogans, well scattered, each facing the east with thin spirals of smoke rising from the central smoke hole. He went to one knee, watching the quiet scene; no one moving around, no lights apart from the flicker of flame behind the entry ways or the smoke holes reflected from the central fire in each hogan. He let his imagination picture the life in the village: children playing, women busy at cookfires, men returning from hunts or tending the flocks of sheep or cattle, life not unlike that of any community, whether among the whites or natives. The thought of being a part of making these people suffer hunger and cold just to get them to leave their homes brought bile to his throat and anger in his spirit. But the reminder of raids on towns and ranches, people killed, children and women taken from their families, added steel to his resolve. Yet he knew that most of these people were not a part of those raids, most were just families trying to make a life. Planting and raising crops, tending and growing herds of sheep and cattle, raising children and teaching them how to become men and women of strength. Why was it that so many must suffer for the deeds of a few? But such has been the way for centuries among many cultures around the world.

He shook his head as he stood to go, motioning to Lobo to return to the horses. Tate lifted his eyes to the starry sky, and started to pray, not just for his own, but for these people and the months before them all. He asked his God to give guidance, strength, and resiliency to all involved.

On a hunch, Tate turned to the west southwest away from the White Cone Mountain, to move across the flat toward the beginning of Canyon de Chelly. Traveling by the light of the moon, he chose to drop into the wide draw of Palisade Creek which made the travel easy. The shadow of round top buttes rose to his left, while flat tops showed their shoulders on his right. Carson had been certain the canyons were not used by the Navajo, but Tate remembered the excursions of Colonels Sumner and Miles, but that was more than a decade past, yet the canyons had been a refuge of the Navajo. He was determined to ride the rim and thoroughly scope the canyons for any sign of the people. With a population numbering in excess of ten thousand, where else could they be?

CHAPTER SIXTEEN
CANYONS

HE TUCKED HIS CHIN INTO THE DRAWN-UP COLLAR OF HIS BUFFALO hide coat. The wind came from the southwest and portended stormy weather. As dark clouds played hide and seek with the big moon, Tate determined to find better cover for his day camp. Crossing the dry wash of Palisade Creek, he dropped into the shallow swale of Whiskey Creek, followed it towards the canyon and turned back to the south at the first fork. A talus slope pushed into the narrow canyon and offered a granite overhang large enough for man and horses alike.

Tate wasted little time stripping the animals and making camp. Aged driftwood in a tangled pile at the sharp bend of the canyon offered an ample supply for his fire and he quickly laid in a store for the day. He glanced up above the overhang and the outstretched limbs of several juniper offered to dissipate any smoke. He fashioned a woven windscreen from another juniper and a scraggly piñon for the horses' protection at the exposed side of the overhang. He stacked some rocks in a semi-circle to protect his fire and to serve as a reflector for the heat. Satisfied, he stood with hands on hips, looking around at the camp. He planned to use this camp for a few days and make reconnoitering surveys of the canyon rim on the south side, then move and search the east and north rims.

Lobo had trotted off on one of his hunting trips, preferring fresh rabbit to dried and smoked jerky or pemmican. But Tate fried up some pork belly and whipped up some Johnny cake for his breakfast and soon sat on a flat rock, enjoying the hot coffee and his meal. When he turned into his blankets, he reckoned on just a few hours sleep, knowing his canyon search would have to be done in the daylight and his schedule would have to change, as would his surveys. He could see into the canyon in the daylight, but he would be more easily seen as well.

The sun was at its zenith when Lobo awakened Tate with his cold nose against his cheek. Tate came instantly awake, looking at the wolf through squinted eyes and seeing the animal belly down beside him, he knew there was no reason for alarm. He reached from under the warm buffalo robe and rubbed Lobo behind his ears, "So, what's the deal? You hungry or sumpin'?"

Lobo just smiled back, tongue lolling, and staring at his friend, waiting for him to roll out and do some exploring. "Alright, alright, I'm gettin' up," answered Tate, pulling his moccasins from under the blankets and slipping them on over his wool socks. He stood, stomped his feet to get the blood flowing, and tossed a couple sticks on the smoldering coals to heat up his coffee. The sun shone warm on his face and he noted the snow was rapidly melting. That was the way of the high desert, one moment it was blistering cold and everything white, and soon the warm sun brought temperatures that quickly melted the snow into the thirsty land. The clear blue sky was totally absent of clouds and Tate was relieved to know his tracks of the night before would soon be obliterated.

He saddled Shady while the coffee heated, downed a cup, and

was in the saddle to start his first survey of the vast canyons. Retracing his route from his camp, he came to the fork with Whiskey Creek but reined up at the sound of animals approaching. He waved Lobo back and backed Shady into a small cluster of piñon. The bleating of sheep told of a flock being pushed into the canyon and Tate leaned on his pommel to peer through the thin branches before him. Lobo padded to the top of the bank and stood looking down on a herd of about a hundred sheep, tended to and pushed by one young man, a Navajo.

When Tate saw just one shepherd, he gigged Shady forward and called out, "Yá'át'ééh"

He held up one hand, palm out with the other hand in sight, showing he held no weapons. The young man stopped and stared, wide eyes showing fright as he looked around for any others. Tate kept his tone mild, and began, "I mean you no harm," using his hands in sign. "I just want to talk a little. Do you speak English?" Tate waited for any response, but the obviously scared young man held tightly to a long stick used to prod the sheep and stared at the white man.

The shepherd slowly nodded his head and spoke softly, "I speak English."

"Good, good," answered Tate as he stepped down and reached in his pocket for some smoked meat. He held out his hand to offer some to the young man and he sat down on a nearby stone. "My name's Tate, what's yours?"

The Navajo cautiously came near and reached for the meat, "I am Big Twin," he answered, taking a bite of the meat and tearing off a piece. In most introductions by the *Diné* the name would be followed by the clans, but the boy was cautious of the man before him.

"Nice lookin' sheep you got there," said Tate, nodding to the woolies. "Takin' 'em into the canyon, are ya?"

"Yes. There is more graze in the canyon. More water."

"Your family livin' down there?" asked Tate.

"Sometimes," answered Big Twin, noncommittally. Suddenly, he stepped back as his eyes grew large, moving the stick before him.

Lobo had come from his perch and padded up to stop beside Tate, looking at the young man. Tate watched the reaction of Big Twin and said, "Don't be afraid, he's my friend."

"He is Má iitsoh!" declared Big Twin, pointing at Lobo.

"If you mean, he's a wolf, yeah. I call him Lobo!"

The Navajo recognized the Spanish term for wolf and frowned at the white man before him, "He is your friend?" he asked.

"Yeah, he is. Been with me most of his life. He's a good protector," answered Tate.

"Má iitsoh is the protector of the Bitter Water Clan and the protector of Abalone Shell Boy and of Doko'o'osliid, the sacred mountain you call San Francisco Peaks. Má iitsoh was given by Changing Woman to our people in the beginning of time."

"You don't say. Well, he's" reaching down to stroke Lobo's scruff, "been my protector for many years, too."

Big Twin looked at Tate, a slight frown wrinkling his forehead, "You must be favored by Changing Woman, or you could not walk with Má iitsoh."

"You speak English very well. Where did you learn?"

"When the black robes came, it was easier for them to teach us Spanish and English than for them to learn the language of the *Diné.* Since that time, our fathers have taught us."

Tate nodded his understanding, having heard about the missions of the Spaniards before. "Well, how 'bout you doin' a favor for both of us, will you? When you take your flock down into the canyon, you need to tell your people that they need to surrender to Fort Defiance." The boy took a step back at the term surrender, but Tate continued. "Now, don't go gettin' all excited. I know Colonel Carson, and he has promised that if your people surrender, no one will be harmed, but they will have to go to Bosque Redondo. If they do, they will be given plenty of food and blankets, so they won't go hungry."

"But some of our people wanted to surrender, and they were shot!" answered the Navajo.

"I know, and that's a terrible thing. But the men that did that have been punished and it won't happen again. And if your people don't surrender, the troops are gonna come into the canyon and many will die. You don't want that, do you?

"You tell your people Má iitsoh," he nodded toward Lobo, "and Longbow," pointing his thumb at his chest, "will make sure they are protected. Can you do that?"

"You are Longbow?"

"That's right, I'm known as Longbow by many nations," answered Tate.

Big Twin looked from Tate to Lobo and back to Tate, "May I touch?" motioning toward Lobo.

"Sure, but go easy, now." He watched as the Navajo cautiously stepped forward, hand outstretched as Tate looked to Lobo and spoke softly, "Easy boy, easy. He just wants to pet you."

The man let the wolf smell his hand, then he reached up to stroke Lobo on top of his head and behind his ears. With a wide-eyed stare, the Navajo moved very slowly, and stepped back as a grin split his face. He looked up to Tate and said, "I will tell my people. I do not know what they will do, but I will tell them."

"Good, good," answered Tate as he stood then remounted Shady. Big Twin had moved back to his sheep, glanced back at Tate and prodded the herd before him to move them further into the canyon. Tate watched, then gigged Shady up the draw to top out on the rim. Lobo trotted alongside as he pointed the grulla to the far canyon rim, where he would begin his search. He worked his way southwest along the rim, stopping and walking to the edge where he would glass the valley bottom. With the fashioned, leather hood that extended over the end of the scope he was certain no reflection would give his location away and he scanned the far wall and canyon bottom for any sign of habitation. Each stop showed new marvels at the handiwork of the Creator, with red rock pillars, multi-hued canyon walls that appeared to be painted in stripes of reds, tans, greys, and whites. The soft sandstone had been worn smooth and carved by the elements giving the appearance of ancient palaces and monuments. The marvels continued to grasp Tate's imagination and brought unsolicited utterances of praise and wonder. While the canyon walls were devoid of any life, the bottom held a variety of trees and bushes, some were fruit trees that had been planted in decades past by ancestors of the *Diné* that now hid within the shadows and crevices of the canyon.

Tate rolled to his back and extended his hands toward the sun to calculate how much daylight was left. He decided to head back to his camp, saving the rest of the south rim for tomorrow. With an early start, he should be able to give a good search and then start to the north rim and maybe Canyon del Muerto the next day. He knew his mission might take more than a week, but from all the signs, the Navajo were in the canyon and that was what Carson needed to know.

CHAPTER SEVENTEEN
DISCOVERY

It was the day after White Fox met her Santa Fe parents that Sean accompanied his sister to Fort Marcy to visit her Lieutenant Whitcomb. She had detected a different mood with the lieutenant when he visited her at their house, and she suspected he had received orders to leave Fort Marcy. She had coerced her brother to escort her to the fort as it wasn't proper for a young lady to visit the post unaccompanied.

"So, just what makes you suspicious of your lieutenant?" asked Sean, grinning at his little sister.

"He's not *my* lieutenant! And I'm not *suspicious!* It's just that he was, well, distracted when we talked, not his usual talkative self and I just thought there was something bothering him. I suspect he's got orders to leave, just as we were getting, you know, acquainted." She pouted a little, trying to be nonchalant in her manner, but she was unsuccessful in fooling her brother, who knew her moods better than anyone.

"You kinda like this 'un, huh?" asked Sean, without showing any concern or joviality.

Sadie stopped walking, turned to her brother, and with a very serious expression and placing her hand on his arm, "Yes, I *more* than like him. But don't go telling Mother or Father. I'll do that *if* we get more serious." It was an admonishing remark but bore the tone of imploring her brother to keep her secret.

Sean grinned at the woman standing before him, realizing all the more that she was no longer his *little* sister, "Don't worry, I'll let you deliver that bit all by yourself."

They started walking again and she glanced at him, "Yeah, a lot you know about it. You went and got married before anyone even met your intended." She swung a playful slap at his arm and they both chuckled at the truth of the past.

They turned the corner to start up the slight slope toward the fort when they encountered the lieutenant coming toward them. He grinned widely, "Well, the two people I most wanted to see! I was just coming to see you," he declared as he took Sadie's hand. Looking to Sean he said, "Come, come, let's go into Mama Ortega's, I've got something to tell the both of you!"

Lieutenant Josiah Whitcomb held the chair for Sadie, then seated himself across from Sean. He looked from Sean to Sadie, leaned forward conspiratorially and started, "I've received orders!"

Sadie put her hand to her mouth as she gasped, "Oh no, Josiah!"

The prim officer looked to the lady beside him, "It's fine, Sadie. It's not permanent, I'll be back." He looked to Sean, "And if I can convince Sean to come with, then I might be back even sooner. I've been tasked with taking the new company of volunteers and a load of supplies to Fort Wingate, then return with some wounded men and dispatches. That's all, but it will take about two weeks, maybe a little longer."

"Oh," replied Sadie, obviously relieved. Then looking to Sean, "What does Sean have to do with it?"

"We need a scout, and the commandant asked if I knew of any that might be available and I said, I might." He grinned as he looked across the table at Sean, "I imagine you've had your fill of listening to the talk of three women, haven't you?"

Sean grinned and answered, "There is no safe answer to that question, but it would be nice to get out of town for a while. However, I did promise my pa that I'd watch over the womenfolk."

Sadie giggled at her brother, "As if we can't watch over our ownselves. But you might want to talk to both Ma and White Fox before you commit yourself. Because if you decide to go, just remember, you have to come back and I'm sure you'd like a warm welcome when you return as opposed to a load of buckshot!"

SEAN SAT atop the point above Bonito Canyon. Below and behind him lay Fort Canby. The bottom of the canyon, some five hundred feet below him, was long in shadows from the slow rising sun that pushed Sean's shadow to the edge of the knoll. The grey line of early morn slowly lifted its skirts as long lances of red and orange began to stretch across the sky. Sean had followed his father's example and met with his Lord at break of day. He knew somewhere to the north and west, his pa was scouting for Navajo somewhere around the Canyon de Chelly. Although they both were attached to Fort Canby, Tate serving under Carson and Sean with Captain Albert Pfeiffer, they seldom were at the fort together.

Sean was remembering his brief time with Sadie and Josiah Whitcomb when he was recruited to serve as a scout, a term he originally thought was to be quite temporary, but he was soon conscripted by the commandant of Fort Wingate to guide the new recruits on to Fort Canby. It was the possibility of meeting up with his pa that convinced Sean to take the assignment, but as so often happens, one thing leads to another and now he was the scout for

Carson's friend, Captain Pfeiffer. That time with Sadie and Josiah had been several weeks ago, but at least the lieutenant had promised to take word to the ladies of his continuing work as a scout and that he hoped to join up with his father.

He picked up a small stone and tossed it toward a tree, as he thought of his wife White Fox, and his mother and sister, all of whom were waiting in Santa Fe, hoping their men would be back for Christmas. But Sean had learned just yesterday that no leaves would be granted for anyone to go home for Christmas, but that the campaign against the Navajos would be pressed forward even more than before. He shook his head as he thought of the few expeditions he had been on with Pfeiffer and the captives taken and homes destroyed. He didn't like it, but he had also seen the destruction and death dealt out by raiding parties of the Navajo. He had tried to balance the scales of understanding and ended by praying that the Lord would soon bring it all to an end.

He rose, picked up the reins of his Appaloosa, Dusty, and motioned for the big black wolf, Indy, to lead the way as he mounted up and reined around to return to Fort Canby. He was hopeful of seeing his pa soon as he considered what some of the men were saying about the possibility of a major assault on Canyon de Chelly.

Tate had finished his reconnaissance of the south rim of the canyon and had packed up his camp and was now slowly making his way around a deep side canyon that cut due north from the otherwise east west lateral of the main gorge. He dipped into the tail end of the arroyo that fed the larger defile, and Shady dug his hooves deep in the soft soil of the far bank to make it back into the trees. He stopped, stepped down, and loosened the girth on Shady, the cinch on the pack-saddle of the bay and let the horses have a blow. They shook, rattling the gear, and Tate poured water into his hat for each to have a drink. Although the air was cool and the snow had been driven into the dry soil by the hot sun of the last two days, it was still obviously winter in the high desert. Temperature in the shade was at least ten degrees cooler and the breeze drove the chill into the collar of his capote. His buffalo robe was tied on the pack, too hot for the sunshine, but very welcome in the night.

He tipped the canteen up and took a long draught, then felt the weight of his second canteen on the pack. It was full but, with one down, he had to find water soon. Hanging the empty canteen on the saddle horn, he ground tied the horses, bid Lobo follow and walked out of the trees, hunkered down on a rock, to take a survey of the side canyon, searching for any water. But he was disappointed, nothing showed sign of a stream or spring or even a tank of standing water. But if the Navajo were there, there would also be water, and he would find it. With a last look to scan the canyon below, he returned to the horses to move further along the rim with his scout.

The further he traveled, the more he saw and the more amazed he was at the work of the Creator. The sculpted pillars and towers formed over eons of erosion appeared as if each one was carefully crafted and allowed to be uncovered by the master artisan, the Creator. He was belly down, enamored with the beauty of the canyon, when movement caught his eye. Several warriors were descending pole ladders, apparently coming from caves that lay beneath his promontory. He watched and counted, six . . . seven . . . eight . . . nine . . . ten, for a total of fourteen warriors, all with weapons that ranged from rifles to lances and bows and arrows. This was more than a hunting party.

He continued to watch as they dropped to the valley floor then disappeared around a talus slope, to re-emerge horseback. Led by a stocky man with long loose hair bound only by a headband in the tradition of an Apache, the band moved to Tate's left, up-canyon, and he realized they took to the side canyon and came out very near where he had stopped and surveyed that same canyon just moments before. The trees obscured his view of them and theirs of him, but he heard them move away, almost backtracking his course. He shook his head and realized he held his breath, hoping they would not see his tracks and come after him. But the sounds of their leaving diminished, and he was relieved, believing he was safe, at least for the moment.

With one last look around, he returned to his horses and started off to continue his search of the valley below. Now he knew there were several different groups within the canyon, and the raiding party that just left was only one of many. He looked to the sky, calculating the remaining hours of daylight and searched for any sign of winter storm, but seeing none and thinking there were at least three hours of light remaining, he continued his reconnaissance.

His next promontory was chosen because he saw the junction on the opposite side with what he had heard called Monument Canyon. As he bellied down with his scope, he was surprised to see a lone spire that stood what he estimated to be almost eight hundred feet tall. The red sandstone stood like a giant lance thrust into the ground with its tip pointed heavenward. The slow setting sun stretched the shadow of the spire back against the grey cliff face making it appear even taller. Tate watched the shadows lengthen like from some giant sundial as the end of the day was being cast in black shadows. He pulled back from his overlook, stepped back aboard Shady and motioned Lobo toward the far edge of the opposite canyon that came from the Canyon del Muerto. He had spotted a ravine with some greenery and thought they might find some snowmelt or other source of water. He had guessed right and came upon Lobo lapping water from a small seep below a cluster of alder and willows. Here he would make camp, and hopefully finish his reconnoiter on the morrow, but for now, food and rest beckoned.

CHAPTER EIGHTEEN
CAPTAIN

DUSTY STRETCHED OUT, ENJOYING THE RUBDOWN FROM SEAN. HE nosed into the grain in the

feed bin, savoring the rarity but he bent his neck and looked at his man, suspicious of the treatment and looking like he was wondering what was in store. Sean had always liked taking time to spoil his Appy, the horse had been a faithful companion and many times taken Sean places most horses would balk at and delivered him from predicaments that could have been deadly. Truly a time when man and horse were best friends, with both enjoying the benefits of that friendship.

"You treat that horse like he was your best friend!" came a raspy voice from the doorway of the livery. It was the unmistakable grating growl of First Sergeant James McKee, "You're like Cap'n Pfeiffer, always spoilin' his horse!"

"This horse has gotten me outta more trouble than I can shake a stick at, Sergeant. He deserves all the spoilin' he can handle." Sean stopped, turning to the seasoned soldier, "You've been with the captain for some time, haven't you Sarge?"

"More'n most. Was with him down at Fort McRae after he had

that little set-to wit' them 'Paches, been with him ever' since! He's a good man, Cap'n is, yessir. None better!"

Sean turned back to his brushing of Dusty but spoke over his shoulder as he asked, "Has he always been such a, well, I guess you could say, angry fighter?"

"You'd be angry too, youngster, if you had to go through what he did," drawled the whiskery faced first sergeant. He was a weathered man, sun-darkened complexion, wrinkled skin, a big drooping moustache that hid his upper lip and most of his lower one too. He pushed his cap back, showing his receding hairline and thinning salt and pepper hair. He took a seat on a tack box, looked up at Sean, "I don't usually tell this, but you've shown yourself to be a good scout and dependable fighter too, so, mebbe you need to know 'bout the cap'n. He had him a real purty wife, they'd been married oh, 'bout seven years, I reckon, an' she was with him down to Fort McRae. One day, she asked the cap'n, . . ."

"ALBERT, could we go to the hot springs? I've just been so, well, uncomfortable with this pregnancy and I'd love to just sit an' soak in those waters. Could we please?" Antonita Salinas had fallen in love with the dashing Captain Pfeiffer almost from the first time they met. He had been working with a freighter out of St. Louis and made trips to Santa Fe where they first met, introduced by Captain Charles Deus of Fort Marcy, who invited them to a party at the fort. They were inseparable and were soon married in a very elaborate ceremony in the church. She wore the most expensive wedding dress she could find and was laden with beautiful jewelry like none had seen before. From her hair ornaments to the white satin with hand stitched roses and the filigree medallions on her necklace, she was the most beautiful of brides. Albert Pfeiffer was determined to give her the best life he could, and soon took a commission as Captain of Company A in the militia of New Mexico.

With a pretty little daughter of six that was the mirror image of her mother, they now expected and hoped for a son. Captain Pfeiffer could never say no to his wife, even if he wanted to, which he didn't, and when she asked to go to the hot springs for a refreshing soak in the mineral waters, he quickly made the arrangements. Although the Apache and Comanche were actively raiding, he thought an escort of six soldiers would be more than enough to provide safety for his family, and with two servant girls, his wife and daughter should be well attended.

The hot springs were only about twelve miles from the fort, and it was mid-morning when they arrived. With several trees and shrubs nearby, it was just moments before the ladies were in the water, enjoying the warmth and refreshing minerals. Across the pool and beyond some more shrubs, the captain was also soaking up the warmth, leaning back against the stones at the edge of the bank, and dozing.

A stifled scream from the ladies side caught his attention, but he thought it was just horseplay or something and called out, "Is everything alright? Antonita? Are you alright?" He grew alarmed and waded to the end of the small pool to look around just in time to see several mounted Apache making off with all four of the women and girls. He hollered as they fled, but none slowed. He quickly looked for the six-soldier escort, saw two men down, another holding his side as blood flowed, but two others had dropped to one knee and were taking aim with their rifles when the captain shouted, "NO! You'll hit the women!" As he shouted, he waddled from the water, grabbed his rifle and took off, naked and barefoot, in pursuit of the raiders. The Apache had taken their horses, and he had no concern for the soldiers, believing they could take care of their own, his only concern was his wife and daughter.

As he ran, bow-legged as he was, he paid no heed to the rocks or cacti in his way. He had gone most of two miles when the Apache reined up to look back. When they saw the man, several of them turned back to attack the captain, who frantically searched for cover and ran to a pile of rock. An excellent shot, he took aim at the Apache in the lead and carefully took his shot, hitting the man's horse that catapulted his rider over his head and he stumbled and fell. The Apache jumped to his feet and took the second shot of the captain in his chest that dropped him where he stood, never to rise again.

Pfeiffer swung his rifle to take aim on another and his next three shots all scored a kill, which caused the Apache to break off their charge and take cover. But it was a hot and merciless sun that bore down on the naked captain, making him even more uncomfortable sitting amongst the hot rocks. Yet every time the Apache sought to attack, his unerring marksmanship took a toll and by mid-afternoon, the attackers made their escape.

As Captain Pfeiffer thought about his family and the Apache, he thought they would not immediately kill the women, for if that's all they wanted they would have done it at the springs. But by taking them captive he was certain they intended to keep them as slaves or wives. With that assurance, he determined to make it to the fort for reinforcements to go after his family. The nine miles would normally be an easy hike for a seasoned soldier, but he had neither uniform nor boots, but his resolve outweighed his handicaps and he started his trek.

When he was still three or four miles from the fort, he was startled by the screaming war cries of three Apache that came galloping up behind him. With no cover, he dropped to one knee and took careful aim, shooting one warrior from his horse, but the others were upon him and he turned to run, taking one arrow in his back, the point of which protruded from his chest, and another in his leg. He stumbled, caught himself with an outstretched arm, then turned to shoot the nearest attacker, killing him and causing the last man to turn and flee.

Captain Pfeiffer struggled to his feet, and staggered on the rest of the way, making it to the fort to the alarm and amazement of the soldiers in the bastions. They immediately shouted to open the gates, and the regimental surgeon was summoned. With the captain seated, the surgeon looked at the man, "This is gonna hurt, but prob'ly not as much as you've already experienced." The surgeon shook his head as he worked to cut the shaft of the arrow just behind the point, then stood behind the captain, placed one hand on his back, and nodding to his assistant to hold the man still, he slowly withdrew the arrow, causing the captain to slump forward, unconscious.

Two days later, the captain opened his eyes, looking around at the inside of the fort infirmary, seeing an orderly, he asked, "Where am I?"

The man in white came near, "Why, you're at Fort McRae, Captain. You've been here two days now. How ya' feelin'?"

"Two days?!" he pushed the covers back, looking around, "Where's my uniform?"

"Uh, you weren't wearin' one, sir."

Memories of the attack flooded back into his consciousness, "My family! I've got to get my family! Get me some clothes, now!" he demanded.

The orderly hesitated, "Uh, cap'n, the troopers done went out after your family, sir."

"They did? Did they find them? Are they alright?" demanded the captain, looking around, hoping to see his Antonita.

The regimental surgeon heard the ruckus and came to the

captain's bed, "Captain, I'm sorry to tell you sir, the troopers did find your wife and daughter and the servant girls. They were all dead, sir. I'm sorry, Captain."

Pfeiffer drew a deep breath, looking at the surgeon, then dropped his head, slowly shaking it side to side. In a whisper he said, "My Antonita, and little Angelina, no, no, no." He turned, buried his face in the pillow and let deep sobs wrack his body. The surgeon turned to leave, motioning the orderly to leave also, and the captain was given time to grieve alone.

The agony of intense pain replaced the grief. The sun-scorched skin was as grievous as the arrow wounds and his suffering continued for many days. It would be two months before he was allowed to leave the infirmary, another month to return to duty.

". . . and ever since that time, he's been fightin' Injuns. Can't say's I blame him none. He's been a long-time friend of Carson an' if the man has a fault, it's his drinkin'. Now, if he was Irish, like me, he'd be able to hold his liquor better, but he's one of them Dutcheys, so, . . ." left off the sergeant, grinning at Sean.

As the sergeant had related the story, Sean had taken a seat on another tack box opposite and listened intently. He remembered his emotions when White Fox had been taken by the Crow and he could hardly imagine how he would feel if he lost both his wife and a child.

"I've been with him when he fought Comanche, Apache, an' more, and I ain't never been alongside anybody else that I'd rather be with in an Injun fight, than Cap'n Pfeiffer. Now, don't you go sayin' nuthin' 'bout what I done said, now, y'hear?" drawled the sergeant.

Sean looked at the grizzled first sergeant, respectful of the comradeship he shared with the captain, and nodded, "Never," answered Sean. “What little I’ve ridden with the man, he’s never given me any reason to doubt him, now I understand why. I believe you’re right, Sergeant, he’s a good man.”

The first sergeant rose, looking around for some place to spit his chaw, finally settling on a corner of a stall and let it fly. He wiped his chin with his sleeve, nodded his head, and walked out of the livery, never looking back. Sean chuckled and returned to his labors with Dusty.

CHAPTER NINETEEN
REPORT

It was just a wisp of smoke, more the smell of smoke, that stopped Tate. He was in the sparse juniper above the north rim of Canyon del Muerto, having finished his reconnoiter of Canyon de Chelly, he chose to circumvent the smaller canyon by making a wide swing to the north and then to the west. He was bound for Fort Canby, about two and a half days ride away. He wasn't expecting to find any Navajo in the trees, it wasn't their way, but the smoke told of someone. He stepped down, ground tied Shady, and with Lobo leading the way, he made a stealthy advance toward what he expected would be a camp.

Tate was suddenly stopped by the cry of a baby. He dropped to one knee, motioning Lobo to his side, and listened. It *was* the cry of an infant! Tate and Lobo looked at one another, both showing confused expressions. He leaned to the side of the tree, trying to see through the branches and saw a lean-to shelter made of both branches and blankets, the tendril of smoke curling upwards just beyond. They waited, and a man went to a pot beside the fire, reached in with a rag, soaked it, wrung it out and turned back to the lean-to. It didn't take much to understand what was happening, but Tate was concerned about the child and what might happen if he approached.

With a motion to Lobo, they returned to the horses and mounted up. They started toward the camp, humming a tune just to appear unthreatening and letting the camp know he was approaching. Once he broke through the trees he reined up, leaned on the pommel of his saddle and spoke, "Mornin' folks!"

Standing before the lean-to was a tall Navajo man, a boy of about ten, and a girl of about six. The man appeared to be unarmed but stood stoic and staring at the intruder. The children stared at Lobo, at once frightened and fascinated.

Tate sat back, and using sign and speaking said, "Heard the baby cry. Thought you folks might use some food an' such. Young-sters look hungry, I got some meat there," he pointed to the haunch of a deer atop the rig on the pack-horse. "I'm gonna get down, don't mean you no harm." He slowly swung his leg over the cantle and stepped down. He walked back to the bay horse and took the hind quarter down, carried it to the fire, and lay it on a large flat rock nearby. Lobo was at his side every step, and bellied down next to the big rock, looking at the children, tongue lolling and with his usual open-mouthed smile.

All this time, the three family members did not move, nor speak, and Tate stopped, hands on hips and asked, "Do any of you speak English?"

"Some," answered the man.

"Good!" responded Tate. He pointed at his chest, "I'm Tate, also known as Longbow. You look kinda busy, would you like me to fix a meal?"

"You would do that?"

"I'm hungry, aren't you?" asked Tate. Then turning to the children, he asked, "Hungry?" while rubbing his belly and smiling. The boy looked from Tate to his father, then back at Tate and nodded his head. The girl stepped behind her father and held onto his leg while peeking around at this strange white man. Tate saw the girl tug on her father's britches and, pointing at Lobo, said, "Ma' iitsoh!"

The father looked at his daughter, nodded his head and put a finger to his lips for her to remain silent.

"Good, good," answered Tate, looking up at the man, "You go 'head on and tend to your woman and baby, I'll get us sumpin' to eat goin' and we'll have us a good meal." Without waiting for an answer, Tate went to the packs and fetched the frying pan, coffee pot, cornmeal, flour, and coffee and returned to the fire. He filled the coffee pot from a canteen and put it on the small flat rock by the flames, then set about making some johnnycakes and slicing some venison. He looked at the boy, "Can you fetch me some green sticks, 'bout so long?" stretching his hands apart about two feet. He drew out his knife, held it by the blade toward the boy. The boy nodded, took the knife and started down the slope toward some oak brush, searching for just the right sticks.

Tate sat back on the big rock, sipping his coffee. Everyone had eaten their fill and the children joined their mother in the lean-to while the man, who Tate learned was named Delgadito or Tall Painful One, joined Tate for coffee.

The Indian looked at Tate, "Why you do this?" he asked, taking a swig of coffee as he waited for an answer.

Tate looked at the proud warrior, dropped his eyes, and chuckled, "Well, I had the meat, you were hungry, so, seemed like the right thing to do."

Delgadito looked at Tate, pondering what he had said, then replied, "You are not like most white men. Most I have known would kill Navajo, not feed him."

Tate considered, "Yeah, there are some like that, just like there are some *Diné* that would do the same thing to a white man."

"Ummm," grunted Delgadito in agreement.

Tate glanced back toward the lean-to and asked, "Your woman gonna be alright?"

"Ummm," nodded the man. "She good woman. Ready to travel tomorrow."

Tate had learned that among the Navajo, a direct question into the affairs of another is considered rude and the people did not ask but waited for the other to tell what he wanted someone to know. If he didn't say anything, all the questions would be to no avail, for they would go unanswered. So, Tate slowly nodded his head, took another drink and waited for Delgadito to share whatever he thought necessary.

After a pause of a couple minutes, the warrior looked at Tate, "We are going to the fort to surrender. We may be killed, but it is better than dying of hunger in the winter."

Tate thought about the man and what he was determined to do, even though he thought he and his family might be killed at the hands of the soldiers, he thought this was the only chance for his family to survive the winter. Tate tossed the dregs of his coffee into the grass, and looked to Degadito, "If it's alright with you, I'll go with you to the fort. I know Colonel Carson very well and he has promised that any Navajo that surrenders will not be killed. And if I go with you, I will make certain you and your family will be safe. But you know you will have to go to Basque Redondo, don't you?"

"I know. But will the soldiers have food for my family?"

"Yes, they have promised to have food for everyone and anything else you might need."

"Good. We will go with the first light," declared the man, standing to go to the lean-to with his family.

. . .

THEY MADE an unusual sight walking into the fort. Tate and Delgadito, side by side leading the horses, the Indian standing as tall as Tate, which was unusual for the Navajo were not a tall people, and the boy beside his father. The woman with the baby in her arms sat on Shady, the little girl behind her mother. When Tate tethered Shady and the pack-horse at the rail before the commandant's cabin, several soldiers stopped to gawk, but no one said anything. Tate looked to Delgadito and motioned for him to come with him, and the two men walked into the cabin to be greeted by the orderly seated at a small desk in the outer room.

"Afternoon Corporal. Carson in?" asked Tate.

"Uh, yessir, Mr. Saint, sir. I'm sure he'll want to see you. Go on in," he said, staring at the tall Navajo.

As the door swung wide and Tate stepped in, Carson grinned and stood with his hand outstretched. He started to speak but saw the man with his friend and looked back at Tate with an expectant expression. Tate chuckled, "Colonel Carson, this is Delgadito. He and his family have come in to surrender and go to Bosque Redondo."

Carson extended his hand to the man, "Greetings Delgadito. I'm glad to hear you've decided to surrender. Are there others with you?"

"No. Others think they will be killed. I will take my family to Bosque, and if what Longbow says is true, I will return to tell my people to surrender."

Tate was visibly surprised to hear Delgadito make the offer to return. That had not been mentioned during their two-day trip from the canyon, but it was good news to both Tate and Carson.

Carson responded, "Good, good. That's all I've wanted. It's much better that they surrender than for us to have to fight."

Delgadito raised one hand, "I do not know if they will surrender. But if it is as you say, I will tell them. It is each man's choice to surrender or not. My brother, Barboncito had said he will never surrender."

"Your brother is Barboncito? I met him and talked with him. He is a good leader of your people, but let's hope he changes his mind. I would hate to see so many people die for no reason." He sat back in his chair, motioned for the two men to be seated, and called for the corporal. When the orderly came into the office, Carson instructed, "Show Delgadito and his family where they can sleep, with the others that have come in, and make sure they have ample food and blankets."

"Yessir, Colonel sir!" answered the orderly.

Carson addressed Delgadito, "The corporal will show you where you can bed down, there are some others that have come in and you'll be with them. If you need any food or blankets, tell the corporal here and he'll get what you need."

Delgadito stood, shook Carson's hand, and left the office with the corporal. Carson turned to Tate, "Good Job, Tate. I didn't expect you to bring in any of 'em, but it's good! Now, tell me 'bout'chur scout, any Navajo in the canyons?"

Tate stood and walked to the map on the wall, it was a crude representation of the larger area but with the canyons clearly marked. He pointed to the beginnings of the canyon and pointed to the places he stopped and observed, what he saw and what he thought. "From all I could see, Colonel, and I know you don't wanna hear it, but there are quite a few groups the canyons. They're not all in one area, some appear to be in caves or other overhangs, some are in the old cliff dwellings, and it appears they've stocked up whatever they could hoard. With 'em all hidin' out, there's no way to tell how many, but I'd say quite a few."

"Where'd you find Delgadito?" asked Kit.

Tate pointed toward the north edge of Canyon del Muerto, "Right 'bout here. His boy told me 'bout a place called Massacre Cave, said his people won't go in there, but many years ago they did. Said there was o'er a hunnert of 'em there when the Spaniards attacked and massacred the bunch of 'em. Said there was thirty, forty, women an' children killed there. Apparently, they believe that wherever someone dies, his chindi or spirit hangs around and the bad part ain't nuthin' to mess with, so they don't go where they died."

"I'm familiar with the story. Happened back somewhere around 1810 or so. That's just another reason why the Navajo believe all other people want to kill the *Diné*." Carson leaned back in his chair, looked at Tate as he sat down, "Carleton's pushin' pretty hard. Wants me to go into the Canyon. Says we ain't gettin' any leaves to go to our families until I have at least a hundred captives ready to go to Bosque."

Tate leaned back in his chair, folded his arms across his chest, "Think he'd wait long 'nuff for Delgadito to go to Bosque and come back to get 'em to surrender?"

"No. That's five, six weeks. He wants it done and soon. So, I'm puttin' together a plan. I'll be countin' on you and Sean to do some scoutin'. You up to it?"

"Will it get us home sooner?" asked Tate, leaning forward, elbows on knees.

"After this is done, you, Sean, and me will all go home, Carleton can put it in his pipe an' smoke it, for all I care. My Josefa wants to see me, I wanna see her an' the kids, and I'm sure Maggie and White Fox are feelin' the same."

CHAPTER TWENTY
PLANS

Barboncito led the band of raiders, sitting on his horse proudly, stiff-backed, holding his Hawken rifle butt on his thigh. His people needed meat and the many patrols and expeditions of the bluecoats had driven what game was left deeper into the Chuska Mountains and beyond. He was intent on striking back at those that sought to destroy his people. They had fought the Mexicans and the Ute for generations, but now they had the forces of Carson against them and the *Diné* were facing starvation as they hid in the canyons, helpless against the fierce winter. Most were almost out of food while many had already exhausted their hoards. Before they left the canyon, he had found the bodies of an entire family, huddled together and frozen. The canyon had been picked clean of any wood for fires to warm the caves or dwellings and most had lost their extra blankets and clothing in the raids of the bluecoats. It was rage that boiled in the hearts of Barboncito and his warriors.

"They are fools!" declared Barboncito as he stood beside his scouts. They were standing on an escarpment, shielded by a stand of juniper, overlooking Fort Canby. The herds of horses and mules were between the fort and their promontory, with a lone sentry dozing at his post. The light of the moon showed the herd numbered several hundred, but Barboncito's band of fourteen warriors could not handle that many. As he surveyed the herd, one of the scouts pointed out several mules in a bunch apart from the others. Barboncito nodded his head and turned back to his band, "Two Toes, you take these," motioning to eight of the warriors standing beside their ponies, "cut through the herd slowly and quietly." He motioned to another, "Walking Man, you take the sentry. When he is dead, your signal like the blackbird, will start the others. I will take the rest, there," pointing to the upper end of the herd, "we will drive them away. We will cross the ridge by the cottonwood spring." He looked to the others, waiting for questions. When no one spoke, he nodded to Walking Man to go for the sentry.

TATE AND SEAN stood at the back wall, looking over those that were gathered before them. Carson sat behind his desk but at his right sat Captain Asa Carey, appointed by General Carleton as the post commander whenever Carson was absent. In front of the desk were Captain Albert Pfeiffer, Captain Eben Everett, and Captain Joseph Berney. Lieutenant Colonel Chaves and Major Rafael Chacon were seated together to the right of Carson's desk.

Carson stood, walked toward the map, but was interrupted by banging on the door and a call from the orderly, "Colonel, Colonel!" Carson frowned, irritation showing, "Come in, Corporal!"

The door swung wide and an excited corporal started,

"Colonel, beg pardon sir, but the Indians have raided our herds, again!" He gasped for breath, "The sentry had his throat slit and they run off about twenty head of mules, sir!"

Carson pounded the desk, sheaves of paper under the rock paperweight and the inkwell and blotter bounced at the impact. Carson grabbed for the inkwell to keep it from spilling and moved it to the side near the blotter and pen. He looked angrily at the corporal, "What's being done?"

"Uh, Major Ayers was the officer of the day and he ordered a squad under Sergeant Herrera to go after 'em, sir!"

Carson stood, fuming, then took a deep breath to compose himself, "Good, good. He's 'bout the best man for the job." He looked up at the corporal, "Have him report to me immediately when he returns!"

"Yessir!" answered the corporal, saluting. Carson returned the salute and dismissed the corporal before returning to his chair. He looked at the officers around him, "That's just what we need! After what we lost in that attack on the supply train, and what Major Sena let the Navajos run off, we're gettin' a little lean of animals. But just so you know, General Carleton says the lack of stock is no excuse!

"His words," Carson reached for the most recent missive from the general, "'It is hoped hereafter, your command will be able to protect its own stock.'" Carson looked up at the assembled officers, "He goes on to say that if the men have to carry their own provisions and gear and walk, we cannot delay the expedition into Canyon de Chelly."

Carson walked to the map, nodded to Tate and said, "First, I want our scout, Tate Saint, to give you an idea of what he saw in the canyons."

Tate stepped to the map and began, "I started out here," pointing to the eastern most end of the canyon at Whiskey Creek,

"I scouted the south and north edges of the Canyon de Chelly and some of the north edge of Canyon del Muerto." As he spoke, he indicated on the map where he had reconnoitered and what he saw, giving both a description of the canyons and the sign of any Navajo hiding within. "If you've never seen the canyon, you should know it is a formidable sight. The walls in most places are near to a thousand feet of sheer cliff or steep sandstone. There are very few places where you can enter or leave the canyon. I guess it to be about twenty-five miles from this end," pointing to the eastern beginning of the canyon, "to the mouth, here." He looked at the men, "There are several side canyons that could hide hundreds of people, caves that are big enough for hundreds more, and cliff dwellings that are totally inaccessible and could hold several hundred. But, according to Delgadito and the young Navajo with the sheep that I talked to, the people are starving and freezing."

A voice came from the group, "You saw and talked to a Navajo with a herd of sheep?"

"That's right," answered Tate.

"Did you take the sheep or kill them? Couldn't the Indians have them to eat?"

Tate stared at the questioning Captain Carey for a moment, then without answering, turned back to the map. "This branch," pointing at the upper portion of the map, "is called the Canyon del Muerto, the Canyon of Death, because the Navajo have hidden there before and the Spaniards attacked and killed well over a hundred that hid in the cave called Massacre Cave." He turned back to the men, "These people are used to being attacked and what we bring is nothing new. They are determined to stay hidden, even if they starve." He looked to Carson, who nodded, and Tate returned to stand beside Sean.

Carson stood before the map, and looking to the officers, "Captain Pfeiffer, you and your company H will leave first and go to the northwest to begin your assault from the head of the canyon. You will move through the canyon until you meet the other forces coming from the mouth. I will lead the rest of the force, companies A, D, E, and K. With Major Ayers and Captains Carey, Everett, and Berney, we will begin our assault from the southwest point or the mouth of the canyon. Your orders, gentlemen, are to take captives or encourage the surrender of the Navajo. Only as a last resort are they to be killed!" He purposely looked at each of the officers to ensure every man fully understood. He looked to Pfeifer, "Captain, you will leave Saturday morning, first light. The rest of us," he looked at the other assembled officers, "will leave at first light, Wednesday!"

The men looked to one another, nodding heads and quietly assuring one another. Carson continued, "Now, it's gonna be colder than a well-digger's hind-end! We've got about six inches of snow on the ground now, and could have more 'fore we leave, so prepare accordingly! If there are no questions, you're dismissed!"

Tate and Sean waited for the others to leave then Tate stepped forward, "You really think you oughta be leadin' this bunch, Colonel? I've been noticin' you ain't been lookin' too healthy!"

Carson plopped into his chair, "Aww, it's this cussed wound I got in muh chest, bothers me when the weather's cold. That's all. But, Carleton ain't give me much choice in the matter. If I wanna go home to Josefa, I've gotta have at least a hundred captives!" He looked up at his friend, "You two," looking from Tate to Sean, "have been a great help to me. I couldn't ask for more, an' if you wanna go home to your women folk, I'll understand, but I'm hopin' you'll see this through." He looked to Tate, hopeful expectancy showing in his eyes.

"We will, Kit. And it ain't cuz Carleton's insisting. It's only because we're friends," answered Tate, reaching out a hand to shake.

The colonel leaned forward, grasping Tate's hand in his, slapping the coupled hands with his free hand and looking at Tate, "Thanks friend. I greatly appreciate it."

Both Tate and Sean stepped back, each giving a slight nod as they turned to leave. As they left the office, Tate looked to his son, "You'll be headin' out in the mornin', so, let's get you outfitted proper, reckon?"

"Sounds like the thing to do, Pa," answered Sean, as they walked toward the sutler.

CHAPTER TWENTY-ONE
MARCH

Sean remembered his discussions with his father about the route and trails to the head of Canyon de Chelly. The snow in Bonito Canyon was drifted deep and the fresh legs of Dusty picked his way through, followed close behind by the big black wolf, Indy. Both Sean and Dusty were used to snow, spending most of his life in the mountains of the Wind River Range in the northern reaches of the Rocky Mountains, and those same mountains were where Indy was born so he was a true mountain wolf. This dusting in the desert was nothing compared to the deep snow and drifts of the high country. As the big Appaloosa humped his way through the wide drift, Indy thought it fun to jump and run in the snow, but Sean was thinking about the bend of the trail just beyond that would turn the expedition to the north.

"Here in the high desert, the snow can be misleading," drawled Tate as he leaned back against the wall of the hay loft. He reached out and drew a long piece of hay, putting the end in his mouth, "where it looks like its nice an' flat, could just be drifts coverin' up a dip or even a prairie dog village, so ya' gotta watch close, or ya' might end up breakin' a leg on your horse!" He crossed his outstretched legs at the ankles, "An' that White Cone Mountain I told you about, what with the snow, it won't look any different than the rest of the hills and such. I noticed when I went through there most o' the hills 'round there had about the same shape, so look closely."

Sean sat opposite his pa and near the big door overlooking the parade ground, he glanced out and asked, "You said it would be easy enterin' the canyon from the creek, that right?"

"Yeah and remember the main landmarks. First the big crater with some hills to the west, then crossing the Sunsela saddle between those two purty good sized timber covered hills. Now from that saddle, ya' might get a little high up and you can see that White Cone Mountain straight north of you. Then the start of the canyon will be west southwest from there."

"How long ya' think it'll take the troops to get to the head of the canyon?" asked Sean.

"Hmm, since they'll be walkin' and in no big hurry, I'd say 'bout eight or nine days. You got'chur buffalo robe, don'tchu?"

Sean chuckled, "Yeah, and it sure looks like I'm gonna need it."

THAT CONVERSATION WAS last night in the warmth of the big hay loft, where they nestled down in the soft, warm hay and slept sound, no concern about Indians or any other danger. But that was last night, now Sean was responsible for more than a hundred men. He looked back over his shoulder to see the dark blue line behind the lead wagon pulled by a four-up of mules. Another wagon followed the column of troops with the only horses ridden by the officers, Captain Pfeiffer in the lead.

The trail held to the bottom of the slope, just below the tree line that clung to the west of the long ridge. As it made the bend around the shoulder of the flat top ridge, Sean looked up at the rimrock that hung near the crest, about four hundred feet above the trail. He had often wondered what would happen if that whole line of rimrock gave way at once and tumbled down the slope; there would be destruction for miles. As he scanned the slope, he saw the deep drifts that held to the many dips and draws that came from the top, ruts carved by run-off now held the wet snow, threatening to let their burdens cascade down on unsuspecting travelers. But he dropped his eyes, chuckling at his own imagination and pushed on, setting his sights far to the north.

With his goal being the big crater basin, Sean kept his eye on the long line of the rimrock ridge to his right. At the end of the ridge, lay the basin and hopefully a camp for the night. He knew the men would be tired, cranky, wet and cold, and Tate had suggested camping at the end of the ridge and the edge of the crater. "There's a nice basin there that'd be good cover from the wind. There's also trees an' such for fire, so, if'n I was you, I'd shoot for that for the first camp. After that, them foot so'jers won't make as many miles in a day, an' you'll hafta find camps sooner."

Sean realized he found it easy just to follow his father's suggestions. But that was always the way of it in the wilderness, men quizzed others that knew the land, mentally recording every description of landmarks and dangers, mapping trails out in their minds, and following the suggestions of those that had traveled this way before. The man that sought to make his own discoveries and not heed what others said was a fool and would more often than not find himself in some predicament that could have been avoided if he had only given heed to others. Anyone that chooses to make his own way without using the wisdom of those that have gone before will usually fail and fail miserably. Man does not have enough lifetime to make all the same mistakes over and over again, wisdom chooses to profit from the mistakes of others and make greater progress than those that have gone before.

When the sun was approaching its zenith, Sean reined Dusty to the cluster of trees on the south facing slope of the draw before him. The warm sun had melted the snow and the slight breeze had dried out the spot just below the juniper that Sean chose for his nooning. He loosened the girth on Dusty, ground tied him near some bunch grass, and kindled a little fire for some coffee. He stretched out to absorb some of the warm sun while it lasted, listening for the water to start boiling. He started to doze, but the chug-a-lug of the water brought him around and he dropped a handful of coffee into the pot, replaced the lid, and waited. Within a few moments, he poured just a little cold water in to settle the grounds, then poured himself a cup and sat back, sipping on his coffee and working on the jerky. He would dip the meat into the coffee, let it soak just a mite, then with a sip of coffee and a chew of meat, occasionally tossing a tidbit to the wolf, and he enjoyed his noon.

Once the coffee was gone and the meat consumed, Sean lay back to bask in the sun, Indy at his side. He knew the wolf and Dusty would be ever watchful and he could doze without concern of any danger, and doze he did, with Indy by his side for added warmth. It was a little less than an hour later when a cold nose on his cheek woke him. He looked around, not moving, and saw Dusty standing, head up and ears forward, looking across the trail toward the break in the ridge beyond. Indy was also watching something, but they didn't appear alarmed, just curious. Sean slowly rose, looking where his friends were watching, and saw three deer, one a bit larger than the others, and Sean thought it was a buck. Mule deer shed their antlers in the winter, and it takes a while for the buttons of growing horns to show and this desert Muley looked to be a good one. He watched, and when their heads were down, he reached for his Spencer, thinking the troops might like some fresh meat.

One shot dropped the buck and startled the does, who disappeared as if they were never there, showing white rumps as they vaulted over the nearby greasewood and ocotillo, making for the timber on the ridge beyond. He made short work of field-dressing the buck, lay the carcass over the rump of the Appaloosa, and started on his way again.

He had stopped for his nooning at the end of the rimrock ridge and pointed his way north and around the tree-line to cross the flat before coming to the big crater. As his father had described, the big crater held what he called a 'shadow ridge' that followed the contour of the crater, and the mountains he described were nestled on the far side. He looked around, saw what he thought would make a comfortable camp and stepped down. Once Dusty was stripped of his gear, Sean picketed him near a patch of grass that showed above the snow. He knew the Appy would paw away the snow and enjoy the grass. He dropped his gear near the trees and lay the deer carcass to one side.

He gathered several arms full of firewood, made a couple fire rings with the nearby stones, and started both fires about ten yards apart. He fetched several green sticks from some willows, then sliced off several steaks and skewered them on the willows to hang over the edge of the fire to start cooking. He whipped up some biscuit dough, used two tin plates to hold and cover the biscuits, then made a slight depression, raked some coals in, placed the plates on top and covered them with more coals and a layer of dirt to have an oven.

The western sky was painted in shades of gold and orange, the only two clouds caught and held the colors on the bottom, and the entire land was cast in a golden aura, when the lead wagon rumbled into the camp. Sean had his frying pan stacked with cooked steaks sizzling at the side of the fire while another round of venison steaks hung near the flames. Captain Pfeiffer walked up to the fire, looked around, and watched at Sean uncovered the tins of biscuits and handed him one. The captain, eyes wide in surprise, gladly accepted and quickly bit into the hot treat, smiled and said, "I ain't never had a scout that could and would cook too! These are great!" he declared, looking at the last bit of biscuit in his hand. "Keep this up an' you'll make some woman a good wife!"

Laughter came from behind him as First Sergeant McKee walked up to the fire and accepted a hot biscuit from Sean. He looked at it, took a bite, and smiled, "You sure there ain't some Irish in you m'boy?"

Sean grinned and answered, "My mum is Maggie O'Shaunessey and she's from County Cork!"

The big sergeant grinned, slapped his knee, and said, "I knew it! Tis Irish ye are and allus will be, laddie!"

All the men laughed and made short work of both the steaks and biscuits. Sean let the rest of the men know there were some steaks already cooked, but the late comers might have to slice and cook their own. When he returned to the fire, Captain Pfeiffer looked at him and said, "What you've done has done more than anything else to lift the spirits of these men. They were all grumbling, tired, cold, and hungry. And to come into camp with a fire going and steaks cooking, well, you might just have spoiled 'em, that's all!"

Sean sat down by the fire, poured himself some coffee, and sat back, "The way I look at it Captain, if there's somethin' needs doin' and I've got the time and wherewithal, then I oughta be for doin' it. These men still have a long ways to go, so if this helps, then fine. But, if I run out of coffee, don't be expectin' a sweet disposition less'n you've got some to replace it!" he cautioned.

The captain and sergeant grinned, as the captain said, "Sergeant, you make sure this man never runs out of coffee!"

"I'll certainly see to it, sir!"

CHAPTER TWENTY-TWO
CAPTIVES

THE SNOW WAS COMING FACE ON, COLD WIND DRIVING IT INTO HIM as Sean pulled up the collar on his buffalo robe, burying his face in the fur. He pulled the brim down on the floppy felt hat to shield his eyes, Dusty hung his head but pushed on through the deepening snow. It was before first light when Sean left the encampment, the storm hitting just after the sun winked for a few moments before disappearing behind the storm clouds. With the wind whistling in his ears, the howl of the storm threatened to drive him back into the trees. Dusty stumbled and Sean reined up, stepping down between Indy and the horse. Shielding his face with his hands, he tried to see ahead, the intermittent wind giving momentary glimpses of the tree line to his left.

Sean led out, fearful of his horse stepping into a hole or other impediment, trailing the reins of Dusty behind him, leaning into the howling wind. His job was to blaze the trail for the troops, but with the storm, there was no way they could see his tracks. He leaned toward the trees, planning to find shelter to wait out the storm, stumbling in the snow. Each step he leaned into the wind, stretching out then burying his foot in the snow that reached to his knees one time, barely to his ankles on the next step. He stretched out again but couldn't free his foot and fell forward on his face. Struggling to rise, he saw the bones then the skull of a mule. Tidbits of meat and ligaments still clung to the skeleton, telling Sean this was one of the stolen mules from the fort. The Navajo had butchered the animal here, undoubtedly, to feast themselves on the stolen bounty. More steps, more bones, but he pushed on to the trees, needing some shelter.

Several more struggling steps and suddenly the wind broke. He was behind a line of trees and a low ridge beyond. Sean fell to his knees; Indy came beside him and Dusty stretched out his nose to see if he was alright. It was relief that brought him down, but now, breathing easier, he stood to draw Dusty near the trees and Indy at his side. Abruptly, he heard the twang of a bullet ricocheting off a stone. He spun on his heels, searching for the source as he grabbed his Spencer from the scabbard and pushed Dusty back into the trees. He dropped to one knee, looking, then he heard the report of a rifle, and dropped to his belly. He raised just enough to look in the direction of the sound, saw a man rise from behind a rock, looking his way. Sean quickly but stealthily lifted the Spencer, eared back the hammer, and squeezed off his shot, the bullet driving the Indian back against a boulder, where he slid to the ground.

Sean jacked another cartridge into the Spencer, cocked the hammer, looking through the blowing snow, watching for any movement, anything that would give away the location of any other attackers. The wind stilled for just a moment and he saw the dark outline of another man, head and shoulders showing above a rocky outcropping. The man was looking for a target but became one as the Spencer bucked and barked, bringing a blossom of red at the base of the Navajo's neck, knocking him behind the boulder.

Again, Sean dropped the lever and brought another cartridge

into the breech, closing the lever he cocked the hammer, and watched. Suddenly another head popped above a boulder, bringing a rifle to bear on Sean. He saw the warrior's rifle belch fire, but the Spencer blasted just as he felt a hard blow to the side of his head. Everything went black and he could feel himself falling yet it seemed so slow, tottering over like a falling tree, he felt his grip on the rifle, but still he fell and then a deep and silent blackness.

"IT APPEARS we might have a problem, Sergeant!" said Captain Pfeiffer. "With this new snow, any sign of Sean's passing is gone."

"It would appear so, sir. You want me to move out ahead an' see what I can find?" answered First Sergeant McKee. "Now that the sun's out, shouldn't be too hard."

"Yes, but take two men with you. When you find the trail, send one back. Meanwhile, we'll push on, hopin' we're on the right trail. He said last night he'd go past that ridge yonder and head straight north, so hopefully you'll pick up his sign soon."

"Yessir, will do sir!" answered the sergeant. He quickly picked two men, ordered them to secure horses and saddles, and follow him. Within moments the trio started on the trail. Once they rounded the point of the low ridge and crossed the saddle of the finger ridge, lying before them was the wide open flat. The dry lakebed on their right now held and abundance of fresh snow, and the flats beyond were sparsely covered with new fallen snow. The wind had carried most of the new fluff into the trees and ridges to the west.

Sergeant McKee took the lead, staying near the tree line, searching both the open flats and the edge of the trees. He looked to his men, "Keep yore eyes on the trees, if that wind was whippin' through here earlier, he prob'ly took shelter yonder," nodding his head to their left where the long low, timber covered ridge lifted its dark shoulders.

They had traveled about five miles from the camp and were starting to swing wide of a long finger ridge, when one of the men shouted, "Sarge! Look yonder! Is that a horse there by them trees?"

The sergeant reined up and turned toward the tree line. There by the trees, almost obscured by his markings, stood the Appaloosa of Sean. He gigged his horse to go to the trees, reined up when he saw the big wolf lying alongside a partially covered, outstretched Sean. His arm was extended, his rifle just beyond his fingertips. Seeing blood on the snow, the sergeant warily looked around, but saw no movement. He turned to the men, "McDougal! Take your rifle, search the area, somebody shot this man!" McKee dropped to one knee beside Sean and brushed away the snow, then rolled him over. A moan escaped the almost blue lips of Sean as he struggled to open his eyes. The hair on the left side of his head was matted with blood and Sergeant McKee reached to examine the wound. A long groove parted his hair, but there was no entry wound, just the mark of the bullet. Blood slowly oozed from the wound, and the sergeant grabbed a handful of snow to wipe it away.

Finally, his eyes fluttered open and Sean moaned again, scowling at the sergeant. "Well it's for sure an' certain you ain't no angel so I must still be alive. How bad is it, Sarge?"

"Just a graze boy, but you'll have a scar, sure enough," answered McKee.

"Hey Sarge!" came the voice of McDougal. "There's three dead Injuns o'er here. Looks like that there scout had him quite a fight!"

"Any sign of others?" shouted the sergeant to his trooper.

"No, but Riley found their horses yonder. He's fetchin' 'em back."

"Alright, c'mon back here," ordered McKee. He looked to Sean, "You feel up to ridin'?"

Sean looked up to see blue sky and asked, "Ain't it 'bout noon time? How's about fixin' some coffee while you wait for the others?"

"Irish coffee?" asked McKee, smiling and patting his side, implying he had a bottle stashed.

"Not in mine, that stuff'd just give me a worse headache!" answered Sean, putting a hand to the side of his head. He brought it away bloody and grabbed some snow to wipe it again. After the second handful, he was satisfied his wound was cleaned and he stood to loosen the cinch for Dusty. He staggered once, caught his balance with a grab at the saddle strings, then finished his task. Sergeant McKee started a small fire, Sean put the coffeepot on, and they sat back to wait for the brew.

"So, what happened here?" asked McKee.

"Oh, the wind kinda blew us over here for some shelter, and I no sooner stepped down an' they opened up on me. I think they were some o' them that stole the mules, I stumbled on a couple carcasses back yonder," he nodded his head toward the flats. "They mighta been left here case anybody was followin' an' I was their first target."

"Well, you sure done 'em in," declared McKee.

"They almost done me in," answered Sean, putting a hand to his head. It came away bloody, so he grabbed another handful of snow to hold to his wound to try to stanch the flow of blood.

Sergeant McKee looked at Sean, "Mebbe I better bandage that for you. Looks like it's gonna keep bleedin' if I don't."

Sean nodded his agreement and sat while McKee did his best. After he was finished, McKee said, "That oughta hold ya' at least till tonight. Then we can take a look at it again, but I'm thinkin' that's all you'll need."

"Thanks, Sarge." Sean stood and went to Dusty, tightened the cinch, slipped the Spencer in the scabbard, then turning to the sergeant, "I'm gonna head on out.

HIGH NOON on the third day out of Fort Canby, Sean stood above the crest of the Sunsela saddle that cut between the two rugged and timbered hills that stood apart from the Chuska Range. He was scoping the trail ahead when he saw movement closer in nearer, the far edge of the trees. He climbed a little higher on the finger ridge, and sat down, using his knees to stabilize the scope and watched, waiting for movement. There, below the trail, that area with greenery. The green showed it to be cottonwoods and alders, maybe even aspen, perhaps a trickle of a spring. He saw movement again and waited. He slowly nodded his head, recognizing several people, all appearing to be women, moving slowly about the spring.

He looked behind at the trail and saw the column nearing, Captain Pfeiffer in the lead. He slipped back down the edge of the slope, careful to not reveal himself to those by the spring and waited by the trail for the captain. It was just a few moments when the captain and first sergeant rode up the trail and seeing Sean, reined up beside him.

"Well, Sean, we're making good time today. If it weren't for those blasted wagons, we'd be doin' a lot better." He looked back at the driver fighting the leads and the mules, negotiating the rugged trail that wasn't meant for wagons, but he made slow progress. "Course the troops don't mind, they can take more breaks, waitin' for them to get up this hill." He looked at the scout, "Were you waiting for a reason, Sean?"

"Yessir." He turned to look down the trail to see if he could see the greenery from where he stood, then pointing, "See that green down there?"

"Yeah, that a spring or somethin'?" he asked.

"Somethin', but it's not the green that concerns me. There's some people there, I'm thinkin' it's some women, maybe some children, of the Navajo. I couldn't tell if there were any men, but as much as I could see, there weren't any."

The captain stepped down, reached for Sean's scope and lifted it for a look. He watched for a moment, "Yeah, I can see movement, but from here I can't tell anything." He looked around, "Lieutenant Sanchez, you and Sergeant McKee, come with me and Sean here. We've got some business to attend to," ordered the captain.

He turned to Sean, "Can you get closer without them knowin' you're there?"

Sean looked at the man, nodded, "Can you recognize the squeal of the red-tailed hawk?"

The captain looked from Sean to the sergeant, and the grizzled veteran grinned and nodded, "You want me to bring your horse along?"

Sean grinned, "Sure, Sarge." He looked to the greenery, calculated a moment, then said, "Give me about a quarter hour, then come along slowly. If you hear my call, it's safe." He motioned to Indy and the two trotted off together, starting down the trail then disappearing into the trees.

With the snow, stealth was easy, except where the snow had crusted with the cold nights and warm days. He danced through the trees, picking his way carefully yet easily made his way near the spring. He slowed, stopped behind a clump of rocks and listened. Low voices, all sounding like women and children, blended with the rustle of branches and movement. He slowly moved to where he could see into the clearing and was immediately stayed. What he saw was a pitiful sight, children trying to snuggle with their mothers for warmth, eyes sunken, cheeks hollow, sadness and fear on their faces. Sean breathed heavily, waited as he watched, then hearing movement on the trail he gave the shrill cry of the red-tailed hawk.

The sound of the hawk caused everyone in the clearing to stop moving and speaking, holding still, afraid they would be discovered. Sean stood and walked slowly toward them, rifle held loosely at his side, the other hand out, palm forward, and he spoke softly. "I'm not here to hurt you. Others are coming, we have food and blankets." He stopped, sat his rifle, butt down, beside him, then used his hands to speak in sign as he spoke, "Anyone speak English?"

One young woman stood, a child of about five at her side, "I speak English."

"Tell your people we are not here to hurt you. We have food and blankets for you, and we will take you to shelter." The woman nodded, turned to the others and translated.

When the captain and the others rode into the clearing, Sean explained, "I told 'em we have food and blankets. I'm thinkin' this might solve a couple problems. You're tired of that wagon, so how 'bout usin' it to take these women and children back to the fort? 'Cause, Cap'n, you ain't gettin' that wagon down in the canyon, just ain't no way! If you put the rest of the supplies in the second wagon, you can let it follow you till you get to the canyon, then send it back, too. Maybe you'll have some more captives for that one."

The captain looked at the Navajo, shook his head, "None of 'em look like they could walk that far, that's for sure. They look like they're starvin' and freezin'!"

"They are Cap'n, they are. That's General Carleton's war for you," spat Sean, turning away and going for his horse. He looked back at the captain, "I'll go 'head on and find us a camp." He mounted up and rode through the trees to return to the trail, shaking his head all the while.

CHAPTER TWENTY-THREE
CARSON

"I'll say one thing for you Kit! You couldn't have picked a worse day to start this expedition!" shouted Tate. Carson rode directly behind Tate as he bucked the snow drifts in the Bonito Canyon. With snow on the level well over a foot deep, the drifts in the canyon often reached three feet and more.

"Blame it on Carleton!" shouted Carson, tucking his chin into his collar, fighting against the wind. Behind him came four oxen-pulled wagons, fourteen officers, and four companies of men. Altogether, just under four hundred men to go against an unknown number of entrenched Navajo on their home ground in a canyon complex that had been described as Hades itself. Carson had done everything he could to avoid going into the canyon, where less than ten years before Colonel Dixon Miles took his column and stated, "No command should again enter it."

He had already dispatched one company under the command of Captain Albert Pfeiffer to go to the east end of the canyon to start his assault, and Carson planned to start the assault of four companies from the mouth of the canyon on the west end. But the elements were certainly against them, snow had fallen intermittently for the last week and a half, and now storm clouds were gathering in the west and threatening to make travel even worse. They weren't even a day out of Fort Canby and things were looking grave.

Once they cleared Bonito canyon, the chosen route was due west into the face of the coming storm and the wind was increasing, reducing visibility to no more than two hundred yards. Yet Tate plunged on, pushing toward the trees for what little wind break they offered. The howling wind and blowing snow showed no mercy on the double column of men. With all four companies mounted, the travel was less challenging than that of Pfeiffer's foot company, but the storm was more intense. Tate's chosen route took him between two long ridges that offered some shelter from the driving wind and he stopped at the edge of the trees, motioning for Carson to give the column the first break of the day. With close to six miles behind them, the horses, oxen and men were already suffering from the wintry blast and were greatly relieved to have the break.

Carson rode back along the line, encouraging the men, but when he came to the wagons, he was surprised to see the oxen of the last wagon, stumbling and struggling to move toward the trees. As he watched, the big lead oxen fell, and rolled to his side, with the yoke pulling the others down also. He rode up, stepped down, and saw immediately that the lead ox was dead, and the other one was struggling with the yoke that appeared to be choking him. Carson hollered at the teamster, and the two worked together to free the second ox that struggled to his feet, trying to pull away, but the teamster settled him down. The man turned to Carson, "Colonel, it's that blasted trail! By the time we get to it, it's ankle deep mud cuz all them horses are trompin' it down, and these hyar ox gotta pull the weight o' them wagons thru it, an' it's wearin' 'em out!"

The wintry weather showed no let-up for the next three days. Originally bound for Pueblo Colorado then on to Canyon de Chelly, a trip that should take no more than three days, required six days of rigorous travel with the loss of more than twenty oxen, requiring the abandonment of one wagon. They made camp just below the mouth of the canyon where the dry sandy bed of an elbow bend of the draw offered a little protection with a cluster of juniper. The entire terrain was blanketed with snow up to a foot deep both within and above the canyon. With the temperature dropping as fast as the sun, the men needed the warmth of fires and food before any assault could begin. But Carson was concerned about the failure of Pfeiffer to be waiting at the entrance of the canyon and was also anxious to see if there was any activity in the canyon. As the column neared the campsite, Kit called for Sergeant Herrera and Tate. When the sergeant came near, Carson looked to Tate, "I need you to take the sergeant and a squad of men and go along the south rim, see if you can find Pfeiffer and if there are any Navajo camped close in." He looked at the sergeant, "Remember, we want captives not casualties!"

"Yessir, whatever you say, sir!" answered Herrera as he snapped a salute and reined around to get his squad.

Tate led off as they started up the slight slope of hard rock, hooves of horses clattering, saddles creaking, and men grumbling. The wind had cleared the rock of snow but stayed behind with the cold to harass the riders, probing their clothing for any weak spots to send spiny fingers of ice down the collars and under the coat-tails. The men grabbed at their collars, hunched their shoulders, and hugged their horses with legs that longed for warmth. The sun was resting on the western horizon, coloring the cloudless sky with lances of gold and red that shared their color with the white blanketed landscape.

The squad followed close behind Tate and Lobo, casting furtive glances toward the canyon rim, cautious of the footing under the snow. Occasionally Tate would stop, step down, and walk closer to the edge, peering over to see into the bottom, but the diminishing daylight hindered his view and he would look to Lobo for any indication of danger. But the wolf showed no sign of concern.

They were nearing a side canyon, Lobo out ahead, when the wolf suddenly stopped, one paw raised, head down, mouth closed and body rigid and unmoving. Tate held up a hand to stop the others, stepped down, and hunkered down to walk to the side of the wolf. He looked to the edge of the side canyon, saw a touch of a glow, probably from a cookfire, and knew there were people there. He turned and waved the sergeant forward with the two men, Lobo beside them, as he dropped to all fours in the snow and moved nearer the edge. They saw the opening of a wide cave like overhang, sheltering a group of many Navajo. There were several women and children, and more than a dozen men.

Suddenly, Lobo growled, looking to their right, and a rifle shot sounded, the bullet kicking snow into the face of Sergeant Herrera. Tate came to one knee, firing his Spencer and the warrior dropped from sight; Tate knew his bullet had scored a hit. The men of the squad who had been standing beside their horses, now rushed forward as other warriors popped up at the edge of the canyon, firing.

The sudden barrage from the squad took its toll, but other Indians climbed over the edge, screaming and charging. The soldiers frantically reloaded their Springfields as Tate fired his Spencer repeater several times. The sergeant used his Colt Navy pistol and within moments, the skirmish was over. Tate and the sergeant stood and walked slowly to the edge and saw just below was a wide shelf of rock had provided the Navajo with a shooting platform, but now held several dead warriors. Sergeant Herrera walked to the rim where he could see into the overhang that now stood empty, the fire nothing but coals. He hollered to anyone near, "If you can hear my voice, come out of the canyon. We do not want to kill you! We only fired on your men because they fired on us! Now, come out of the canyon, and we'll take you to get food and blankets!"

Tate looked at the man, "That might work, if any of 'em can understand you."

But Tate was surprised when he saw several of the women and children coming up the steep draw, and approaching the soldiers, hands held up above their heads. He shook his head and walked back to retrieve Shady and mounted up. He looked to the sergeant, "We ain't gonna find Pfeiffer now, you'll need to take these captives back to the camp."

CARSON ASSEMBLED his officers at his fire. The men had overseen the deployment of the companies and the arrangement of their shelters, now as dusk was settling in, the need was for warm food. Carson had his cook prepare a meal for all the officers with meat cut from the downed oxen, and the men were seated on boxes and rocks around the fire as the colonel began to lay out his plan.

"I am concerned about Captain Pfeiffer, I had expected him to be here at the mouth of the canyon by now, but maybe he had some difficulties in his travel. However, at first light, we will start our advance. Tate and I did a little reconnoiter on the south rim, looking for another way into the canyon, but with walls nigh onto a thousand feet an' straight up an' down, weren't no other way in, 'ceptin' this way here." He pointed toward the mouth about a mile and a half distant from their camp. "We did see some Navajo on the far side, but none near at hand. I also sent Sergeant Herrera with Tate to scout out the south rim a ways with a squad of men, and we heard some gunfire from that direction, so maybe he's made some contact," he looked in the direction of the south rim, barely visible in the diminishing light, "and he should be back just anytime now.

"So, Captain Carey, you will take companies B and C and move along the south rim. Captain Berney, you will take companies A and D and move along the north rim. I will accompany Captain Carey." Carson moved away from the fire, frowning and looking in the direction of the canyon. He saw movement, men on horses and others approaching.

"Hello, Colonel," came the cry from one of the mounted men. "Sergeant Herrera reporting sir!"

He drew near and Carson saw the face of the man in the firelight, and ordered, "Step down, Sergeant! What happened?"

"We got into a little skirmish with some of 'em," he tossed his head to indicate some of his men still coming, "the others are bringing in 'bout a half-dozen captives. We killed eleven of 'em, tried to talk but they weren't in a listenin' mood, I reckon. We got some sheep and goats too, thought mebbe they'd make for some fresh meat if we need it."

Carson turned back toward his fire, "Hey Cooky! You got 'nuff for these men?"

"I reckon so, Colonel, sir. Send 'em on over!" answered the cook, grumbling all the while.

"Sergeant have your men come to the fire for some warm food, they deserve it. Now, I've got to let the others know what's happened, so they'll have an idea about tomorrow." He looked around, "Where's Tate?"

"He decided to go a little further, see if he could find Pfeiffer. I don't think he'll be gone too long, but it's lookin' purty light out, so . . . "

Carson walked back to the fire, told the others about the sergeant's scout and the men rose to congratulate the sergeant on his success. Carson poured another cup of coffee, sat by the fire and stared into the flames, concerned about Pfeiffer and now Tate as well.

CHAPTER TWENTY-FOUR
TSAILE

JUST BEFORE PFEIFFER AND COMPANY CAME UPON THE NEAR-FROZEN band of Navajo, he and Sean had scoped the distance from the ridge above Sunsela Saddle. The landmark they sought was known as White Cone mountain, but with all the nearby mountains under a fresh blanket of snow, every cone shaped mountain fit that description. Sean pointed out the nearest, just north of their position, but Pfeiffer focused on the more distant of the three, believing the chosen route to the eastern end of the canyon was further along than they had traveled.

Once Pfeiffer had taken charge of the surrendered band of women and children, Sean mounted up and pointed Dusty toward the cone-shaped mountain now about fifteen miles away. He lifted his eyes to the sun that had disappeared behind some dark clouds, guessing there to be about three hours of daylight left. Before he had traveled another mile, more clouds gathered, and the wind told of a coming storm. He hunched his shoulders, turned up his collar, and shielded his eyes with his hand, searching for a site with cover for the following troops. With a landmark of a lonesome knoll, he pushed into the face of the storm, seeking that shelter he knew the troops desperately needed.

Sean was hunkered into his coat, hat pulled down, as he trusted the long-legged Appaloosa to pick his way to the lee side of the rim-rock ridge that held a skirt of juniper and piñon. The Appy tugged at the reins as Sean gave him his head. He knew the horse was following the lead of the black wolf, Indy, and they could find their way better than he, what with the swirling snow that only offered an occasional glimpse of the trail before him. But the animals never erred and when Dusty stopped, Sean felt the break from the wind. He lifted the brim of his hat, causing snow to fall into the collar of his coat, chilling him even more, but he was relieved to see the tree line, and stepped down. He led Dusty into a cluster of juniper, stripped the gear off, breaking off a branch to brush down the horse. Indy had dropped to his belly under the low limb of the largest juniper, and Sean used several branches to weave a better windbreak for the animals.

Once they were settled, he stepped away, kicking at the snow for some dry wood and gathered it for a fire. He usually made a small, hat-sized fire just big enough for the coffee pot and a small frying pan, but this time he built it big. The troopers would need some kind of beacon to find the camp in the blowing snow and they needed the shelter from the merciless storm.

Sergeant McKee rode point, searching the white for any sign of tracks left by Sean, usually seeing shallow dips that were quickly filling up with the wind-blown drifts. But he plodded on from one to another, keeping his eyes down to watch for anything that resembled a track. A brief let-up of the wind made him lift his eyes and the winking light ahead promised a fire. The crusty sergeant grinned, knowing that was the way of their young scout, always watching out for them.

. . .

In the middle of the night, the storm lost its force and whispered itself away. The howling of storm winds was replaced by honks, snorts and growls of tired sleeping troops. Morning came with clear skies and the slow rising sun shared its shades of pink with the blanket of snow, and when the colors gave way to brightness, the crystalline snow sparkled like the angels had sprinkled diamonds on the Creator's handiwork. Even the grumpiest complaining trooper was hushed to silence by the awesome beauty that lay before them. But the silence was short-lived as growling stomachs demanded attention and cold toes needed blood stomped into them.

Sean left the griping garrison behind as he and Dusty followed a scampering black wolf that buried his nose in the snow, tossing it into the air, and jumping after it. Sean chuckled at the antics of his four-legged friend, and even Dusty seemed to be full of new-found energy and stepped higher than usual, as his pace quickened on the trail. It proved to be a good day's travel, the snow mostly blown away from the trail, making the troopers' long walk easier than most days had already been. With a short break for nooning, the shallow ravine of the Tsaile Creek, that Sean thought was Whiskey Creek, snaked across the trail before them and with uplifted eyes, hand shading from the bright sun, the beginning of the canyon lay just a few hundred yards to the west of the trail.

With dusk fast approaching, Sean pushed Dusty across the ice-covered creek, pointing him to the base of a tree-covered mesa for the night's camp. He knew the captain would want the troops rested up and well-fed before they started the assault on the canyon come morning. After finding a basin that surrounded a small knoll below the ridge, he stripped the gear from the horse, picketed him, and with scope and rifle in hand and Indy at his side, he climbed to the top of the butte for a good look-see of the area.

The promontory on the butte was about two hundred and

fifty feet above the valley floor, offering him a good view of their camp just below and the beginning of the canyon about a mile to a mile and a half distant. He sat between two scraggly piñon that shaded him from the lowering sun and prevented any reflection off his glass, and carefully followed the contours and twists of the upper end of the canyon. Twice he saw thin, wispy spirals of smoke, but neither lasted for long, telling of cookfires rather than blazes for warmth. Those could be a band on the move or just a group that showed extra caution before their hide-outs. As he moved the telescope, he watched for movement as well as smoke, anything that would betray the presence of people.

He lowered the brass tube, rubbed his face, and began to lift the scope for one more scan, when something caught his eye just below the rim of the bluff. There, movement in the trees near his campsite, he lifted his scope, saw Dusty also staring in that direction with ears up and nostrils flaring. He moved the scope and saw three figures, Navajo men, stealthily approaching the camp. The leader stopped, motioned to the others in the direction of the tethered Dusty, and they moved closer to the horse. Sean dropped the scope into its bag at his waist, and motioned to Indy, "Go, get Dusty!" The wolf leapt from the bluff into the deep snow below and bounded toward the horse.

When the warriors were about ten yards from Dusty, Sean fired a shot into the ground at their feet. All three stopped, looking to the butte top and scampering behind trees for cover. But as the leader turned, a flash of black fur barreled into him, knocking him to the ground. With teeth sunk into the man's neck, the big wolf shook his head side to side, ripping out the man's throat. Sean was on one knee, watching for the other two, then saw the back of one as he ran through the trees, trying to escape. He searched the trees for the other, when suddenly Dusty reared up, pawing at the air while on the ground before him was the other warrior, grabbing at the lead rope, and slapping at the horse.

Sean bounded down the slope of the butte, arriving just as Navajo jumped on Dusty's back and slapped the Appaloosa's rear with his bow. But the horse would have none of it. He dropped his head, between his front feet, kicking at the treetops with his hind feet. The man wasn't as good a horseman as he thought himself to be as Dusty again put his nose between his hooves and kicked high with his hind feet. As the Navajo started falling forward, Dusty reared up, pawing at the clouds and stretching his head high, he fell back on the man, crushing him beneath his powerful body. The Appy quickly rolled to the side and came to his feet, just as Sean came through the trees, rifle at the ready. But the man did not move; his head had hit a boulder hidden beneath the snow, and blood now painted the wintry blanket. Sean looked to Dusty, now standing, trembling and snorting. The big horse was shaking his head side to side, threatening the man that had attacked him, but the Indian was dead.

He walked to his horse, hand outstretched and talking in low tones, "Easy boy, easy. You're alright, easy now," and he wrapped his arms around the big horse's neck, burying his face in the frosty mane. He looked through the trees to see the wolf astraddle of his prey, and he called to the beast, "Indy, c'mere boy." The big wolf turned to look over his shoulder to the familiar voice, and with another look at the mutilated man, he padded through the snow, rubbing his bloody snout in the wintry covering to clean his fur, then came to Sean's side to share in the attention. With one arm under Dusty's neck, and the other hand on Indy's scruff, Sean chuckled to himself, then said, "You two are the best friends a man could have, yessiree bob!"

The column soon arrived, and Sean took the captain and Sergeant McKee for a quick look at the head of the canyon while there was still a little light left in the dimming dusk. The captain's only comment was, "That thing starts out purty narrow, I reckon it widens out down there a ways," which was a much a question as not.

"Yessir, I had a purty good look from up on the bluff yonder, and it widens and deepens purty quick. From what Pa told me, it's nigh unto twenty-five mile from here to the mouth of it. Don't think we'll make it in a day."

"Nope, an' I don't like the idea of spending the night in there either. But, we'll just have to see how it plays out tomorrow." He lifted his eyes to the sky, "Don't appear to be no storm clouds movin' about, so, maybe that's a good thing."

"Well, at least there's two less we have to be concerned about," said Sean, nonchalantly.

The captain looked at his scout, "Run into some, didja?"

"Well, ya might say they run into muh friends," he answered, pointing to Indy.

When the captain looked at the wolf, for the first time he noticed some blood on his jowls and looked to Sean, "You mean, . . ."

"Ummhumm. Couple of 'em tried to steal Dusty here, an he," nodding to Indy, "took care of one and Dusty here done in the other. I just sorta watched."

CHAPTER TWENTY-FIVE
START

SEAN WALKED THROUGH THE DISARRAYED CAMP OF THE TROOPS, stepping lightly as to not awaken them. The lazy sun was well below the eastern horizon, and only a thin, grey line held the promise of its return. Sean climbed to the top of the knoll to spend a little time with his Lord and maybe get an early look at the maw of the canyon. Indy lunged up the slope, playfully mocking his two-legged friend and stood at the top, tongue lolling as he watched and waited for Sean. They went to the promontory of the day before, Sean seating himself on the broad, sandstone slab and turning to the east to look to the silhouetted line of the horizon. He thought of White Fox, dropped his eyes, smiling, then lifted his eyes to the tail of the Milky Way, looked over his shoulder to the lowering moon, and began to pray.

As the first light of early morning lay upon the countryside, Sean lifted his telescope to trace the snake-like canyon for sign of life. The twists, turns, and deepening gorge brought to Sean's mind the passage from Revelation that spoke of the angel laying hold on the dragon, Satan, and casting him into the bottomless pit. As he scanned the canyon, Sean chuckled at the thought of going into what resembled the bottomless pit and definitely had the twists and turns of a dragon or serpent. He also thought of the times he and his teacher father had read about the dragon Argonautica that guarded the golden fleece, as written by Apollonius of Rhodes, and the dragon of Beowulf. He laughed at himself, thinking about dragons, knowing that was no way to start a day. One last scan showed two spirals of smoke deeper into the canyon, but he could see no activity. He rose, motioned to Indy, and the two slipped down the slope of the bluff to join the others for some coffee and breakfast.

Sean was welcomed by a strain of music coming from the camp of the men. He recognized the sound of a Jews harp, and he smiled at the sounds from a concertina, a relatively new and unusual instrument some called a squeeze box, especially in the wilderness in the hands of a trooper. He listened to the words, smiling as he heard,

Come dress your ranks, my gallant souls, a standing in a row,
Kit Carson he is waiting to march against the foe;
At night we march to Moqui, o'er lofty hills of snow,
To meet and crush the savage foe, bold Johnny Navajo.
Johnny Navajo! O Johnny Navajo!
We'll first chastise, then civilize, bold Johnny Navajo.

Sean looked to Captain Pfeiffer as he approached the fire and saw the captain smiling as well. Sean asked, "Who's responsible for that?" nodding his head in the direction of the singers.

The captain chuckled, "That was the bandmaster, Lucian B., he came up with it back at the fort." He frowned, thinking, "Ya know, I don't think anybody knows his last name, he's always been called Lucian B.!"

He lifted the coffeepot to Sean, watched as he filled his cup, then motioned for the scout to sit down. Three others were already seated: First Lieutenant Peter Bishop, Pfeiffer's second in command, Lieutenant Stephen Coyle, and First Sergeant James McKee. All were nursing their hot cups of coffee, holding them with both hands and savoring the warmth and aroma. The captain looked to the men and began, "I'm dividing our company into three groups. Bishop, you'll take first platoon and first squad from second, I'll take third platoon and second squad from second, and Coyle, you'll take fourth platoon and third and fourth squads from second. Bishop, you'll lead off, I'll follow, and Coyle, you'll bring up the rear. Now, once the canyon opens up, Lieutenant Bishop, I'll move up with you, but you'll take the right side and hug the wall, I'll do the same on the left. Lieutenant Coyle, you are to relieve anybody that gets in trouble and will be responsible for any captives. Sarge, you'll be with our scout, Sean."

"Uh, Captain, will we be camping in the canyon?" asked Lieutenant Bishop.

"Yes, we will, providing we find a suitable place. So, the men will need to pack their bedrolls with 'em. As you've probably guessed, the wagon won't be goin' into the canyon."

He looked to the east and the colors of the sunrise, "We'll move out in half an hour!"

The others stood, finished off their coffee and dropped the cups for the cook's helper, and went to organize their troops. Sergeant McKee remained seated next to Sean and looked to the younger man, "So, what kind of trouble is the laddie gonna get us in today?"

Sean chuckled at the man who was running his fingers through the salt and pepper hair and grinning at the scout, "Oh, I'm sure I'll find enough trouble to keep an old man like you busy enough!"

"Old man?! Watch your tongue boyo! I'll give you more'n enough trouble all by meself!"

The captain laughed at the two, then spoke to the sergeant, "Be sure to pack your Sharps, Sergeant. I'm thinkin' it might come in handy today."

"Aye, and I'm agreein' with you there, Captain!"

THE LONG SHADOWS of the ridge-riding junipers stretched into the bottom of the ravine that held the frozen waters of the Tsaile Creek. With the sun just above the eastern horizon, the shadows darkened the gorge and held the cold in the bottom. Snow covered the frozen stream, but Sean rode on the right, McKee on the left, both with rifles across the bows of their saddles. The horses picked their way through the crusty snow, each step sounding, and often reverberating, in the narrow defile. Sean lifted his eyes to the white rimrock that clung to the ridge edge overhead, an unusual formation that appeared as if frozen from eons past. Piñon and juniper held tenaciously to the steep slopes, sharing their footholds with ocotillo, cholla and prickly pear cacti.

Sean spoke softly, just loud enough for the sergeant to hear, "One good thing," he started.

"I'm glad you can find something good, what is it?" asked McKee.

"Won't be seein' any rattlesnakes! Too cold for 'em."

The sergeant chuckled, looked to Sean, "What about snow snakes?" asked the sergeant, trying to appear serious.

"Nah, too low for 'em, they like the high country," explained Sean, soberly.

"Well, them foot soldiers behind us will be glad to know that."

The gorge was deeper, the white rimrock now in layers of feldspar and limestone on the steeper slopes, but still the juniper and piñon held to the sidewalls. The narrow bottom often forcing both Sean and McKee to step down and lead their horses on the snow-covered frozen stream. The walls seemed to push in, crowding them closer and making them fight their way through the manzanita and buckbrush at the stream's edge. As the canyon seemed to widen just a bit, Sean and McKee started to mount up, but a flash of color and movement caught Sean's eye, and he dropped to one knee, putting a hand on Indy's scruff to hold him back. McKee saw Sean stop and dropped as well, trying to see where the scout was looking. Sean looked to the sergeant, motioned with four fingers, pointing past the brush.

McKee craned around until he could see some Navajo, huddled together by a small fire, their ragged clothes little enough to cover them and not enough for warmth. Sean stood, speaking in a calm voice, "Do not move! We will not hurt you."

The woman jumped to her feet, eyes wide and looking at Sean, then back to her brood. A man who appeared sickly, and two youngsters in rags, were all three trying to share one thin blanket. The woman chattered in Navajo, motioning to her family and back to Sean. She stepped back as if to shield them.

Sean spoke again, calmly and slowly walking forward, weaving through the brush, his rifle held ready. "We won't hurt you." He motioned with his free hand as if feeding himself, "We have food," then pointing to the children, "eat!" He had kept hold of Dusty's reins and now turned to his saddlebags to retrieve some smoked meat. With his rifle cradled in his arm, he walked forward and handed the woman the strips of meat. Her eyes widened, and she cautiously accepted the offering, looked to Sean, and quickly turned to give the meat to her family. While Sean approached the Indians, McKee had turned back to tell the captain about the Navajo, and now the two men walked up behind Sean, the captain holding a blanket and some hardtack.

Sean made sign language, and the woman apparently understood, and a bit of a smile broke on her face as he told her, "Other soldiers will take you to a wagon at the head of the canyon. They will give you more food and more blankets and take you to the fort for protection."

She enthusiastically nodded her head and signed to Sean, "We are grateful. We were too weak to go to the fort and we thought we would freeze or starve here."

Sean answered, "You will be fed, and will be safe."

Again, she nodded and turned back to explain to her family.

WITH CLOSE TO three miles behind them, the canyon finally widened enough for the two columns of men to move side-by-side along the bottom of the canyon, with the frozen stream between them. Suddenly, from a ledge high up above the captain's platoon, rock began tumbling down with some striking the soldiers who moved across the stream. The lieutenant shouted, "There, on the ledge! Squad one, fire!"

Sean had just sighted the Navajo when the barrage from the lieutenant's squad pushed the warriors back. Several Indians shouted down at the soldiers, taunting them. Although the troopers didn't understand the words, they recognized the tone and intent. The Navajo continued to throw rocks and hurl insults but were back from the edge of the ledge and not visible to the soldiers. More rocks were thrown, but the ledge was at least six hundred feet above the canyon floor, and the soldiers easily dodged the rocks. The lieutenant looked to Pfeiffer, who hollered, "Fire another volley, then we'll move out. We'll do the same for you!"

The platoon with the lieutenant readied themselves and at the command, the rolling thunder of the volley racketed across the canyon, echoing down the gorge, followed by the scuffling sound of the soldiers pushing through the brush and around the bend.

The second volley was unnecessary, and the three columns were soon reunited. Another sharp bend and the canyon opened where a smaller side canyon joined. Pfeiffer ordered a halt and nooning with several of the soldiers stationed to watch the walls and rim for any attackers.

They pushed on as the canyon widened. The stream made a sharp cut back to the east at a junction with two smaller chasms. With a wider, flat bottom, the gorge yielded a cornfield and orchard of peach trees, which Pfeiffer order to be cut down. As the soldiers hacked away at the trees, several rifle shots came from a huge cavernous overhang high up the cliff wall. From below, it appeared as nothing more than a big hollow, but it burrowed into the cliffside, offering shelter for many. When the shots echoed across the gorge, the soldiers ducked for cover, and the captain hollered for Sergeant McKee. When the gruff, old Irishman came alongside, the captain ordered, "McKee, get as far up that slope yonder," pointing to the slope opposite the big cavern, "and put that Sharps to work!"

"Yessir, Cap'n, sir!" he answered. With a wave of his hand to Sean, the sergeant started climbing the slope, weaving in and out among the scrub oak and piñon. Sean followed, Indy at his heels, Spencer in his hand. The sergeant found a bit of a shoulder with some broken off slabs of sandstone and sat down to take his shots. Sean joined him, taking a position behind another slab.

"Cap'n ain't happy 'bout them fellas yonder keepin' our sojer boys from cuttin' down them trees." He laid the Sharps on the stone, shaded his eyes for a better view as he squinted, and with a slow nod of his head, "There's two or three of 'em, there by that streak coming from up top. See 'em?"

"Yeah, I see 'em," answered Sean. He pulled out his telescope for a closer look, "And the one on the left sees us, you might wanna take him first," suggested Sean, looking to the sharp-shooting sergeant. He had no sooner glanced that way than the big Sharps bucked and roared, spitting smoke and lead, bouncing the blast off the opposite cliff face. As Sean looked through the scope, he saw the Navajo shooter, stand up, hands over his face as he fell backward to never rise again. The second shooter stared at his friend and turned to shake his fist toward McKee, shouting incoherently. He lifted his rifle, but before he could shoot, the Sharps roared again and took its toll on the second shooter. Sean saw the Indian tumble backward as the big .52 caliber slug pushed its way through his chest.

Another Navajo stood, throwing rocks and insults at the soldiers below, shaking a fist toward McKee, shouting more insults. When the Indian bent to fetch the rifle dropped by the second shooter, Sean looked to McKee, saw he was readying another shot, then lifted his scope to view the third warrior. Just as McKee drew a bead on the would-be shooter, Sean saw a squash blossom necklace, an open neckline, and realized it was a woman. He turned to speak to McKee just as the Sharps bucked again, and Sean turned back to see the shooter fall.

"That does it! Three shots, three shooters! Cap'n oughta be happy with that!"

Sean looked at McKee, started to speak, but thought better of it, and rose to return to the canyon bottom with the troops. When they returned to the captain's side, the sergeant reported, "Done and done, Cap'n, sir!"

"I saw that, Sergeant." He looked from McKee to Sean and back to McKee, "Anything different 'bout that last one?"

"What'chu mean, sir?"

"Anything different?" he looked to Sean, who dropped his eyes. "I thought that last one might be a woman," said the captain.

"A woman? All I saw was a Navajo raisin' a rifle and gettin' ready to shoot me!" answered the sergeant, brow furrowing in confusion. He looked to Sean, "You had a scope, was it?"

Nodding his head, Sean answered, "Afraid so, I had turned to tell you, but you fired 'fore I could say anything. But she was a warrior, and all you did was kill a warrior that was tryin' to kill you."

The sergeant appeared deflated, shoulders drooping, as he turned away, going to his mount to replace the Sharps in the scabbard. It just wasn't something a man was to do.

CHAPTER TWENTY-SIX
BASE

CAPTAIN PFEIFFER CHOSE TO MAKE CAMP WHERE THEY WERE, THE junction of three canyons offered more space and the few alder and cottonwood by the stream, plus the fallen stone would provide cover. But to show proper caution, he sent several groups of three and four men to scout the surrounding canyons and cliffs for any Navajo. Sean and Sergeant McKee were sent to scout the big cavernous maw that was used by the shooters, suspecting there would be more.

It was a difficult climb. The steep slope held few piñon, and those were scraggly, some with roots showing as others held stubbornly to cracks in the sandstone walls. The ancients had carved footholds in the sheer cliff, and Sean started climbing, Spencer slung over his back, as McKee stood back watching the ledge overhead. Sean stretched from handhold to handhold, each one just a little further than the last. He hugged the rough surface, reaching with his moccasined toes for another foothold. He looked up to the ledge above him, stretched for it, and pulled himself up and over. He looked around quickly, then stood to motion McKee to follow.

Once both men were atop the ledge, the sergeant took the lead and as the ledge narrowed, he stretched out his arms to hug the wall, sliding his feet along the rough surface of the ledge, his heels hanging off the edge. As he rounded the belly of the bulging cliff, he saw the big cavern and froze in place, searching for any movement. Satisfied there was none, he scooted the rest of the way off the ledge and gained solid footing at the corner of the cavern. Sean joined him, and both men swung their rifles off the slings and held them, Sean with his thumb on the hammer, ready to ear it back and shoot. But there was no one, only the bodies of the three shooters, still lying where they fell, blood pooled and dried around them.

"They didn't even take their dead!" said McKee, surprised.

"No, the Navajo are different than most others, they don't like touching the dead. Even when one of 'em dies in their hogan, they knock a hole in the back, close up the doorway, and never enter it again. Somethin' about the Chindi, or spirit of the dead," explained Sean, looking around the big cavern. "Ya know, Pa was tellin' me 'bout this cave, or at least one like it, I think they called it Massacre Cave. Seems the Spaniards wiped out a bunch o' Navajo, somethin' like a hundred or so, back around the turn of the century."

"You keep talkin' like that an' I'm gonna start seein' ghosts!" declared McKee. "How's about we scram?"

"Suits me!" answered Sean, heading toward the far side. From below they had seen a gravely runoff that came from the rim and ran down the slope at the edge of the cavern, probably the way the rest of the Navajo had disappeared. As they worked their way, Sean saw the tracks of several people, all moccasined and all sizes, that had been here and left recently, after the snow. But the far side of the trail was obliterated by snow and gravel.

With an early start, as the first morning shadows kept the

canyon in darkness, the troopers spread out across the canyon bottom, each man carefully picking his way. With barely a mile behind them, the leaders stepped into the bright sunlight that lanced across the narrow bottom from the side gorge that split the rim and gave access to the canyon floor. But the sunlight also gave a small band of Navajo an advantage. With the brightness in their eyes, the soldiers were caught unaware, and arrows and rifle shots startled them as they dropped to the ground behind a slight rise in the canyon bottom. "Anybody hit?" asked the lieutenant, looking down the line at his men. No one responded, as each man looked right and left at his companions. The lLieutenant ordered, "Sergeant Chavez, take your squad around this point," he pointed to his right where a dry run-off creek bed joined the willows in the bottom, "work your way forward. I'll take a squad and come on their right, from behind that wall!" He motioned to the towering sandstone wall that sheltered the branch canyon. "Go!"

Both groups, hunkered down below the low ridge, quickly worked their way to the designated points. The lieutenant was higher and could see where the sergeant was in the dry creek bottom. He waved at the sergeant, then stepped to the edge of the white sandstone, looked around as he hugged the cliff face, then opened the ball with his pistol shot. The Navajo were scattered across the mouth of the smaller canyon, most behind slabs of sandstone, but all were surprised when the lieutenant fired from the cliff's edge. Their movement, seen by the sergeant and his men, made them easy targets and the first squad opened fire with their Springfields. The rifle shots racketed through the smaller canyon, each blast magnified by the confined space and echoed back and forth, making each shot sound like dozens. The short pause as the soldiers reloaded prompted the Navajo to jump and run, but the second squad with the lieutenant stepped around the cliff face and fired a volley, dropping two of the attackers and causing the others to flee, leaving behind the two wounded and two others that chose to surrender by standing with rifles over their heads.

"Sergeant," shouted the lieutenant, "Secure the captives, check on the casualties! We'll cover you!" As the sergeant and his men rose from the creek bottom, the second squad stood, rifles held ready, searching the smaller canyon for any other attackers.

Within moments the sergeant returned, "Three captives, sir. One wounded, but we fixed him up. He'll be alright."

Captain Pfeiffer rode up behind the lieutenant, looking at the captives and then to the officer, "Good work, Bishop. Any of our men hurt?"

"None, sir," answered Lieutenant Bishop, holstering his sidearm.

"Then let's keep moving. My platoon will take the lead, but don't be too far back. With the canyon this wide, we'll need to stay up with one another."

"Yessir."

WITH EACH SIDE canyon came another attack and brief skirmish, but most often the Navajo fled up the narrow canyons and made their escape. However, there were a few captives taken and an occasional attacker killed. Of necessity, the captain sent a squad into each side canyon to search for any groups that might be taken or convinced to surrender. Whenever hogans were found, they were burnt. Water holes were filled in with rocks, gravel, and debris. Other shelters were destroyed, as well as any orchards. Occasionally storage bins fashioned from rock and mud were found, mostly empty but they were destroyed anyway.

"Captain, sir," began a somber looking corporal, "Uh, we found a bit of a cave up that canyon yonder, and uh, well sir, we found some Navajo."

"How many? And where are they?" asked the captain, looking about.

"Uh, they's still in the cave, sir. They was plumb froze to death, sir. They was six of 'em, sir, didn't have but two blankets and they was all skinny like, an', well, froze stiff sir." The corporal dropped his gaze, kicked at the snow at his feet, and looked back up at the captain, expecting more orders.

"I see," answered the captain. He took a deep breath that lifted his shoulders, looked back at the corporal, "You and your men fall back in with the rest. We'll be stoppin' soon for noonin'."

"Yessir," answered the corporal, snapping a salute to the captain. When Pfeiffer returned the salute, the slump-shouldered corporal nodded to his men, and they went to their place in the column.

When the two columns rounded another sharp bend, they were startled by a rain of rocks from high up the cliff-face. A few rifle shots came from the ledge near the top, and the men below sought shelter on the far side of the canyon. The ledge that held the attackers was at least seven hundred feet above the canyon floor, and the attackers appeared to be jumping from ledge to ledge, finding more stones to throw and hurling insults in Spanish at the soldiers. Many of the men were Mexican Volunteers and clearly understood the vulgar invectives and threats. Captain Pfeiffer also understood, having married a Mexican woman, and he shook his head at the insults. He looked to his men, "Alright men, two ranks, first rank, ready, aim, fire!" Fifteen rifles roared, rattling the entire canyon, and the ricocheting bullets could be heard bouncing off the rocks, chipping at the sandstone, drawing screams from wounded Navajo. Before the echoing stopped, the second rank fired, and the roar reverberated and sounded almost like the blast of a cannon. When the sound dwindled, there were no more threats or rocks that came from the ledge.

As Pfeiffer looked around, he could make out some fields and several fruit trees lined out in the smaller canyon. He ordered all the mounted officers to ride their horses through the fields repeatedly, then marched the men through and had them cut down all the fruit trees. Satisfied, they moved out again and started down the canyon. With two more skirmishes, with no casualties or captives, and almost two more miles of canyon behind them, they came upon a waiting Sean and Sergeant McKee. Pfeiffer reined up beside them, "Any trouble?"

"No trouble, Captain. But there's somethin' you wanna see, and there are some Navajo camped there, but I think they might come along peaceable like," answered Sean, looking from the captain to a nodding McKee.

The captain looked at both men, waved his hand, "Lead on, then."

The sheer sandstone walls rose eight hundred feet above them, colors looking like waves on a seashore, with swoops and ridges of harder rock showing less wear than the softer stone that washed from under the shoulders of hard rock. The sun had done its work on the snow in the bottom of the canyon and the shod hooves of horses clattered and bounced as echoes from cliff face to canyon wall. On their left, the wall gave way to a clefted overhang and dropped off to a narrow ridge of rock that marked the confluence of two canyons. Here the canyon bottom held more brush and shrubs, thickly carpeting the floor of the gorge with alders and stubby cottonwood interspersed with willows.

As they rounded the point, Pfeiffer was cautious of another attack, but was stunned by the cliff wall that rose straight up, bellying out towards the canyon bottom and holding several dark stained streaks of seepage from above. But the canyon wall held a greater surprise as at the bottom edge, tucked under the massive bulging cliff, lay several stone dwellings, not unlike those found in other canyons but higher up in the cliffs. As the captain sat staring, movement caught his attention and he saw figures scampering for cover among the remnants of the ancient stone dwellings. He turned to look at Sean, "Has anyone approached them?"

"Not yet, sir. But they know we're here."

Pfeiffer looked at Sean, then Sergeant McKee, back toward the ruins and said, "Alright then, let's go."

The three men, leaving the others behind, rode closer to the ruins, side by side, and the captain stopped, called out, "We will not harm you! We have food and blankets!"

No one answered. And the captain said the same thing in Spanish, which caused a few faces to appear, staring at the men. He continued, "Come with us, we have blankets and food for you. We will go to the mouth of the canyon where there are more soldiers and more food."

Slowly, they began to come from behind the walls of the ruins, most were women and children, but there were two white haired men and two young men. Eleven in all, several in rags, the sight making the captain shiver with cold. He turned to Sergeant McKee, "Go on back and get some blankets and any food you can round up." He looked back at the Navajo, "And any of those officers or others with horses, have them come here and get these kids, maybe some of the women, and let 'em ride."

Sean looked at the captain, then at the Navajo and seeing a girl of about ten that stood by her mother, shivering, he stepped down and walked to the two. He spoke in Spanish, "You," pointing at the woman, "get up there," pointing to the saddle, "I'll hand up your girl."

When they were mounted, he reached into his saddlebags for some smoked meat, handed a piece to both of them, then unwrapped his bedroll and put the blanket around the girl's shoulders and around her mother as well. Both looked down at the big wolf that stood beside the man, then to the man, and the girl said, "He's a wolf!"

Sean grinned, "He's my friend."

THEY MADE QUITE a sight walking into the camp of troopers. Officers walking beside horses carrying Navajo women and children, troopers walking behind. But the camp held very few soldiers, but several wagons, and mules and horses picketed by the trees. Captain Pfeiffer walked to the nearest fire and saw a man cooking, and asked, "Where is everybody?"

The cook looked up, "Oh, sorry suh! I thought you was Colonel Carson's men coming back. They all went scoutin' the canyon. The colonel went thataway," he pointed over his shoulder at the south edge, "An' Cap'n Berney went thataway. They's s'posed to be back for supper, suh!"

Pfeiffer grinned, "You gonna have any to spare," nodding toward the big pots hanging over the fire.

The colored cook said, "Yassuh, sho nuff!"

"Good! I've got some hungry men."

The cook looked at the men straggling into the camp, and answered, "Lawdy, suh, I ain't got 'nuff for all of y'alls."

"Don't worry, Cooky, just me and a couple others. That'll do." He turned back to motion to Sean and the other officers and Sergeant McKee to join him. They had delivered the Navajo to the far wagons where the men were handing out blankets and more. Sean was the first to the fire, smiled as he reached for a cup to get some coffee, and sat down with the steaming brew and said, "Ahh, now everythings gonna be alright."

CHAPTER TWENTY-SEVEN
MISSION

"This is the problem we're facing," began Tate as he drew in the dirt at his feet. He made an image like a crooked "Y" with an additional branch below the junction. "This part," pointing at the two main branches, "is the Canyon de Chelly," then pointing to the additional branch below the junction of the others, "and this is Canyon del Muerto. For anyone to take the north rim of Canyon de Chelly, he'll have to find a way to the top from below. Otherwise, he'll just be scouting the north rim of Canyon del Muerto." Tate looked to Carson for his response.

The colonel stared at the crude map scrawled in the dirt, then up at Tate. "Do you know of a place that might allow the men to make it to the top?" he asked.

"Possibly. There's a spot right here," pointing to his diagram, "but I think the men will have to climb it and lead their horses. It's too steep to try to stay mounted, but, maybe . . ."

"That means you'll be with Berney." He looked from Tate to Captain Joseph Berney, "Captain, are you willing to try it?"

"Sir, if our scout thinks it's possible, we can certainly try it," answered the career officer from St. Louis. This was his first hitch in the west and he never ceased to be amazed at the diversity and magnificence in the countryside that was totally different than anything he had ever encountered in his life. His entire life, before enlisting, had been spent in the city, and now every day was an adventure in an amazing wilderness. He was a man that never backed down from a challenge and had proven himself an excellent officer and was well respected by his men. He looked to Tate, "Will you be with us?"

"All the way. But, our most difficult part may be the first mile or two in the bottom of the canyon, before we try to make it to the top. I've seen sign of Navajo throughout and they might be lying in wait for us," explained Tate.

"We'll be ready," replied Berney, looking from Tate to Carson.

Carson looked at the captain, considering the sincerity of the man, then nodded his head. "Alright Captain, we'll move out at the same time and parallel you from atop the south rim. So, if necessary, we can give you some covering fire." He looked to Tate, "Be on the watch for any sign of Pfeiffer. I expected him to be here by now, but . . ."

"I understand Kit," answered Tate, nodding.

THE SUN of the high desert had done its job, driving the moisture from the snowfall into the thirsty ground, but the cold of the night and early morning kept the ice on the edges of the shallow stream that came from the canyon. Tate and Captain Berney rode side by side leading the double column of riders into the canyon. The shallow creek, most often no more than eight or ten inches deep, held ice on its edges and the column was forced to make several crossings as the stream wove from one side of the canyon to the other, cutting its own channel through the sandstone gorge. Sumac, elderberry, and willows lined the banks, adding to the obstacles to their progress, but the troops pushed on, always watchful of the canyon rim that seemed higher and higher with each step.

The many overhangs, steep cliffs, and variegated colors continued to amaze Tate and he enjoyed looking at the marvels of creation. The clatter of hooves rattled back at the riders that followed the twisting route of the creek. Tate pointed high up on a red cliff, "See that up there?" he asked, indicating an overhang with a deep shadow.

"Yeah, is that a cave or somethin'?" asked Berney.

"There's a lot of 'em through here. Some are caves, others just overhangs, some are tunnels that go way back in the rocks. That one, with no ledge below the opening is probably never used. But others," he looked around for more, "like up there," pointing on the opposite side, "with that ledge, gives 'em better access."

"So, you're saying they could be just about anywhere, that right?"

"That's right."

Tate had no sooner spoken than a rain of rocks came from high above them, followed by shouts of threats and insults, although the Navajo were too high to be understood clearly. He gigged Shady to the far side, crowding the captain before him as more rocks came from above. All the troops had followed Tate's example, and as Berney looked high above, he hollered back for right hand man, George Strong. "First Sergeant!"

The seasoned sergeant rode quickly to the captain's side, saluted, "Yessir!?"

"Get a couple sharpshooters an' answer those Navajo with some lead!" ordered the captain.

It only took a moment for the sergeant to comply with the order and the report of two Sharps boomed across the canyon. Shooting almost straight up, at the ledge that was close to a thousand feet above, was a challenge for even the most experienced shooter, but the men showed their expertise as a shout of surprise echoed across the gorge, and the hail of stones ceased. They stayed against the far wall for a few moments, but satisfied the threat was over, they pushed on.

The mouth of Canyon del Muerto was opposite a wide talus of rock and sand that rose like a wide shoulder extending from the south rim. Atop the rim Tate spotted the troop with Carson and Captain Carey. The men had dismounted, and several stood at the ridge, watching those below. Tate led out and around the talus and rounded a long finger ridge that extended into the canyon bottom. Less than a half-mile further, he saw what at first appeared to be two side canyons, but the narrow one ended in the deep shadows. He looked up the wider of the two that showed promise, but the end held a sharp-edged overhang of dark red that promised nothing but a dead end. He started to turn away when something on the left wall caught his eye. Gigging Shady into the canyon for a better look, he sat back, shaded his eyes, and stared at ancient Anasazi cliff dwellings. Tucked under the belly of the cliff, a long line of ancient stone dwellings clung to the long ledge, shadows at the openings with nothing moving.

Tate motioned for Captain Berney to come alongside, and when he pointed out the dwellings, the captain was transfixed at the sight. "I don't know if there's anyone up there, but you might want to have some of your men check, just in case," suggested Tate, "I'm going to take a better look up that other cut back there while you do that."

With a wave of his hand, Tate sent Lobo before him as he followed what appeared to be a faint trail into the narrow defile. Thick brush hid the path and he paused, looking about, then stepped down. He looked at the cliff face, seeing it split and tuck back in behind the brush. He pushed aside the thick sumac, pulling some away and, as he suspected, he found a dark cave just big enough for a riderless horse to pass through. As he stepped in, he saw a dim light around the slight bend, just enough to see the interior of the cave that appeared more as a tunnel. With Lobo before him, and leading Shady, he cautiously worked his way through. Once around the bend, the bright sunlight poured through the far end, about thirty yards away. Lobo was already at the opening, looking back to see if Tate was following.

With a careful look around, Tate stepped from the tunnel into a small, vertical-sided basin with the remains of a trail at the end. It would be a short but steep climb, but he was certain he could climb it and Shady could follow. With the lead rope tucked in his belt, he started up the abrupt slope, using hands and feet to push his way up and over the rough sandstone ledge. He heard Shady digging at the dirt behind him and he scampered out of the way as the grulla dug deep and pushed his way over the edge. Lobo had bellied down to watch the other two struggle with the climb he easily made and now watched as their sides heaved from the exertion. Tate looked at the wolf, laughed, and said, "You think it's funny, don't you!" Lobo rose and walked casually to the man's side, nosed his hand and waited for his friend to rub behind his ears as was his custom. Tate ground tied Shady near some bunch grass, motioned for Lobo to stay with him, then turned back to the tunnel to lead the others to the top.

When Carson and Carey saw the troops on the north rim, they resumed their search from the south rim. Carson had repeatedly expressed his concern for Captain Pfeiffer and his foot troops. Pfeiffer had the more difficult mission with his company of foot soldiers marching to the east end of the canyons and making the foray through to the mouth where Carson had camped. So far, there had been no word nor sign of Pfeiffer's command and the Colonel was determined to find them. Carson had always been apprehensive of the canyon and even now was here under protest of the direct order from General Carleton.

Less than two miles further, the column was halted when the forward scout reported back. "Colonel, sir! I think this is where Sergeant Herrera had his skirmish with the Navajo. We found some wounded up there," nodding to the canyon rim, "they need some medical attention, sir."

"Thank you, Corporal," answered Kit, then turned to Captain Carey, "Get your medics up there and see to 'em." He lifted his eyes to the thickening cloud cover, "I think we're 'bout to get more snow, so we'll prob'ly need to turn back." He stood in his stirrups, shaded his eyes and motioned with his chin, "Ain't that the east end yonder?"

The captain looked where Carson indicated, "Could be, Colonel."

But what Carson thought was the Chuska Mountains, was actually the tail end of that range that was nothing more than the Defiance Plateau. But the captain was not anxious to be caught in a blizzard at the edge of the canyon where there was no protection nor shelter to be had, much preferring his tent back at the base camp. Where Captain Berney was an adventurer and relished each new experience, Carey was a dedicated career West Pointer that preferred his comfort to adventure and always managed to work any predicament into his advantage and ultimately his comfort.

Both columns turned back, and the storm hit before they reached camp, but all were determined and soon rode into camp. Already with several fires going, additional shelters erected, and Pfeiffer's company ready to welcome them back. Standing at the bigger cookfire, holding a steaming cup of coffee with his heavy campaign coat with collar standing tall, Captain Pfeiffer lifted his cup to Colonel Carson as he rode up and stepped down. Handing the reins of his mount to his orderly, Carson stepped to the fire, snatched up a cup, and poured himself some coffee. He looked to Pfeiffer and asked, "So?"

The captain chuckled, "Come to find out, Colonel, we were so anxious, we went too far and came down Canyon del Muerto, not Canyon de Chelly!"

Carson nodded, sipped some coffee, "And?"

"And we brought in a few prisoners, killed some warriors, sent some near-frozen women an' children back to the fort, and destroyed several fields, hogans, and stores. There's still a bunch of 'em in that canyon, but gettin' 'em outta there, well, that's another story."

"Ummhumm, that's what we're findin' out." Carson took another swig of coffee, sat down to warm his hands at the fire. They were joined by Tate, Sean, and Captains Berney and Carey. As the men waited for Cooky to finish the cooking, they discussed the mission so far, and all agreed they would need to go through Canyon de Chelly in the same way Pfeiffer came through Canyon del Muerto.

Carson looked to Pfeiffer, "Dependin' on the weather tomorrow, I might send you and your men back to the fort with the captives. You have done more'n your share what with all your boys hoofin' it." He looked to the others, "I think we've got enough men that we can clean out this bigger canyon in a couple days."

"Clean out?" asked Pfeiffer. "Colonel, you could have two, three times as many men as you do, and you still couldn't 'clean out' that canyon. Now, you'll be able to destroy crops, hogans, take their livestock, and ruin their water, but there's too many places for 'em to hide for you to clean 'em out." He paused, looked at the fire, "How many Navajo you s'pose there are in there?" nodding toward the canyon.

Carson considered a moment, "I've thought about that a lot, an' it wouldn't surprise me if there's four or five thousand of 'em."

Captain Pfeiffer grinned, "My guess would be two or three times that many!"

The others scowled at Pfeiffer, and Carey asked, "You really think so?"

"Maybe more," said Pfeiffer. The others fell silent, considering what the captain had said. Most were surprised at Carson's number, but were very doubtful of Pfeiffer's. But if he was right, this was going to be a long campaign.

CHAPTER TWENTY-EIGHT
SIEGE

"It is better to die than to surrender to the bluecoats!" declared Barboncito, his words sounding like a growling threat as his voice rumbled in the confines of the hohrahn. The structure was atop Fortress Rock in the Canyon del Muerto, built for the winter of hiding from the white man. Several such structures were atop the big rock, most dug into the soil, using the few carried in logs to support the roof of bark and dirt. The shelf around the inside of the circle served as seats or sleeping platforms, but now held the leaders of the band atop the rock.

Many of those gathered mumbled their agreement, nodding their heads as they waited for others to speak. Manuelito stood, "What Barboncito says is true, but our people are starving and freezing. Carson and his bluecoats are camped at the mouth of the canyons and some have already come through our sacred lands, killing and destroying. They will not leave unless we surrender or are all dead."

Draws a Bow, though not a leader was a respected warrior of the people, stood to speak. He looked around the circle at the leaders and elders of the people who sat somberly waiting, "If we all die, what good is it? Who will feed our children and our women? Or are they to die as well? We have few weapons and those we have do little against the many guns of the bluecoats. And the Ute and the Mexicans come against us also. One of our young men who watches the sheep spoke with the scout of the bluecoats. This man told him the soldiers do not want to kill us, but will give food and blankets, but we must go to Bosque Redondo. He said the bluecoats will protect us from the Comanche, the Ute, and the Mexican." Draws a Bow was younger than most of those gathered, but his words were heard by the others who had also listened to the promises of the soldiers.

Chief Lambskins Hat sat erect, shoulders back and chest thrust out. Without standing he spoke, "There have been others that have listened to the words of the bluecoats and went to the fort to surrender, but they were killed! Why should we believe them? There have been others that were killed after they surrendered, and to go to Bosque Redondo is to leave the sacred lands of our people! Would we give the four sacred mountains to the soldiers? Or should we fight until the last man to honor Changing Woman and to keep Dinetah?"

Lambskins Hat was the most respected of the medicine men or singers of the Diné and his fiery words were heard and stirred the hearts of the leaders who were anxious to hear any words that would give them hope. He continued, "It is not of our people to tell another what he must do, each must make his own decision, but here, atop Tsélaa, where our ancestors hid from the Spaniards, are more than two hundred Diné and the Dinetah is our home."

Manuelito stood, and in a voice that pronounced rather than incited, said, "We will fight until we can fight no more. When our children cry for hunger or from cold, we will fight. If they no longer cry, then our children and our women must be given to Mother Earth." He looked around the circle of leaders and elders, dropped his gaze to the floor and seated himself on the shelf bench. No one moved nor spoke for several moments until Lamb-skins Hat said, "I will consider what we must do to walk in beauty."

"Captain Berney and his men brought in several captives from his scout of the north rim, we brought the wounded from Herrera's fight and a few others from the south rim. But we know there are many more within the canyons. Today, Captain Berney will take his troop into Canyon del Muerto, Captain Pfeiffer reported several Navajo camped atop one of those islands of rock and he believes they can be talked down. Major Ayers, you and the rest of the troop will go into Canyon de Chelly, you'll move quickly and destroy every field, hogan, water source, food storage and whatever else seems fitting. I want these people to know the only way they will survive is to surrender and go to Bosque Redondo!" He stopped abruptly, looking over the heads of the assembled men that sat around the fire, enjoying the first cup of coffee for the day.

As the colonel stared, the others stood and looked to see a small band of raggedly dressed Navajo slowly approaching the camp, their leader in front with hands held high, one holding a white flag of truce. Carson mumbled, "We'll I'll be, that's the fella what said he'd go tell his people and come back, and so he did!"

He looked at the other officers, "That man met up with us on the rim, said he wanted to come in with his people and submit. I didn't trust him but sent him back to tell his people and come in by mid-morning, and here they are!" He grinned at the others, "So, as you meet up with others, tell 'em 'bout this!"

He sat his coffee down and walked toward the leader of the group then stuttered a step as he looked beyond the small group to see several others following. A quick glance and rough count told him there were at least sixty people in the two groups. He extended his hand to the leader, smiling, "Welcome, welcome. I'm glad you came!" He turned toward the men, "Sergeant Strong! Take these folks to the wagons and get 'em some food and blankets!" The sergeant hopped to, went to the leader and motioned for the people to follow him, and took them to the wagons and began handing out the blankets. He tasked another sergeant to disburse the foodstuffs and the people soon were seated around a fire with the other Navajo, chattering and warming themselves.

Carson returned to the fire for some more coffee and looked to the men. "Well, that's good. But I expect today's mission to be even more productive!" He looked to Berney and Ayers, "Get your men ready and mounted! You move out in fifteen minutes!"

"According to Captain Pfeiffer, that looks like the rock island he talked about. And there's smoke, so there's people up there." Captain Berney paused as he looked around, then turning to his first sergeant, "Sergeant, search around that big rock for any source of water. Then we'll station ourselves, you and half the men on that side, I'll take the others and position ourselves on this side. Whenever you can take a shot at those up there, do it. We want them to know they are not getting off that rock without surrendering!"

"Yessir!" answered First Sergeant Bailey, quickly reining around to gather his men and position themselves. With the wider bottom of the gorge, they could have some shelter against the far wall, and out of range of the rock throwers. He knew the captain would do the same on this side and if there was water to be found, they would place guards around it so the Navajo would have no access. As he began to position the men, he entertained a passing thought that this might be a drawn-out mission that could take several days, so he looked for a location that would also make a good camp.

Bailey stepped down, looking around at the brush and flat between the creek and the cliff face opposite the big rock formation. His men were picking their spots, thinking of the best location for their bedroll, when big rocks, the size of a man's head, began to hail down from atop the fortress.

The clatter of stone on stone, brush breaking, ice at the edge of the stream cracking, and the shouts of men filled the gorge bottom with a cacophony of noise. Horses whinnied, some struck by the rocks, others struggling at their leads trying to escape the clamor. One man, frustrated at the onslaught, lifted his rifle and fired, the lone shot adding to the racket, each sound echoing back and forth between the sandstone cliffs. From high above came shouts and curses, most in Spanish, few understood, war cries rising into screams. More soldiers fired their rifles, but with the Navajo showing only small portions of their bodies and their perch being almost a thousand feet above the canyon floor, the rifles had little effect.

A lull in the noise prompted Sergeant Bailey to shout orders, "Draw back! Here beside the cliff!" The men looked to the familiar voice, scampered for the undercut. Once gathered together, the sergeant chided the men, "Don't you fools know that shooting almost straight up, it's mighty hard to hit anything? 'Sides, that's over three hundred yards and ain't very many of you can hit a standing target at that range! Now, save your ammunition till we have a better fight!" He stomped around, slapping his hat against his leg, then stopping, he looked at a group of three men, "Vasquez, Martinez, Smith, get some firewood, if you can find any, and get a fire started," he pointed to the undercut, "there! And get some coffee going!" He looked at others, "Phillips, O'Hara,

Lopez, get the horses picketed," he looked around, "there, up that draw!"

He heard shouting and firing from the other side of the rock and looked back to the men, "Corporal Leyba, you're in charge till I get back. I'm checkin' on the captain!" He started around the point, stopped and watched as more rocks rained down from high up on the rocky formation. The captain and his men were well protected, having taken cover well away and up the draw into the throat of the smaller canyon.

The captain waved Sergeant Bailey over and the men sat down, looking back at the towering butte. "I don't know how they got up there!" exclaimed the captain. "Look there, on that backside, you can see carved handholds, but they only go up part way. That's still too far to get up easily." He shook his head, wondering. He looked at the sergeant, "Your men settled in?"

"Yessir. One man took a pretty good hit from them rocks they chucked at us, but he'll be alright. Have quite a knot for a while, but he's layin' back by the fire, takin' advantage of his injury." He looked to the captain, "How we gonna get 'em off there, Cap'n?"

"I sent a couple sharpshooters up the draw here, they're lookin' for a place they can get up on top there, either side, someplace they can shoot from. Maybe they can make it a little hot for the Navajo, an' they'll be willin' to come off there." He reached for an offered cup of coffee from one of the men, "You have any other ideas, Sergeant?"

"Well, sir, them Navajo oughta be purty hungry, ya reckon?" asked the sergeant, watching the Captain nod in agreement. "What if we got some fires goin' and fry up some bacon. Let that drift up to 'em, might make 'em think about comin' down, ya think?"

"I like it, Sergeant! See to it with your men, I'll do the same here. And, we found the water over there," pointing to a cleft in the cliff face, "and we'll keep a guard on it. I think we'll be stayin' the night here, so plan accordingly."

"Yessir," answered Bailey, snapping a salute and turning away to return to his men.

"WE ARE GOING to leap-frog our way up that canyon! At first contact or location of a field, hogan, or water source, the lead company will set about taking captives and destroying whatever is there. The other companies will pass on and at the next contact, the lead company will set-to, and so forth. I want us to make it through the length of the canyon with all possible haste. At the fork, the two lead companies will divide and continue. It will be necessary when captives are taken to send them back with an escort, but don't cut your forces too thin! Any questions?" asked Carson, looking from man to man, looking for any indication of problems. All the men sat, shaking their heads and looking to one another.

"Good, good. Now, I've already sent our scouts, Tate and Sean Saint, into the canyon. They will mark any possible hostile locations, either by waiting for you at the location, or marking it so you'll have no question. Major Ayers, your company A will lead off, Captain Carey, your company D will be second and Captain Everett, company E, will bring up the rear." He looked at the men, and added, "Good luck and God speed." The men rose as one, saluted, and turned to assemble their companies for the mission.

Within moments, the troops were readied and with a nod from Carson, Major Ayers gave the order, "Fo'rd Ho!" and within less than thirty yards, "At a canter, Ho!" and the entire remaining regiment leaned forward as the horses quick-stepped into a canter, riding four abreast. Carson beamed as the troops disappeared into the mouth of the foreboding canyon, and his pride showed as a broad smile split his face. It was an impressive sight to see close to three hundred cavalry, armed and eager, heading into battle. The clatter of hooves, rattle of sabers, the jangle of canteens and other gear, and the occasional shouted order echoed back from canyon walls and the tension and excitement grew.

CHAPTER TWENTY-NINE
CONTACT

Lobo and Indy trotted side by side into the darkness of the canyon. The fresh snow padded the footfalls of the horses that followed, and the men that rode had accustomed themselves to the dim light of the blue moon of winter. They watched for any indication of fires. They knew the Navajo were short on wood, but there would still be small cookfires, the Indians choosing to make the small fires before the light of day when rising smoke would give them away. They knew the bluecoats seldom fought in the dark and had never seen them move before daylight. Believing themselves to be safe, and needful of cookfires for what little food they had left, the early morning before first light would be the safest.

At every glow of a fire, Tate and Sean would rein up and make an arrow with rocks or branches to show the location for the troops. The sign would also have a smaller arrow pointing toward the cliffs if necessary, or other sign to indicate the location. Within the first three miles, they made four signs, two with an H pointing to hogans and one with a smaller arrow and a C to indicate caves high up on the cliff face. At about the two-mile point, a large, rocky-top butte that stood as a sentinel extending from the north edge, appeared to have several fires and they made three arrows, spaced apart, each with a smaller arrow to indicate up high.

The first side canyon held cornfields and hogans; a small, spring-fed stream coming from deep within, and the scouts laid out additional arrows. Wild Cherry Canyon held fruit orchards, and Sean and Tate both shook their heads, knowing the trees in the orchards that had stood for decades and gave fruit to generations would be destroyed. They moved on until they came to the fork of the canyons. Another solitary butte stood at the junction of three narrow valleys but there was no indication of anyone atop it. From the fork with Canyon del Muerto, the two scouts had ridden about eight miles, and the sun was stretching the shadows across the canyons, when Tate said, "Let's have us some coffee, ya reckon?"

"Sounds mighty good to me," answered Sean. They walked to a cluster of stunted cottonwoods that sat back from the bank of the frozen creek and stepped down to give the horses an overdue break. Both men loosened the girths, and picketed the horses close by where they could paw for some grass, the tops showing above the few inches of fresh snow. Sean gathered some wood from beneath the taller trees, dropped it in a pile beside his pa, who was building a little pyramid of kindling, and stood with hands on his hips looking up at the thin spire that stretched high above the canyon floor. Tate saw what Sean was looking at, said, "They call that Spider Rock. Seems that has something to do with the beliefs of the Navajo."

"Ain't that sumpin' though?" asked Sean, shading his eyes from the morning sun that seemed to be stretching the long shadow of the spire down the length of the canyon. The bigger shadow of the lonesome butte behind the spire lay like a black gate across the entrance of the south fork known as Horse Track Canyon.

With little flames licking at the kindling, Tate stacked some bigger sticks, sat back on his haunches, and answered, "All of God's creation is something, wouldn't you say?"

"This is an amazing place," drawled Sean, looking around at the massive canyon walls with the streaks of colors, and the pillars and formations of the side canyons standing like a palisade of protection for the ancients that had inhabited the canyon so long before. The gurgle of the coffee brought his attention back, and he sat on the sandstone slab, reached for the pot, and poured his cup full. As the two scouts enjoyed the brew, the rattle of distant gunfire told of the soldiers behind them. Tate dropped his eyes, slowly shaking his head, wondering about the many Navajo and what the outcome of this mission would portend.

Major Ayers spotted the first sign, the rock arrow in the snow that pointed to the small cut in the south wall, and with hand signals, he moved his column to the south edge, letting Captain Carey and the others pass him by, keeping to their pace that had now been slowed to a trot. Ayers shouted, "Sergeant!" and First Sergeant John Harvin came to his side, "Take First Platoon, destroy that field and then burn that hogan!" Both men looked to the canyon maw and easily spotted the field and hogan, the sergeant instantly barking orders to the platoon and gigging his horse forward. As the platoon charged toward the field, the blanket at the hogan was flipped aside and a man stepped out, lifted his hands, and stepped forward. Behind him came a woman and three youngsters and the family walked toward the major and the rest of the column. Within moments, smoke rose from the burning hogan and the woman turned, hand to her mouth as she began to sob, seeing her home destroyed. The oldest boy took his mother's arm and turned her away to go to the soldiers.

Captain Carey was at the lead of the long column of two companies, and kicked his horse to a canter, signaling to the rest to do the same. The stream bed made two sharp turns back on itself, before lining out into the sun. A large butte extended into the canyon, but the blinding sun showed only a towering shadow and the captain followed the frozen stream, lined with snow-covered brush on either side. A sudden barrage of gunfire came from atop Refuge Rock, splitting the column with Captain Carey taking his men at a gallop past the point of the butte to take cover beyond a talus slope. Captain Everett took his men into an overhang to the rear of the butte and behind an outthrust of sandstone. Everett's men were quick to return fire, but the butte top was about seven hundred feet above and most of the bullets struck the cliff face below the rim.

Once around the talus slope, Carey quickly dismounted his men and shouted an order, "Form a skirmish line on this side of the creek, behind that brush!" he pointed to the creek that twisted across the canyon bottom. Once the platoon of men was in place, "Fire!" The barrage sounded like a cannonade with the echoing multiplying the salvo. The men immediately reloaded, and the command came again, "Fire!" The volley was startling, and the whining of ricocheting bullets added to the dissonance.

Suddenly, the canyon was filled with the clatter of hooves and the shouts of men as Major Ayers and his company of cavalry came at a gallop around the bend of the canyon. Those with sidearms waved them overhead as the men shouted and when they neared the butte, the pistols racketed their firing like a continuous volley. The major was leaning into the charge, the mane of his horse whipping at his face, and the bugler, riding just behind the major, added his trilogy of notes to the discord as he blew the thrilling sounds of the cavalry's charge.

Major Ayers expertly led the way, reining his mount to the far side of the stream bed to miss the entrenched skirmish line of startled troopers. As he passed, he shouted, "Get Captain Everett out of his hole and have him follow me!" Captain Carey stared flabbergasted at the passing major and automatically saluted the man as he flew by, grinning all the while.

The flying charge of Major Ayers motivated Captain Everett, who mounted his men and came from the overhang at a run to follow the major. Before Captain Carey had the chance to fire another volley, he heard the echoing charge of Everett as the company of cavalry rounded the point of the butte, with Captain Everett waving at Carey as he passed. The captain stood, watching the second company of men pass him by and he momentarily forgot his position, but a random shot from atop the butte ricocheted a bullet from a nearby rock and brought him back to his purpose. He turned to the men, "Ready! Aim! Fire!" and his frustration was momentarily vented with the rolling volley that thundered through the canyon.

He dropped to his knees behind the brush, looked askance to the first sergeant at his side, then asked calmly, "Any ideas how to get them down from there?"

"Well sir, I'd say get a couple men up there to shoot down on them. Place a couple more here and on the other side, and the rest of us catch up with Major Ayers!"

The captain looked at the leather-faced sergeant, let a slow grin paint his face, and said, "Do it!" He stood and ordered the rest of the men, "To your horses!"

Major Ayers and his company reined up once they were well past the bend in the canyon that shielded them from the fracas at the butte, and he heard the approach of the company of Captain Everett. He sat, waiting for the captain, and saw the sign left by the scouts, pointing into the next side canyon. When the captain rode up, Major Ayers pointed at the sign in the middle of the fresh snow that showed only the tracks of the scouts and asked, "Isn't it your turn?" looking at the junior officer, grinning.

The captain looked at the mouth of the side canyon, "Wonder what we'll find in there?"

"Well, the way I see it, you can either send in a couple scouts, or you can charge in like the place was on fire and you are the firemen!"

The captain looked at Major Ayers, shook his head, "You're having too much fun."

The major laughed, "You didn't get a kick out of that little charge back there?"

With a chuckle, Carey nodded his head.

"Then have at it!" suggested the major, pointing to the side canyon.

The captain looked at him, then at the canyon, and called, "Bugler! Sound the charge!" The men of his company grabbed at their sidearms and kicked their horses to follow the captain as he headed into the canyon. The major gave him just a moment, and with a hand signal, motioned his men ahead, looking into the canyon as they passed. With no gunfire coming from the small gorge, the major chuckled and spoke to the first sergeant, "We'll have to remind the captain that he's the only man to lead a charge into a dead-end and empty canyon!"

But the canyon wasn't empty. An orchard of peach trees, a cornfield with dried and sagging cornstalks, two hogans, and an adobe brick storage bin waited with two families of cold and starving Navajo standing with arms up to surrender to the bluecoats. Captain Everett quickly assigned a platoon to destroy the farm and hogans, and four men to escort the families from the canyon.

. . .

TATE AND SEAN stood by the small cookfire, watching the approach of Major Ayers. The pace of the troopers had slowed to a walk as both men and horses had tired. The major walked his horse toward the two scouts, looked at them as they stood drinking their coffee, then stepped down, "Got'ny more of that?"

"Sure Major, we can spare a cup or two," answered Tate as he bent to retrieve the pot and another cup for the major who dropped to the sandstone slab and removed his cap. He ran his fingers through his hair, lifted his face to the warm sun, and accepted the cup of Java. He took a long drink, visibly relaxing, and looked to Tate, "How much longer does this canyon go on?"

Tate chuckled, "Well, Major. You're about half-way. Then, you've got to go back!"

The major shook his head, "Don't remind me. It looks like it goes on forever!"

"Major, I think we can do a better job of scouting from up on top. There's a place back up this draw that we can climb out and if we split up, we can ride the rim and stay ahead of your men, maybe do a better job of keepin' you out of trouble," suggested Tate, tossing the dregs of his coffee aside and readying to leave.

"I think you're right. If we make it to the end of these canyons, would it be easier to get back to the main camp from up on top, or go back the way we came?"

"Probably shorter to go back through the canyon. Might pick up a few stragglers as well. We'll probably join up with you."

"Then we'll see you at the end!" declared the Major. He stood and watched the father and son scouts ride into the south fork that was called Horse Track Canyon. Without a look back, the two men disappeared around the first bend that took them around the sheer face of the white sandstone cliffs.

CHAPTER THIRTY
RETURN

MILLIONS OF STARS WINKED THEIR LIGHTS IN THE CLEAR DARK NIGHT. The moon had waned to less than half, and the cicadas rattled their applause of the majesty of night in the high desert. At the base of Fortress Rock, the soldiers of Company K, First Regiment, New Mexico Cavalry, added their disharmony of snorts, snores, groans, and restless tossing to the din of the darkness. Captain Berney had strategically stationed the guards, each out of sight of the occupants of the top of Fortress Rock, whose vigilance assured the safety of the sleepers as well as the security of the spring-fed pool in the cleft of the rock. Without first-hand knowledge of the stores of the Navajo atop the butte, the one thing the captain was certain of was that there was no source of water nor means to store water on the butte's rocky top. His strategy was to force the people to come down from their lofty perch because of their need for water, then they could be taken as captives and marched to Fort Canby and ultimately to Bosque Redondo.

BARBONCITO, Manuelito, and chief Lambskins Hat counseled

together and devised a plan. They selected Draws a Bow to lead the people to get water. Before the sun dropped in the west, the young warrior had concocted a plan and had many women weaving yucca ropes and readying water jugs. He chose several men to put his plan into action. As night fell, he waited until the deepening darkness brought a quiet to the butte, then in whispered moves, the people lined out as Draws a Bow directed their action with hand signals as he walked to the edge of the butte. He bellied down, listening to the sounds below, then motioned for the people to begin.

Draws a Bow spoke softly, "You, and you, move the pole ladder over the side, quietly!" He watched as the long pole slid to the edge, then teetered over with four men clinging tightly. Bits of sand slid beneath the pole and trickled off the edge, but there was no sound. Slowly they lowered the pole, feeling for the small ledge that would hold it in place. The people had used multiple pole ladders to mount the butte that rose almost a thousand feet above the floor of the canyon, but to lower more than one ladder without discovery would be impossible.

One after another they formed a human chain with three boys, of about twelve summers, going down the pole first. They were followed by three women, then men, each stopping on a notch of the pole. Below the pole, the people hung like a chain, some finding the occasional carved out foothold, but most were held by hands and short yucca or rawhide ropes. Once in place, the water jugs, held by the yucca ropes, were lowered down the human chain. The boys knew their job and silently lowered the jugs into the water, allowing just moments for them to fill, then began the hand over hand retrieval. With each of the members of the chain, holding tight to the hand of the one above, those atop the butte lifted the jugs, emptied them, and lowered each jug again. Without a sound, the jugs were repeatedly lowered, and all the containers atop the butte were filled with fresh water.

As the people returned to the top, they were met by others, happily greeting them and thanking them for getting the water. Barboncito came to the side of Draws a Bow, "You have done well."

"Yes, my chief. The people have done well. Now we have water, but little food. And we will need to do this again and again until the soldiers leave, but will we live through the cold nights with no food?" responded Draws a Bow.

"Lambskins Hat says he will show the bluecoats the power of the people. He said he will call on the spirits to do what we cannot."

Draws a Bow stared at this man, the orator and leader of the people, his expression showing his alarm and asked, "To call on the spirits is to use witchcraft!" His words were almost a whisper, afraid for anyone nearby to hear them, for all the Navajo people were fearful of Skinwalkers and other spirits of the dead.

Barboncito dropped his eyes, looked at the people nearby and back to Draws a Bow, "Each must do what he believes is what is needed. He is a Hataálii and knows things we do not."

WHEN THE FIRST light of early morning darkened the shadows of the canyon, Captain Berney rolled from his blankets to the smell of coffee. When the attending corporal saw the captain stirring, he poured a cup and brought it to the captain, "Mornin' cap'n."

"Mornin' corporal, anyone else stirring?"

"Not yet, cap'n. But I did see the glow of a fire atop the butte before the sun came up. I don't think them Navajo are too worried 'bout us down here."

"You could be right. But unless they have water up there, I

expect they'll be comin' down soon." The captain stood by the fire, looking to the canyon and the towering butte. Most of the men were still in their blankets, and his two Ute scouts were camped apart from the soldiers near the frozen stream and the manzanita brush. He saw both scouts looking to the butte, animatedly talking with one another. When they started toward the captain, he poured himself another cup of coffee and waited.

"Captain, the Navajo on the rock are not going to leave!" stated the older of the two, the one known as Long Walker.

"Oh, why do you say that?" asked the captain.

"I think they have water and will not come down."

"Where would they get water up there? Surely there's no spring or well, not up there," asked the captain, lifting his eyes to the butte top. As he did, he saw movement, and what he thought was a stone thrown over the edge. He reflexively took a step back, pointing at the butte, causing the two scouts to turn and look. As they watched, what they thought was a stone, exploded in a splash of water at the base of the butte. "Now what . . . why'd they do that?" asked the captain, of no one in particular, shading his eyes to see where the water jug had burst.

Long Walker looked at the captain, "To show you they have water, as I said."

The captain looked from the Ute to the base of the butte, then considered for a moment, "We'll stay another night, they might be tryin' to convince us just so we'll leave." He looked at the two men before him, then asked, "You think you could get up on the rim somewhere, get a better look at what they're doin' up there?"

Long Walker looked to his fellow scout, Rides a White Horse, to see him nod in answer to the question. Walker turned to the captain, "Yes, we will go."

"Alright, take a look, come back and report it. I mainly wanna know if they have food and water, understand?"

"Yes," answered the scout, turning away.

TATE WAS SEATED on a slightly tilting sandstone slab atop a rugged butte that extended into the canyon. He guessed he was about halfway from the fork of the canyons where he left Major Ayers and the east end of the north fork. He had seen movement and walked out on the point, leaving Shady ground tied in the piñons and now sat with scope in hand, elbows resting on his knees as he searched the canyon bottom. Less than a half-mile down, Major Ayers and his company of cavalry were moving up the canyon. But directly opposite Tate's position, he saw several Navajo scampering up a broad talus slope, with those in the lead, trying to mount the sandstone cliffs above them. But the melting snow from the night before had been turned to ice by the cold winds whipping down the gorge, and the handholds used before were iced over. Tate lifted his scope upwards from the frantic Navajo and saw the maw of an overhang and cave that had been their refuge.

A few people were at the mouth of the cave, looking down at those below. Tate surmised, those in the canyon bottom had gone in search of wood and food, but no one carried any bundles or anything that said their search was successful. Now, they had undoubtedly heard the approaching cavalry and were trying to return to their sanctuary, but Tate could tell, there was no way they would escape the major.

Major Ayers spotted the Navajo atop the talus slope and quickly realized what they were doing. He turned to his first sergeant, "Sergeant! First squad, fire above those people, stop them!"

The order was hollered out, "First Squad, dismount! Form a skirmish line!" the sergeant pointed before him, and when the men were positioned, "One round, above those Navajo. Ready, Aim,

Fire!" The Springfields sounded their threatening chorus, and the splang of ricocheting bullets answered back. The Navajo turned to look at the soldiers below, and Major Ayers cupped his hands to his mouth and shouted, "Stop! We will not hurt you! We have food and blankets! Come down now!" He commanded the sergeant to repeat his words in Spanish, and the dark-skinned sergeant copied the captain with cupped hands and shouted the translation. The Indians had stopped, looked at one another, and one matronly grey-haired woman started down the slope. After a few steps, she stopped, turned to look at the others, said something, and turned back to walk down the slope. Her words had prompted others to move, and within moments, all the people were walking down the slope toward the soldiers.

Tate, still watching with his telescope, grinned and counted, coming up with a tally of twenty-three that were surrendering to the major. Satisfied, he stood and returned to Shady to finish his scout of the north fork of the canyon. He was hopeful the cavalry would complete their search today and make short work of their return in the morning.

THE NIGHT BEFORE, Carson had walked through the camp of the Navajo, speaking to several of the men, telling each one that if they wanted, they could return to the canyon to tell any of their people to surrender and come to the camp. He reminded them that food and blankets awaited, and they would be fed through the winter. Although few immediately accepted the offer, he did see several walking from the camp and were allowed to leave.

Now Carson stood at the cookfire, looking into the flames considering all that had happened on the mission. He looked up to see a group of five Navajo approaching, hands held high as they cautiously drew near. Carson went to them, "Welcome. Good, good," he said, offering his hand to the leader. He called to a sergeant, standing at another of the cookfires, "Sergeant! Take these to the wagons. You know what to do!" He turned to the Navajo before him, "This man will get you food and blankets, and take you to the others."

Throughout the morning, several small groups walked into the camp. Some with cavalry escort from the troops in the canyon, others coming of their own accord, having been told by others of the good treatment they would receive. Carson was pleased with the results and looked forward to the return of the troops from their foray into the canyon.

When dusk had chased the sun below the western horizon, Major Ayers, Captain Everett, and Captain Carey and the father and son scouts, had all returned to the main camp. The troops brought in an additional twenty-two stragglers, and all were anxious for a good meal and night's rest. Carson spoke to the officers, "Gentlemen. You've done a marvelous job, I'm proud of each and every one of you. Although Captain Berney, according to the message he sent by one of his men, will be spending the night in hopes of more surrenders, the rest of us will start back to Fort Canby at first light. The word has spread among the *Diñe* that they will be treated kindly, and I believe many more will surrender. Some of those that came into camp have returned to their families to bring them into Fort Canby, and we can most certainly declare this mission a success! So, be ready at first light, and we'll move out!"

Captain Carey stood and looked at the other men, then turned to Carson, "Colonel, I'm sure I speak for the rest of the men when I say it's been an honor to serve with you, sir." He lifted his cup, "To the Colonel!" The rest of the men stood, lifted their cups and answered "Hear! Hear!" and took their cups as if they were sipping the finest champagne in town and drank to the Colonel.

BUT ABSENT FROM the group was Captain Berney and his company. With a quiet day, unusually quiet in the mind of the captain, with no shouted threats, hurled stones, or rifle fire from atop the butte, he had only the word of his two scouts that the Navajo were still there and still alive. The scouts had reported there were no cookfires, no unusual activity, but with the many Hohrahn dug into the butte top, the people stayed inside. So, as they reported, it was entirely possible they had ample supplies of food and water.

After receiving the report from the Ute scouts, Berney called his officers and first sergeant together. He looked from Lieutenant Brady to Lieutenant Cronin and to First Sergeant Bailey, "From all we can determine, there's no indication that any of those up top have any inclination to come down. I thought by guarding the water down here, they would soon run out and give up, but the scouts say there's no sign of surrender." He lifted his eyes to the darkening sky, "It's too late to start back now, so I'm thinkin' we'll leave at first light."

The sergeant arranged the guard schedule and posted the first guard at the spring, then turned in with the rest of the men. The captain sat by the fire, enjoying the solitude and downed another cup of coffee. He lifted his eyes to the night sky, enjoying the clear cold night and the myriad of stars overhead. He turned to go to his blankets, but as he moved from the fire, he heard sounds from atop the butte. In the night, sounds carry and what he heard sounded like a chant or singing, but he saw no glow from a fire and was not concerned as he rolled into his blankets for the night.

. . .

Draws a Bow had an interest in holy things from the early days of his youth. Whenever he had the opportunity to be a part of a sing, he carefully watched and listened to the Hataáli, considering and wondering if he might be called to learn from the singers. To pursue that path for his life would require many years of learning from the different singers that knew the ways of the people. Now, atop the butte with the others, he had watched the man who was the most respected Hataáli of the *Diné.* Draws a Bow had watched Lambskins Hat the last two nights and had recognized the singer was doing the Anaa'ji or Enemyway, but he also thought Hóch'íjí or Evilway. With his eagerness to learn, he stayed at a distance, trying to stay hidden, as he watched and listened. If it was either it would be complete after this, the third night of the chant.

As the respected singer continued with his sand painting and his chant, the night wore on and Draws a Bow dozed. But before the first light of day showed in the east, the young warrior was jolted awake when the cadence of the sing changed, and the volume increased. He looked to see Lambskins Hat standing, but with a bow in his hands and he was drawing an arrow, flames licking at the point, and aiming it at the stars. Draws watched as the singer let the arrow fly, all while the man missed not a beat in his chant. The arrow arched high above and slowly bent the arch to start what seemed a slow descent to the canyon floor. The dim flame of the arrow disappeared into the depths of darkness of the gorge below, but sudden shouts came from the blackness as soldiers and others stirred and shouted.

Lambskins Hat turned to look directly at Draws a Bow, "I have unleashed the evil spirits of the wind to guide the arrow into the heart of a cavalry officer. This will drive them from our Dinetah!" The chief turned away and walked to his hohrahn.

. . .

THE ARROW FOUND its mark in the chest of Lieutenant Michael Cronin. One moment he was sleeping, then startled awake to the searing pain of an arrow of fire buried in his chest. His eyes flared wide, he tried to speak, but grasping the shaft of the arrow, he drew one shallow breath and died. Nearby the two Ute scouts had jumped from their blankets, to see the Arrow protruding from the chest of the officer, and shouted, "Aaiiiieeee!" and quickly turned back to roll their blankets and retrieve their horses. The racket had awakened Captain Berney, and he came to the side of the lieutenant, looked at the scampering Ute and asked, "Where you goin'?"

Long Walker spoke excitedly and fearfully, "This," pointing to the dead man, "is of the evil spirits of the night. We must leave now, or we will all die in this canyon of death!" Without waiting for a response, the Ute turned, swung aboard his mount and the two kicked their horses to a gallop and left.

The captain looked around, lifted his eyes to see many of the stars snuffing their lanterns, and knew morning was near. He turned to the first sergeant standing near in his stocking feet, "Get 'em ready! We're movin' out!"

"But cap'n, what 'bout coffee an such?" asked the sergeant.

"We're leavin'! We'll stop down the canyon a way and have some coffee then. Move!"

CHAPTER THIRTY-ONE
CANBY

Carson stood at the window of his office, looking out at the encampment of the Navajo. Their camp lay on the outskirts of the cabins and houses of Fort Canby, between the fort and the long ridge of mountains to the east. A cup of steaming coffee in his hand, his glassy-eyed stare stirred his memories of the past year and the many excursions into Navajo country, culminating in their campaign in the canyons. He spoke, somewhat wistfully, "Well Tate, I'm happy to say that I think our mission is over, at least for us, not them," motioning to the distant camp by the lift of his cup. He turned and went to his desk, setting his cup down and leaning back in his chair, clasping his hands behind his head and looking to his long-time friend. "You ready to go home?" he asked, letting a broad smile paint his face, but with a bit of a mischievous glint in his eye.

"You know the answer to that, Kit. Now, Sean here, I've practically had to tie him down to keep him from skedaddling out of here!" declared Tate, looking from Carson to his son sitting beside him.

Sean twisted in his seat, "Ya can't blame me, I ain't never been away from my wife this long, before."

Both Tate and Carson chuckled at the younger man, and Carson said, "How 'bout we take outta here in the mornin'?"

Both Tate and Sean slid forward to the edge of their seats, both expecting more than just an announcement of the trip to return home. And Carson took a deep breath, leaned forward with his elbows on the desk and added, "Carleton said I couldn't have that leave until I could bring in at least a hundred Navajo. So, we'll be takin' most of those," nodding his head to the window and the distant camp, "with us. We'll have a company of cavalry with us, and we'll let the boys in blue take 'em on to Bosque, and we'll go to Santa Fe."

Tate grinned, looked from Sean to Kit, "Where we gonna leave the Navajo?"

"We'll take 'em to the post at Los Pinos. The troops will get resupplied there, maybe get a few more wagons, then they'll go on to Bosque Redondo."

"How many are out there?" asked Sean, nodding his head toward the encampment.

"Last count, just over two hundred. But more are comin' in all the time. We'll have ten wagons, mainly to carry the old, children and women. But most will have to walk. A couple of wagons will be carryin' the rations and such. We should make it to Los Pinos in a little over a week, another three days to Santa Fe. And another three days before I can make it home to Josefa!"

Tate stood, prompting Sean to stand as well, reached out to shake Kit's hand, "Well, my friend, look at it this way, in about two weeks, you'll be home with your family. But us, now, we'll be with our family, but it'll take three times that long before we get home!" The men chuckled as they shook hands, and Carson said, "The sooner started, the sooner finished!"

. . .

THE FOURTH DAY out of Fort Canby, Tate and Sean were well ahead of the wagons, scouting and hunting for some fresh meat for the troopers and the Navajo. The wagon road, well used by freighters shipping supplies between Fort Wingate and Fort Canby, followed the wide valley between the series of flat-top mesas to the north and the slow rising ridges and buttes to the south. The hunt the day before along the mesas yielded a lone buck that didn't go far among so many, and the two scouts were hugging the low buttes to the south, hopeful of a more fruitful hunt. When they came to a narrow valley that cut between the low buttes and pointed to the timber covered plateau to the south, Tate suggested, "Sean, you swing around these buttes thataway," pointing to the south, "and I'll go in this little valley. If I remember right, we'll meet up yonder, 'bout two or three miles or so. I believe the Bluewater creek that comes from that cut yonder," pointing to the notch in the distant plateau, "comes out on the other side of these little buttes. We'll meet up there."

"Alright Pa, if'n either of us get anything, I reckon we'll hear the shootin'."

"And if you get a chance, get on top o' them buttes and have a look-see with your scope."

Sean nodded as he watched his pa rein Shady to his right and he and Lobo started down the narrow valley. He gigged Dusty forward, motioned to Indy, and laying his Spencer across the pommel, they started along the edge of the buttes. Low rising, sparsely covered with piñon, sage, greasewood and cacti, little cover was offered for desert muleys or bighorns, but both animals depended on their eyesight and speed for their protection. After rounding the first low butte, he pointed Dusty to a dim trail that led to the top of the highest of the buttes and Sean thought he might have a view of the entire range from up high. The long-legged Appaloosa easily mounted the round-top, but Sean reined him up before reaching the crest.

The sun had made quick work of the snow, leaving just a few patches that hugged the narrow draws on the north slopes, but the round-topped butte held a rocky knoll shaded by two scraggly piñon. He tethered Dusty to a tree, giving his a little shade from the high sun, and with Indy at his side, Spencer cradled in the crook of his arm, and the scope in his free hand, he took to the rocks, seating himself for a good survey of the landscape. He began a systematic search, watching for any movement or sign of water or grass that might attract deer or sheep. He made a full sweep, searching every dip, rockpile, draw, and ravine that was visible from his promontory. Nothing moved until he saw a scampering coyote that took off after a jackrabbit. The little puffs of dust disappeared into an arroyo, and Sean looked elsewhere.

The knoll he was on, dropped away to a shoulder and another slightly less knoll, but one that had a better view of the valley beyond. He rolled off his perch, catching a glimpse of a rider entering the smaller valley and he grinned, believing it was his pa. He retrieved Dusty and walked to the farther knoll, again tethering the Appy to a tree and hunkering down to go to the crest of the knoll. Seating himself in the shade of a small piñon, he extracted the scope from the case, and began his search of the more promising valley that held both water and graze. He started with the small stream that came from the deep cut in the higher plateau, thinking the deer would be near the water and greenery, maybe taking shade among the manzanita.

Movement caught his eye, and he focused on what he anticipated would be deer. But three riders, riding in single file, came from the cut alongside the stream and stopped as they entered the smaller valley. Sean watched as they talked, pointing up the valley, then apparently in agreement, they moved forward, now side by side. He could make out they were Mexican by the sombreros and saddles. Each man had the look of a vaquero with pants decorated down the seam flared at the boots. Tapaderos covered their stirrups, and rifles lay across the bows of the saddles. If they were hunting, it wasn't for meat.

Sean turned, moving his scope up the length of the valley and spotted another rider, easily identified as his pa, coming towards the three men. He watched his pa lay the Spencer across the pommel of his saddle, check the load and cap, cocking the hammer. Sean grinned, knowing his father had spotted the riders and was preparing himself. He looked back at the three vaqueros, saw them gesturing toward his pa, then he dropped the scope, calculating the distance to the bottom of the valley and about where the riders would meet. He looked below his perch, saw another promontory about thirty yards closer, and he looked to Indy, motioned to the wolf and the two wove their way through the few trees and sage to the new position.

Sean stationed himself on the big flat rock, belly down, knowing he was shielded by the nearby juniper, and readied himself for a shot, if necessary, but he was almost certain it would be necessary. He calculated the distance at about four hundred yards, downhill, but in the open and sunny valley bottom.

Tate reined up, motioned Lobo behind a bunch of greasewood, turned Shady slightly crosswise of the trail and waited. The three men came on, one just a bit ahead of the other two that flanked him, all with their rifles across the bows of their saddles and grinning. He took note of the men, dirty, unshaven and tobacco-stained teeth, and with the wide upturned brim of sombreros.

Their attire had at one time been rather festive, but now showed considerable wear and uncared for with stains and tears showing. But their rifles were clean and well used, each man holding a newer Henry repeating rifle, which Tate thought were only available to the northern troops in the war.

"Greetings Señor! How are you this fine day?" said the man in the lead, grinning and nodding as he spoke, but in a manner that showed anything but genuine friendliness.

"Good. You?" responded Tate, looking from man to man. As he sat with Shady slightly turned, his Spencer was pointed right at the leader, and Tate saw the speaker noting the position of the rifle.

"Oh, we are fine, señor! We come to see you!"

"To see me? Why?" asked Tate, suspicious of the three.

"Because you are with the wagons and the Indians!" stated the man, looking at his two partners who nodded and chuckled as they looked at Tate.

"Oh, and just how does that concern you?" asked Tate, somewhat gruffly.

"Oh señor, because there are women and children among them, and we would have them. We like the Navajo women and children; they are worth many pesos to us!" He paused as he looked to Tate, "And we will take them!"

Tate grinned, appeared relaxed, and said, "You ain't takin' anything!"

The leader frowned, eyes pinching, and he started to lift his rifle, but the big Spencer bucked and roared, the bullet taking the man at the third button of his shirt, caving in his chest, blossoming red, and knocking the man from his saddle. In the next instant, both riders were bringing up their rifles, but a boom from high up the mountain came almost at the same time the second rider grabbed for his Henry. But the big bullet busted the pommel and split with one piece tearing into the man's thigh, just below his crotch. The other ripping across and into his lower belly, spilling blood and guts onto the leather seat of the remains of the saddle. He grabbed at the shattered horn, but slid off the side, unable to grip the bloody pommel.

Tate grabbed at his holstered Colt Navy pistol, and started to bring it up, but a flash of grey came from the ground and knocked the shocked man from his saddle and bore him to the ground. The big wolf landed, teeth in the man's throat, and he tumbled end over end, tearing out a big chunk of the man's neck as he fell. He quickly sprang to his feet and pounced on the man, but a choking scream was muffled by the blood that spurted from the torn neck, and the man's eyes flared with the last thing he ever saw being the bloody teeth and gaping maw of the mouth of the big wolf.

Sean quickly retrieved Dusty, mounted him as they started down the slope. The big Appaloosa dropping to his haunches as he slid down the steep hill, picking up and putting down his front hooves, guiding himself down the gradient. When they bottomed out, Sean leaned down on the horse's neck as they ran to the side of Tate and Shady, coming to a sliding stop beside them. He looked around, saw all three men down, then looked at his pa, "What was that all about?"

Tate put his hands on the pommel, leaning forward, then looked to his son. "It seems they were planning on taking some of the women and children from the train."

"Slave traders!" spat Sean. "Not'ny more!" he proclaimed.

"Nope!" answered Tate, then turning to Sean, "I sure was happy to hear that Spencer bark from up there. What were you doin'?"

"Scopin' for game, like you said. But I didn't think I'd be huntin' two-legged game!"

Tate stepped down and walked to the downed men, picked up a rifle, examined it and jacked a round into the chamber, then lowered the hammer without firing the rifle. Sean had also stepped down and now stood beside his pa, "That's one of those new Henry's, isn't it?"

"Ummhumm. There's two more," he nodded to the other bodies, "Take the rifles and pistols, and anything else that might come in handy."

"We gonna bury 'em?" asked Sean, looking to his pa.

Tate lifted his eyes overhead, saw three turkey buzzards circling, then looked back to Sean, "Well," then nodding to the birds, "They gotta eat too, but I reckon the proper thing is to bury 'em."

THE TRAIN STOPPED at Fort Wingate, resupplied for the remainder of the trip, and started on again. The word had spread among the Navajo and over three hundred had surrendered at Wingate, and more were expected. "Apparently, Kaniache and his Ute are doin' a lot of raiding on the scattered Navajo farms and villages. Got 'em all scared and they're comin' in to surrender, even knowing they're goin' to Basque Redondo. They're plum afraid of the Utes!" declared Carson as he rode beside Tate. "I'm not happy with Kaniache, but their raidin' is driving the Navajo in to the forts, so . . ." he left the thought hanging. He looked to Tate, "But after what you told me 'bout them Mex raiders, I don't know which bunch is worse, but the thought of those Mexicans planning on hitting a troop of cavalry, tells me they had more than just the three of 'em. And if that's the case, I'm wonderin' if they'll be hittin' the troops as they take the Navajo to Bosque."

"Could be. That'n seemed to be pretty sure they could take 'em, and the thought of what they could get sellin' the women and children, seemed to be a pretty good motivator."

"Yeah, there's a lot of things on the wrong side of the law that appeals to some folks," drawled Carson, shaking his head at the thought.

CHAPTER THIRTY-TWO
SANTA FE

THERE WAS NOTHING UNUSUAL OR SPECIAL ABOUT THE THREE MEN that rode into Santa Fe that day, except for the two wolves that trotted before them. They were dirty, unshaven, tired, and little different than the horses they rode. Weary hooves dragged in the dirt, dust clouds lifting at every footfall. The dim light of dusk was fading, and a few lanterns were winking as they parted, with no more than a nod and a wave. One pointing his horse toward Fort Marcy, the other two toward a wide porch in front of a house set back from the roadway, sitting quietly beneath a towering cottonwood, the only tree in the yard. A slow creak of a rocking chair on the plank porch stopped, and a woman rose to her feet, touching the porch post as if in need of support for trembling legs. When she stepped from the shade of the porch, red hair cascaded over her shoulders as she tenuously stepped off the porch, and nary a breath did she take. Two steps more and she broke into a run as she recognized the riders that reined up at the gate of the fence. Her breasts heaved as she gasped and filled her lungs. But words did not come as the big man, whiskered, dirty, smelling of dust and sweat and worse, grabbed her and lifted her to him. They smashed lips together, grasping one another as tightly as they could, and then leaning back, laughed in harmony.

But another had appeared from the darkness and two others buried themselves in a long-awaited embrace. Long black hair coursed down the back of the woman, who stood in a simple gingham dress but barefooted, as she clung to her man. She lay her head on his chest and mumbled into the folds of his coat, "I hope you are Bear Chaser. White Fox has waited long for her man to return. If you are not Bear Chaser, don't tell him." She giggled as she looked into familiar eyes and smiled.

"Well, don't just stand there! The whole neighborhood is going to think who knows what! Come in here! Right now!" ordered a redhead woman, looking a lot like the older one hugging the dirty traveler, and standing with hands on hips as she hollered loud enough for almost everyone in Santa Fe to hear.

Maggie leaned back for a better look at her man and said, "Look at you! You've been riding on the bank of the Rio Grande for what, three days? And not once did you think about jumping in to get rid of some of that road dust, not to mention the smell!" She playfully slapped Tate on the shoulder as they started up the walk to the porch.

"Woman, don't you know it's wintertime?"

"What does that have to do with anything?"

"The river's froze over and it's not fittin' trying to wash with ice!"

"What? Have you gone soft on me? We'll fix that! We've got a genuine copper bathtub right in there and the both of you are gonna put it to use!"

Tate looked to Sean, "How'd we ever get along without these women to take care of us?"

White Fox chimed in, "You didn't!"

. . .

FATHER AND SON sat across the table from one another, looking at the other. Both were attired in new white linen drop-shouldered shirts, wool britches, and were clean-shaven, hair trimmed and looking almost the mirror image of one another. They laughed as the women set dishes piled with food before them, then sat down beside their men. Sadie was at the end and smiling at her family but with an expression that told of more than just happiness that her pa and brother were home. Everyone joined hands, and Tate led them in a prayer of thanksgiving for all the blessings, their safe return, and the future before them. As he said 'Amen' the others chorused an 'Amen' and lifted their eyes to one another, everyone filled with thanksgiving and happiness they were all together.

As they ate and talked, catching up on all that had happened and the many little things that would normally be shared experiences and were now only shared memories, there were occasional watery eyes, smiles, and laughter over distant moments. As the conversation lulled and everyone enjoyed the feast, Sadie spoke up, "Uh, Josiah will be by tomorrow, and," she looked straight at Tate, "he has something he wants to ask you."

Tate stopped, fork held before his open mouth, he looked at his daughter and his eyes showed a slight squint, then he looked at Maggie, a question in his expression. He sat his fork down, sat up a little straighter, saw Sean across the table watching him with a wide grin and a smile on White Fox's face, then he looked at Sadie. "And just what does the Lieutenant want to ask me?"

"Father," she started, using a term never before used, "that is between the two of you. And, he is not a Lieutenant, he is a captain!"

"Captain, is it? Well, apparently he's been up to quite a lot in my absence." He felt Maggie's hand on his leg as he spoke, but he continued, enjoying the moment of mischievousness. He squinted his eyes and lowered his head just a little so that he stared at his daughter in much the same way that Lobo would before he attacked, "What have you been up to while I was gone?"

Maggie pinched his leg under the table, and it was all he could do to keep from laughing, "Well?" he growled.

Sadie put the napkin to her mouth, then lay it beside her plate, knowing her father was staring at her and waiting for a response. She leaned forward, assumed the same pose and expression as her father and said, "You don't fool me! I know you, remember? You tried this when you tried to keep it a secret that you had a new pony for me, and when we found that little bear cub, and I know you're not as mean as you act! So, quit trying to bully me and be happy for me, father!" She sat up, smiled prettily, and crossed her arms and waited.

Tate tried to stay sober-faced and scowling, but he knew exactly what his daughter was up to and he was happy for her. He sat up straight, fussed with his napkin trying to growl all the while, then stopped and let a smile paint his face. He stood and walked around the table, "Then give your *father* a proper welcome home!" as he held out his arms and waited.

She jumped from her seat and into his arms, giggling and crying at the same time as the two embraced. When he leaned back to look at his little girl, he said, "I know if you chose him, he must be alright. But . . ." and he drew out the pause, "that doesn't mean I'm going to let him off easy, after all, you're our only daughter and this won't happen again!"

THE WOMEN BUSIED themselves cleaning off the table as Tate and Josiah rose to go to the porch. As they seated themselves, Sadie brought cups of coffee to them both then retreated inside. Tate looked to the rigid captain, "So, you want to make Sadie your wife, and you're going to continue in your career as an officer?"

"Yessir. My father was a career officer and he did quite well. I believe that the army can provide us a good life. The war seems to be winding down and there will be ample opportunity for good officers. We've talked at some length about a life in the military and all that it requires. I know we'll probably move around some, but usually, after a certain rank, those moves don't come as often, and it can be a good life."

Tate looked at the man, noted his nervousness and tried not to smile, "There's something else that concerns me, young man."

"Oh, and what is that sir?"

"How are things between you and the Lord?"

The captain turned to look at Tate, frowning a little, then asked, "I'm not sure what you mean, sir."

"Simple enough. How are things between you and the Lord?" asked Tate, looking at him.

"Well, alright, I guess. I hadn't really thought about it. I've gone to church before, when I was young, that is."

Tate looked at him, "Ummhumm. Well, let me ask you this. Let's say you have to go out on an expedition, and you run into some renegade Comanche and one of 'em puts an arrow in your gullet. Then what?"

"Uh, you mean, if I die? Well, Sadie would get my benefits, such as they are."

"No, I don't mean that. I mean, what happens to you?"

"Oh, I hadn't really thought about it. I guess, really, I've tried not to think about it."

"Do you believe the Bible?"

"Yessir, I do. Doesn't everybody?"

Tate picked up the Bible lying beside the chair, sat it on his lap and answered, "The Bible tells us that whether we think about it or not, one day, when we die, we will step off into eternity. And what we do here will determine whether we go to hell or heaven." He leaned toward Josiah a little, "Want to know more?"

The captain was no longer nervous, but now his interest overcame his concerns and said, "Yessir, I do. I guess I've always wanted to know, but . . . well, go on."

Tate opened the Bible, "There is a very simple plan that God gives us so we can understand the most important and most basic thing about Him and His Book. It's here in the book of Romans, so I'll show you the verses here so you can understand and decide for yourself. The first is here in chapter three, *"There is none righteous, no not one.* And again, down here," he pointed to the next page, *For all have sinned and come short of the glory of God.* So, the first thing you need to know is that we're all sinners. You understand that, don't you?"

The captain dropped his head and chuckled, "Boy, don't I!"

"Now the second thing you need to know is here in chapter six, *For the wages of sin is death; but the gift of God is eternal life through Jesus Christ our Lord."* Tate looked at Josiah, then added, "See, because we're sinners there's a penalty and that penalty is death. Now, Josiah, that's not just dying, everybody dies, that's eternal death and hell forever. That's the penalty."

Tate watched Josiah drop his head and mutter, "That's bad," he shook his head then lifted his eyes to Tate, "I remember my grandma talking about that. She talked about how terrible things were in hell and that we didn't have to go there, but I don't remember what else she said."

"That's easy enough. It tells us right here in this verse and again in chapter five, *But God commendeth his love toward us in that while we were yet sinners, Christ died for us.* See, God loves us and doesn't want us to go to hell. So, He sent Christ to pay the penalty for us. And because He did, now we can have that gift He spoke of here in chapter six, . . .*the gift of God is eternal life through Jesus Christ our Lord.* So, now, instead of facing eternal death, we can have eternal life!"

"Wow! That's so simple and that's what my grandma talked about. But, wait, how? How do we get that eternal life?"

Tate smiled, "That's the easy part. Remember, He said it was a gift. And like any gift, it doesn't work unless you accept it. So, all you have to do is accept that gift, and fortunately over here," he turned a few pages of the Bible, "in chapter ten he tells us, *That if thou shalt confess with thy mouth the Lord Jesus and believe in thine heart that God hath raised him from the dead, thou shalt be saved.* And in verse thirteen *For whosoever shall call upon the name of the Lord shall be saved."*

"Is it really that simple? All I have to do is ask?"

"Ummhumm. When I started, remember I said it was simple. But the key to it all is back there where it said *believe in thine heart.* It's not something like when a gambler puts an ace up his sleeve to pull out whenever he needs it, or like trying on a new shirt for size, it's got to be from deep in your heart. You have to truly believe."

Josiah lowered his head, then lifted his eyes, "I do! I do believe!"

"Then all you need to do is *call upon* Him and we do that in prayer. So, if you want to do this, I'll lead us in a simple prayer and if you mean it, you can say the same prayer." He paused and looked at the man, who looked back and nodded his head.

Tate lowered his eyes and bowed his head and began, "Our Father in Heaven, we come to you now . . ." and led the two in a simple prayer where Josiah asked God's forgiveness for his sins and asked for Christ to become his Savior. When Tate said, "Amen," he was echoed by Josiah and the two men looked at one another, smiled and shook hands.

. . .

It was a simple but beautiful ceremony conducted by the padre at the chapel. Several of the captain's fellow officers were there and on Sadie's side, her family and the extended family of White Fox. At the conclusion, there were long goodbyes and many tears as would be expected. Tate, Maggie, Sean and White Fox had everything packed and ready for their departure and Sadie and Josiah were going to stay in the house in Santa Fe. After the overly long stay in Santa Fe, they left with four pack horses, having arrived with only two. It was mid-day when the small entourage rode from the historic town, each one turning in their saddle for a last look and wave to Sadie.

When Maggie daubed at her tears, Tate looked, smiled, and leaned over to give her a hug and said, "How 'bout we go home?"

She smiled and answered, "I've been waiting to hear you say that for a long time!"

From behind them, "Hey you two! You gonna neck or ride? I hear the mountains callin' and we wanna go home!" Everyone chuckled and gigged their horses to a trot. They knew they would be chasing springtime all the way as they traveled north to the Rocky Mountains, but that was home, and home beckoned.

EPILOGUE

Although dependable records are sketchy, Carson's departure from Fort Canby on January 26, 1864, with the 240 Navajo, was just the beginning of what would later be called the "Long Walk" of the Navajo. The miserable conditions forced the *Diné* to surrender and go to Bosque Redondo, just to survive. Yet of the between 11,000 and 12,000 Navajo that left Forts Canby and Wingate for the Long Walk, 8,846 actually arrived. With the harsh winter, little clothing and food, the crossing of the Rio Grande river without boats or ferries, and walking somewhere between 350 and 500 miles, depending on the route, many were lost. Time and again raiding Mexican, Ute and Comanche took captives, even while they marched under guard of the cavalry, and others starved, froze or escaped. Although official records state that only 336 died on the march, over 2000 were unaccounted for and one can only surmise as to their end. It is known that some escaped to return to the canyons, but no one knows how many actually perished.

Barboncito, contrary to his earlier declaration, did surrender, but later led an escape of about 500 from the Bosque. Manuelito, one of the last holdouts, also surrendered with his people, but he later escaped. The two leaders later went to authorities and bargained for the release of the people.

Although Kit Carson is blamed or credited with the Long Walk, his only direct involvement was the first 240 that he escorted from Fort Canby to Los Pinos. If there is any blame to be given, it should lay at the feet of General Carleton, on whose orders Carson acted.

A LOOK AT: TO KEEP A PROMISE (BUCKSKIN CHRONICLES BOOK 1)

BY B.N. RUNDELL

The power of a promise made and a promise kept is realized when Jeremiah Thompsett comes of age and accepts the responsibility of fulfilling his mentor's long-held dream. Raised by an escaped slave in the midst of the Arapaho nation in the Wind River mountains, he now must track down the slave catchers that killed his adopted father and stole their cache. The Vengeance Quest takes him and his companions through the mountains and across the nation to fulfill the promise of freeing the family of slaves held dear to his mentor and adopted father.

Accompanied by Broken Shield and Laughing Waters, his Arapaho friend and his sister, the trek through the mountains and to Fort Union is fraught with hazard and ambush. It is here he is joined by Scratch, the crusty mountain man who joins him on his journey downriver and across country to find Ezekiel's family and to seek to free them.

AVAILABLE NOW

ABOUT THE AUTHOR

Born and raised in Colorado into a family of ranchers and cowboys, B.N. Rundell is the youngest of seven sons. Juggling bull riding, skiing, and high school, graduation was a launching pad for a hitch in the Army Paratroopers. After the army, he finished his college education in Springfield, MO, and together with his wife and growing family, entered the ministry as a Baptist preacher.

Together, B.N. and Dawn raised four girls that are now married and have made them proud grandparents. With many years as a successful pastor and educator, he retired from the ministry and followed in the footsteps of his entrepreneurial father and started a successful insurance agency, which is now in the hands of his trusted nephew. He has also been a successful audiobook narrator and has recorded many books for several award-winning authors. Now finally realizing his life-long dream, B.N. has turned his efforts to writing a variety of books, from children's picture books and young adult adventure books, to the historical fiction and western genres.

Made in the USA
Coppell, TX
27 April 2023

16055070R00146